Cathy

Encounters With the Holy Spirit

Book 2 of the *Buddy* series

Arthur Perkins

SIGNALMAN PUBLISHING

Cathy: Encounters with the Holy Spirit
by Arthur Perkins

Signalman Publishing
www.signalmanpublishing.com
email: info@signalmanpublishing.com
Kissimmee, Florida

© Copyright 2014 by Arthur Perkins. All rights reserved. No part of this book may be reproduced or transmitted in any form or by any means, electronic or mechanical, or incorporated into any information retrieval system, electronic or mechanical, without the written permission of the copyright owner.

Scriptures are taken from the King James Version of the Bible
unless otherwise noted.

ISBN: 978-1-940145-19-8 (paperback)
978-1-940145-20-4 (ebook)

DEDICATION

As in my previous Christian novel *Buddy*, I dedicate this work to my wife, Carolyn, the joy of my life. We both dedicate this work, above all, to our God, and to our four daughters and their families.

Cautionary Notes to the Reader

As with all Christian novels, this book reflects the author's particular vision of God. Given the numerous differences in our backgrounds and the manner in which each of us has come to know and appreciate his God, and, above all, the pronounced myopia that afflicts our view of the spiritual realm, our individual understandings of God will differ. I don't know to what extent the Holy Spirit has influenced my own perceptions, so I cannot claim any special understanding as to His nature above that which is common to all Christians. If the reader chooses to view God in a different way than I, he certainly is entitled to consider his own vision to be as accurate as mine. This difference of opinion should not prohibit the reader from enjoying my book, which, after all, is just a novel.

Yet my particular vision, being so very useful in bringing me closer to my God, urges me to share it with others in the hope that if they have not yet experienced the joy of loving God with all their hearts, this novel will encourage them in that direction.

My next caution is more specific and includes a warning of a very real danger to the superficially-informed individual. An assumption is made in this novel that the Rapture will occur at the end of the seven years' Tribulation that will occupy the seventieth week of

Daniel (Daniel 9:24-27). This matter, however, is by no means settled, nor does it represent a boundary between Christians and non-Christians. I know many committed Christians on both sides of this particular fence. At one time or another, I also have been on both sides. As a matter of fact, until very recently when I had the opportunity of hearing Irvin Baxter's highly rational explanation of his post-tribulation stance, I had wholeheartedly endorsed the prevailing pre-tribulation viewpoint.

My reasons for my earlier acceptance of a pre-Tribulation Rapture were twofold: first, the narrative of the Book of Revelation begins with the Church, wherein the first three chapters are concerned with nothing but the Church, after which John (representing the Church, as many think) is taken up to heaven in the Spirit and nothing more is said of the Church on earth; second, Paul suggests in 2 Thessalonians 2 that there will be a "holding back" of rampant debauchery until a removal, after which the world shall experience a general falling away into gross godlessness. This "removal" is commonly attributed to the removal of the Holy Spirit from active intervention in the affairs of man, which itself, given the indwelling of the Holy Spirit within each Christian, suggests the removal of the Church from earth.

In my mind, Irvin Baxter effectively neutralized both reasons. As to the first, the sharpness of the break with the preceding three chapters may merely indicate, as Baxter suggested, a transition of the narrative from the present into the future. And, as he also noted, the Church on earth is indeed represented in several chapters of Revelation prior to Jesus' return to earth. Most notable to me is Revelation 14:9-13. Regarding the second reason, Baxter suggests that it makes more sense in the context of the passage to attribute the "holding back" to the timing of God rather than to the removal from earth of the Holy Spirit. As a matter of fact, there is much to suggest that a departure of the Holy Spirit from earth is contradictory to the nature of that beloved Entity.

Yet further, the Rapture certainly involves resurrection. Revelation 20:1-6 speaks of the first resurrection, suggesting that it occurs at the end of the Tribulation (after the great temptation of the mark of the beast has occurred).

Regardless of which theological stance regarding the timing of the Rapture is correct, in my view there is a significant danger of pinning one's hope on a pre-Tribulation Rapture. Consider the following: if the Rapture actually occurs at the end of the Tribulation, then those who adhere to pre-Tribulation view may be in the midst of the Tribulation without recognizing that it has already begun. Consequently, they may be tempted to accept the mark of the beast without understanding that it is indeed the foretold mark.

For that reason it is important to keep an open mind regarding end-time events, especially recognizing that a post-Tribulation Rapture is a distinct possibility. It also is important to read Revelation Chapter 14 to acquire an understanding of the penalty one incurs for accepting the mark. I, for one, anticipate drawing the line of acceptance of any cashless system, refusing it when it reaches the point of identification being tagged anywhere in the body, regardless of whether or not it overtly represents a specific system suggestive of an antichrist. I also pray for the strength of the Holy Spirit upon me and you if things come to that point in our lifetimes.

INTRODUCTION

With the passage of years, the mutual love and respect that Earl and Joyce held for each other continued to deepen and mature into something quite beyond the prevailing superficial, self-oriented and tenuous cohesion of the modern marriage. Often, after a long workday when he was in bed holding Joyce around the waist, he would silently thank God, not only for giving him a second chance at love, but for adding to it from their encounter with a drunk driver the physical challenges that made their relationship so special, the opportunities these hardships gave to grow into a selfless mutual devotion. That very selflessness toward their complementary others, in turn, drew them both ever closer to the ultimate family of God.

The loss of his right arm became more trivial with each passing year. Earl had lived with its absence long enough that he no longer considered it a handicap. As a matter of fact, he rarely thought of it. He wished at times that he had attempted to overcome the difficulty that it had presented with regard to his favorite activity of hang gliding, and once in a while he'd still have a nostalgic flashback to where he'd be lying prone in his harness high above a beautiful scene made all the more striking by the colorful wings that had become such a natural part of him. But now he was getting old enough that these memories were fading, so this didn't matter so much either.

The same could be said for Joyce, who now drove and walked as and where she wished. She was fully comfortable with the loss of her legs, and there wasn't much that held her back from what she wanted to do, although she missed at times her therapist Maggie and her fellow patient Cindy, whose wit and laughter helped so much toward her recovery from their life-threatening accident. But her marriage to Earl more than made up for that minor loss. Most important to her, their life together seemed to have become the Christian ideal in which two individual souls truly became one. It was a full life, in which her mother, getting quite elderly now, continued to be a vital part. With Earl's retirement from work becoming imminent, the three of them were starting to plan toward a traveling adventure by recreational vehicle. They had made the first rounds of the RV lots, peering and poking inside the luxurious interiors and collecting brochures, which they read at their leisure with an anticipatory thrill.

Earl's only real regret, in fact, was the prolonged absence of Wisdom. After finally allowing him to come to a conscious understanding of Her loving guidance behind the scenes, She had maintained a separation from conscious contact, not to return, at least as far as he was aware. He feared that Her intimate interaction with him might be gone for good, and at times the loss became an intensely-felt void. His fondest memory of Her was of one of Her last appearances to him, when She described the joy and beauty of life at the spiritual level. The difference, She said, was like an old black-and-white movie that was suddenly infused with color. As for humans, they had no idea what lay beyond their larval stage, when, as spiritual beings, they would suddenly blossom into creatures of magnificent beauty, just like caterpillars turn into butterflies.

Buddy was gone from their lives too, but for that Earl was pleased if not actually happy. After saving Earl's job and credibility following the crisis with Pastor Wilson, Buddy had gone on to achieve a measure of fame in his own right in the Special Olympics and became something of a poster-person for the possibilities open to those afflicted with cerebral palsy. Re-united with his natural parents and with Mary, the former Activities Director, at his side as his live-in caretaker and events agent, he had established a new life away from the Midtown Nursing Home. Earl and Joyce continued to conduct a Bible study at Midtown, for which Laurie the new Activities Director was grateful. Yet Buddy was deeply missed by all who had known him.

The only material negative they could see in an otherwise bright future was the deterioration of their beloved country. Under the leadership of a new and radically different administration whose appallingly self-serving policies trampled heavily on traditional Christian values, the United States was descending ever more rapidly into a police state whose government threatened daily to morph into an overtly repressive dictatorship. The politicians, from the president on down, were to be blamed for rampant corruption, but the public itself was the most guilty of all by permitting the removal of Christianity from public life. Even now, the churches that remained were in large part worthless for the shallowness of their understanding of God and the indifference of their worship. A few megachurches held onto their self-devoted membership only by promising the largesse of a Santa-Claus God. The few Churches that continued to hold fast in the face of the decline in faith were in danger of becoming so reactionary that the basic message of the love of God toward man would be eclipsed by the clenched-jaw firmness of their stance.

Earl and Joyce both had read enough of the Bible to know from the history of Israel that when a society that is chosen by God casts Him out of public life, as Anne Graham Lotz has so wisely suggested, He is polite enough to depart altogether, leaving it to its own inadequate devices and foolishness of choice. History also teaches that this society from which God has removed Himself will decline quickly and dramatically into chaos, misery and slavery. For much of its existence as a nation, the United States of America had considered itself to be chosen of God. There is much in its history to vouch for the truth of that assessment. For the past few decades, however, leaders entrusted to the running of the American government have opted to remove God from public institutions and public life while the Christian community passively stood by and watched it happen. Now there are indications that God has packed His bags, has quietly reached for the door handle, and already has stepped outside.

Out of this deteriorating situation, Earl and Joyce were offered the challenge of their lives. The prospects for the survival of their bodies are bleak, but the offer isn't about their bodies. It's about their immortal souls. They were familiar enough with the Bible to have read Jesus' admonition in Matthew 10:28 more than once:

And fear not them who kill, the body, but are not able to kill the soul; but rather fear him who is able to destroy both soul and body in hell.

They would have occasion to cling to that verse for support.

Chapter One

Earl lifted his head from the patch of garden that he was weeding and looked up at the blue sky, almost shining in its radiance. This was one of the times that it came back to him – the smack against earth of running feet, the sudden void as the cliff receded behind, pushing his harness prone and moving his hands down to the basetube as the vista opened up below, the air whispering past his wings as they held him aloft. A pang of desire – a need to fly – gripped him, but he tamped it back down with heartfelt thanks to God for the many blessings that he and Joyce had received. He reflected on the intimacy that he'd enjoyed with Wisdom, and of how that had led to the companion joy of truly knowing Jesus.

And his loving intimacy with Joyce, he felt with gratitude. Alicia remained in his mind, but he was capable now of remembering with happiness their times together without experiencing the crushing pain of her loss.

Earl had two favorite projects at home that occupied his mind and energy when he wasn't working in the yard or spending time with Joyce. One was his preparation for their weekly Bible study at the nursing home. At this point in time he was delving into Luke's

Book of Acts, which recounted the amazing adventures of the Apostles, those who had been eyewitnesses of Jesus, after the Holy Spirit filled them at the first Pentecost following Jesus' crucifixion. He was particularly fond of this book for the freshness and hope it exuded, and his lesson flowed into his mind as if God was talking directly to him.

He continued to update his blog with irregularly-spaced postings, although this second task wasn't as urgently demanding as it was when he was facing opposition to what he considered to be vital insights into the nature of God. In this more relaxed environment he prepared his postings with happy, loving care. At this time of relative peace in his life, he was concerned less with theological opposition than what he perceived to be a growing indifference to Scripture within the Christian community that paralleled the ever-increasing dumbing-down of the schoolchild generation, along with the deliberately inculcated self-centeredness and lack of mental discipline that was more suitable for a regime of oppressive control than for freedom and liberty. As far as he was concerned, it was absolutely imperative for the Christian layperson to have a good working knowledge of the Bible in order to fend off the numerous false teachings that were afflicting many of the long-standing Churches. He and Joyce could do only so much, but at least those he reached with his blog and to whom he spoke in the nursing home would be well-grounded in the Word.

After agreeing to disagree with mutual respect regarding Earl's views on the Holy Spirit, Earl and pastor George Mason gradually eased back into a warm friendship. "After all," George had said to Earl one Sunday after Church services during a friendly discussion of Earl's near-persecution, "the gender of the Holy Spirit isn't a Christian show-stopper like rejecting the deity of Jesus or denying the existence of the Holy Spirit altogether. You claim to love the Holy Spirit. I'm good with that, particularly in the face of so many truly destructive issues that the Church is facing these days, and which I'm increasingly forced to address."

Pastor George now was speaking to one of these issues at Sunday service. "Beginning this morning," he addressed his congregation, "we're going to be spending time in the Book of Revelation. There are many reasons for turning to this book, the most important of which is that it is beginning to appear that we are entering that time of which the book speaks. In addition, despite the promise of God to bless those who read it, it is a book that largely has been neglected by the modern Church for its supposedly negative connotations, which actually are negative only for those who insist upon placing their faith and allegiance on the material world. Unfortunately, the Church's attempt to emphasize the positive to the exclusion of the negative is largely responsible for the poor state that the Church finds itself in today. The modern Christian expectation for loyalty to God is the reaping of physical rewards, like pink Cadillacs and gold-plated Rolex watches. This attitude stands in direct opposition to Jesus' clear statements, echoed by His Apostles, that His kingdom is spiritual rather than physical. When Jesus spoke of blessings, He meant those saved souls to which He would credit His devoted servants, and the joy that would come from the unity of love among those servants and between them and God.

"Turn with me, please, to Matthew 6:24." After a short pause, George started reading words that Jesus had spoken:

No man can serve two masters; for either he will hate the one, and love the other; or else he will hold to the one, and despise the other. Ye cannot serve God and mammon.

"If that isn't plain enough," George continued, "turn now to John 18:36, where Jesus is speaking to Pilate after His arrest:

Jesus answered, "My kingdom is not of this world; if my kingdom were of this world, then would my servants fight, that I should not be delivered to the Jews; but now is my kingdom not from here."

"That pretty much says it all. But just in case you still don't get the picture that a pink Cadillac isn't in every Christian's future, let's go to one more reference." After pausing for the laughter to die down, pastor continued: "Now we'll go to Philippians 1:29:

For unto you it is given in the behalf of Christ, not only to believe on him but also to suffer for his sake.

"Oh, my!" George exclaimed. "that doesn't sound very good."

"No, it doesn't," a beefy, red-faced man mumbled indignantly. Earl had noted that he hadn't laughed with the rest of the congregation when pastor had referenced the earlier verses. Now the man arose, pulled his wife up with him, and stepped awkwardly out into the aisle, where they made a hasty exit. George paused to let them go. He made no comment regarding them, but continued with his sermon.

"But it's a lot better than some may think." That got a laugh too, from the way it dovetailed so naturally into the event that had just taken place. "It may seem counter-intuitive, but historically, the Church has thrived in the face of persecution. Conversely, the Church has always been its worst and least obedient to God when Christianity has been the accepted norm in a society. But even at the personal level it's better than you think. There's love and joy in serving the Lord, and the more difficult it is, the more love and joy is bestowed on those who continue to stand firm in their beliefs while maintaining their compassionate natures in the process. This isn't about a psychological quirk that we humans have. It's about God - specifically the Holy Spirit, who indwells Christians and actively and continuously bestows the love of God upon the obedient ones. It is the Holy Spirit who not only gives us the courage to serve God, but joy in doing so. Now let's get to the heart of the sermon, the Book of Revelation. I've taken so long to get to this point that I'll save the Scripture itself to next week, but I do want to give you an understanding of the book's source and the circumstances under which it was written.

"First of all," he continued, "it's not 'Revelations' with an 's' on the end. It's singular – Revelation – because it is the revelation of Jesus Christ to the Apostle John, who had been banished by the Roman emperor Domitian to the small Island of Patmos on the Aegean Sea between Greece and Turkey. Unlike the other Apostles, John wasn't killed in the name of Christ. Paul had been beheaded and Peter had been crucified upside-down at his own request, having considered himself unworthy to die in the same manner as his Lord Jesus Christ. But not John. John was actually released on the death of Domitian in 97 A.D., whereupon he returned to the Church at Ephesus. John lived to the age of a hundred. Interestingly, this difference of fate was foretold by Jesus in John 21, verses 18 through 23. Let's go there now. In His threefold forgiveness of Peter's threefold denial of Him, the resurrected Jesus had just commanded Peter for the third time to feed his sheep and He continued to address Peter:

> *Verily, verily, I say unto thee, When thou wast young, thou girdest thyself, and walkedst where thou wouldest; but when thou shalt be old, thou shalt stretch forth thy hands, and another shall gird thee, and carry thee where thou wouldest not. This spoke [Jesus], signifying by what death he should glorify God. And when he had spoken thus, he saith unto him, Follow me. Then Peter, turning about, seeth the disciple whom Jesus loves, following; who also leaned on his breast at supper, and said, Lord, who is he that betrayeth thee? Peter, seeing him, saith to Jesus, Lord, and what shall this man do? Jesus saith unto him, If I will that he tarry till I come, what is that to thee? Follow thou me. Then went this saying abroad among the brethren, that that disciple should not die. Yet Jesus said not unto him, He shall not die; but, If I will that he tarry till I come, what is that to thee?*

"According to John," George continued, "while he was in exile on the Island of Patmos, he was in the Spirit on the Lord's day when Jesus appeared to him and spoke to him, giving him insights and messages. Later during a continuation of that event, he saw visions of heaven as well as the spectacularly modern earth in the latter days. The Book of Revelation is John's record of that event. I can hardly wait until next week, when we get into the Scripture itself. Now, please turn in your hymnals to number 147, Charles Wesley's great and moving hymn, *And Can it Be?*'"

"That was a wonderful sermon," Joyce said to Earl as they left the Church. "It's good to see George showing his backbone. We need to hear messages like that."

"How about that couple that left? I wouldn't want to be in their shoes when things get real bad. In fact, I wouldn't want to be in their shoes when they have to face God."

"Actually, I feel sorry for them. They've been badly misled, probably from one or more of the 'positive-thinking' or 'prosperity' televangelists."

"Probably. But they could have been misled as well by any of a number of Churches in our own community."

At the Bible study that Sunday evening, Earl recounted to the group the fear and uncertainty that had possessed the Apostles and other believers as they waited in the upper room for the Holy Spirit as Jesus had promised them. Ten days had passed since they last saw Jesus rising up into heaven and this was now the morning of Shavuot, a feast first established by God through Moses that some called Pentecost for the fifty-day interval between the celebration of First Fruits (the day of Jesus resurrection) and this feast. It was originally celebrated by Jews as the giving of the Law, but after the coming of Jesus, Gentiles also have celebrated it as the birth of the Church through the indwelling of believers by the Holy Spirit. As in the past, they were preparing to read the Book of Ruth, a long-standing Jewish tradition. This link was cherished by Earl, who, because of his view regarding who Ruth and Naomi represented in the story, saw great significance in it. "Suddenly" – Earl dramatically jumped from his chair to the wide-eyed astonishment of the assembled residents – "a mighty wind came rushing, right inside that upper room, and the Holy Spirit came in power and glory to dwell within every person there. They spoke in languages that even they didn't know, but others would understand. When they left the room, some skeptics who were unable to comprehend what had just happened thought that the Apostles were drunk."

He turned to peer into the face of a totally absorbed listener, a pre-teen girl named Catherine who, like Buddy, was afflicted with cerebral palsy. "Cathy," he asked, "do you think they should have known about the power of the Holy Spirit?"

Cathy

She struggled to respond. Their group was so tightly-knit that her struggle was no embarrassment, either to her or the others. Eventually, she mastered a vehement nod. "You're very right," Earl told her. "Jesus spelled it out very clearly in John Chapter 3, when He was talking to Nicodemus. Here, I'll read it to you:

There was a man of the Pharisees named Nicodemus, a ruler of the Jews. This man came to Jesus by night and said to him, Rabbi, we know that you are a teacher come from God; for no one can do these signs that You do unless God is with him. Jesus answered and said to him, Most assuredly, I say to you, unless one is born again, he cannot see the kingdom of God. Nicodemus said to him, How can a man be born when he is old? Can he enter a second time into his mother's womb and be born? Jesus answered, Verily, verily, I say to you, Unless one is born of water and the Spirit, he cannot enter the kingdom of God. That which is born of the flesh is flesh, and that which is born of the Spirit is spirit. Do not marvel that I said to you, You must be born again. The wind blows where it wishes, and you hear the sound of it, but cannot tell where it comes from and where it goes. So is everyone who is born of the Spirit.

Earl looked up from his reading, first to Cathy and then over to their friend Laurie, the Activities Director. She gave him an encouraging smile that conveyed her pleasure with their effort to bring the light of Christ to the nursing home.

"Okay, then," he said. It's nine o'clock in the morning, and the wind of which Jesus had spoken suddenly came into the upper room to infuse those who were there with the power of God. Can you imagine the pandemonium in that little place? But these believers in Christ now had a mission, to spread the light of Christ to a dark world. They soon sorted themselves out and came out among the people in the area." He turned to Acts Chapter 2 and read aloud:

When the Day of Pentecost had fully come, they were all with one accord in one place. And suddenly there came a sound from heaven, as of a rushing mighty wind, and it filled the whole house where they were dwelling. Then there appeared to them cloven tongues, as of fire, and it sat upon each of them. And they were all filled with the Holy Spirit and began to speak with other tongues, as the Spirit gave them utterance. And there were dwelling in Jerusalem Jews, devout men, from every nation under heaven. And when this sound occurred, the multitude came together, and were confused, because everyone heard them speak in his own language. Then they were all amazed and marveled, saying to one another, Behold, are not all these who speak Galileans? And how is it that we hear, each in our own language in which we were born? Parthians and Medes and Elamites, those dwelling in Mesopotamia, Judea and Cappadocia, Pontus and Asia, Phrygia and Pamphylia, Egypt and parts of Libya adjoining Cyrene, visitors from Rome, both Jews and proselytes, Cretans and Arabs – we hear them speaking in our own tongues the wonderful works of God. So they were all amazed and perplexed, saying to one another, Whatever could this mean? Others mocking said, They are full of new wine.

But Peter, standing up with the eleven, raised his voice and said to them, Men of Judea and all who dwell in Jerusalem, let this be known to you, and heed my words. For these are not drunk, as you suppose, since it is only the third hour of the day. But this is what was spoken by the prophet Joel: And it shall come to pass in the last days, says God, That I will pour out of My Spirit on all flesh; Your sons and your daughters shall prophesy, your young men shall see visions, your old men shall dream dreams. And on My menservants and on My maidservants I will pour out My Spirit in those days; and they shall prophesy. I will show wonders in heaven above and signs in the earth beneath: Blood and fire and vapor of smoke. The sun shall be turned into darkness, and the moon into blood, before the coming of the great and awesome day of the Lord. And it shall come to pass that whoever calls on the name of the Lord shall be saved.

Earl closed his Bible and looked at the eager faces. "Remember how afraid Peter was when Jesus was arrested? Three times somebody came up and identified him as one of the Apostles. And each of those three times Peter denied knowing Jesus, even to the point of swearing at his accusers." Earl paused for dramatic effect. "But now," he said with a joyful grin, "Peter is no longer attempting to rely on his own will. He's become a new man. The Holy Spirit is now living in him, just as the Holy Spirit comes to live inside every Christian." He pointed to Cathy, and then to each of the others, saying "To you, and to you, and to you. . .

"Possessing the power of God inside him through the Holy Spirit, Peter has now become a giant of a Christian, capable now of fulfilling Jesus' plan for him when, in thrice commanding him to feed His sheep, He forgave him three times for his denials. Indwelt by the Holy Spirit, Peter feeds the Word of God to the crowd assembled at the Pentecost, in the end saving three thousand souls. This is the first of three major events in which Peter did indeed feed others with the Word, fulfilling Jesus' threefold commandment at the lakeshore after His resurrection. It's in John 21:

> *So when they had eaten breakfast, Jesus said to Simon Peter, Simon, son of Jonah, do you love Me more than these? He said to him, Yes, Lord, you know that I love you. He said to him, Feed my lambs. He said to him again a second time, Simon, son of Jonah, do you love Me? He said to him, Yes, Lord; you know that I love you. He said to him, Feed my sheep. He said to him the third time, Do you love Me? And he said to him, Lord, you know all things; you know that I love you. Jesus said to him, Feed my sheep.*

"The next time that Peter fed Jesus' sheep with the Word is recounted in Acts 4, where this time Peter saves five thousand souls through the Word of God. The third big salvation that Peter offered through the Word was to the Gentile world through Cornelius the devout Italian. It's noted in Acts Chapter 10, which we'll get into a bit later. Other big events happened in the meantime, which I'm sure you'll find very exciting. I sure did."

He looked at them fondly. "It has been good to be with you again," he said as he turned his head lovingly toward Cathy. "We'll be looking forward to seeing you next Sunday. In the meantime, have a wonderful week in the Lord and we'll be praying for each and every one of you." He rose from his chair and walked over toward Joyce.

"Did you see Cathy's face when I was reading Scripture?" Earl asked Joyce as he put on his raincoat. The children were moving back to their rooms. Laurie was among them, wheeling Cathy.

"She's a doll," Joyce agreed. Wouldn't it be nice to spend time with her? I don't mean that what you're doing isn't great, it's just that it would be nice to have some one-on-one time with her, get to know her better." She paused, trying to get to the essence of what she was trying to say. "Make her feel loved."

"Yes, it would be nice," Earl replied without hesitation. "There's no better time than right now to get it started. Let's talk to Laurie about it." They headed for her office.

When Laurie returned to her office after putting Cathy to bed, Earl and Joyce were waiting for her. "We have an idea," Joyce began, "no, more than that. We seem to be led to spend more time with Cathy, away from here. Maybe we could pick her up some Saturday morning and take her to the zoo or something. Do you think that might be all right?"

"I don't see why not," she replied. "Except you just might not know what you're getting into, even for a day's outing. In the first place, she has bathroom needs. Do you think you can handle that, Joyce? It can get pretty strenuous, and I know you're comfortable with your prosthetics, but that might be too much of a load for you."

"I can try. After all, it isn't the first time that we've taken a handicapped person out for a day."

"Oh? But with cerebral palsy?"

"Yes, cerebral palsy. Severe. And what we'd be doing with Cathy wouldn't be anything like what we did with Buddy when Earl took him hang gliding."

Laurie stared at Joyce, her mouth open. Finally she spoke. "Let

Cathy

me get this straight. Earl took Buddy *hang gliding*?" Her frown turned into a broad smile when she finally understood. "You mean, he took this fellow up to watch them fly. That was nice of you," she said, turning her eyes to Earl. What..."

"No," Joyce interrupted. "You got it right the first time. What I meant was that Earl took this severely-afflicted individual hang gliding with him. They flew together. Seven times off a thousand-foot cliff. Later I flew with Earl too. It's quite beautiful."

Laurie buried her head in her arms on the desk. Presently she raised her head and gave Earl an accusing look. "How on earth did you manage to get this – *Buddy* – out of his nursing home? As a matter of fact, how did *you* manage to escape *your* institution?"

Earl shrugged. "Things were a lot less regulated back then. And I had two arms at the time. And I'll tell you something else. It made Buddy's day. It made his life, in fact. Not only did he love the experience, but it gave him the confidence to excel in the Special Olympics. Some day I'll explain to you how I know it wasn't me that did it, but the Holy Spirit."

"Anyway, Laurie," Joyce hastened to add, "It's been years since Earl went hang gliding last. We're not planning on anything close to radical like that. All we want to do with Cathy is take her to the zoo or something like that."

"Well, if you can give me your word that you won't be trying stunts like that with Cathy, I guess you can take her out." The frown remained. "But I'm still concerned with your ability to handle Cathy's special needs," she said, pointing to Joyce. "Let's take this slow. Next Saturday both of you come in and watch the nursing routine. The Saturday after that you can get some hands-on experience with me and a nurse supervising. If you're still willing after that, we can talk about where we go from there."

"Fair enough," Joyce said.

"Okay," Earl echoed, and they bid Laurie goodbye.

"Why did you have to mention Buddy?" Earl asked Joyce when

they were in the car heading home. Did you see the look she gave me?"

"It's the truth," Joyce replied. "As Christians we can do no less than tell the complete truth, whatever the consequences. Actually, I'm surprised that you asked me that question. Not only that, but I was trying to get across to her that if we could handle that with Buddy, we pretty well can handle anything with Cathy."

"No, you're right," he said. "I'm just upset about her change in attitude, and whether that'll have an impact on whether we can take Cathy out of the nursing home."

"Don't be. Everything that happens to us is up to God."

"Right you are. Thanks."

Chapter Two

Within the White House of the United States is an obscure room that, for years at a time, would remain untouched except for occasional visits of the cleaning crew to dust the furniture and freshen the air. Most presidents never gave it a thought, their minds being occupied by weightier matters than the mere use of a room.

The ambiguity of the room made it the perfect place for the current president to use as his private domain, having no intention of ever leaving this residence – until recently, that is, when his interest turned toward larger possibilities. His first act upon deciding to occupy the room for special use was to change the furniture, replacing the various chairs, sofas and tables with objects of equivalent function but more suited to his taste in comfort. Beyond that, he directed the search and acquisition of objects that expressed the uniqueness of his being. Somewhere along the way he had been enlightened with regard to his roots, and those elements of his forbears that expressed the nobility of his family he had collected and kept. Now he had the ideal venue by which he could display these objects for his personal pleasure and gratification.

At the present time the president sat in his favorite overstuffed chair next to an elegant sixteenth century end table on which were placed an ornate golden lamp and a very large crystal-cut glass of Johnny Walker Blue King George V Scotch Whisky, provided from the deep and generous pockets of the American taxpayer.

The glass of whisky had been full when the president had first arrived in the room. He picked it up again and knocked back a good mouthful of the spirits, bringing the level down below half-full. He did have some leaning toward the Muslim faith – as much as a person possessed by the enormous quantity of self-interest that he did could care about any religion of which he wasn't its grand master – but that inclination wasn't sufficient to compel him to observe its moral edicts. He smacked his lips and waited until the rich glow suffused his body, and then looked about him, at the red velvet of the walls, the opulent silk curtains, the fireplace in which a cheerful log fire burned brightly, endowing the room with warmth and the faint smell of maple. His eyes drifted to a corner where a pool table and a poker table stood, both richly covered in green velvet.

The sight filled him with another glow that augmented the first and then supplanted it: pride of the most magnificent kind. He had reached the pinnacle of power, verified by the furnishings of this grand room and the comfort in which he sat. He lacked one comfort, correcting that oversight by extracting a large Cuban cigar from a pocket of his silk nightjacket. Reaching deeper, he lifted out a solid gold lighter. Then, having taken care of the pleasant chore of lighting the cigar, he leaned back in his chair and pulled rich tobacco smoke into his lungs, reveling in the instant high.

I'm living as a king, he told himself. *Indeed, I am a king. Royalty.* But the thought didn't satisfy him as it had in the past. Instead, it led to a new and troubling thought: his kingship wasn't unique. He was but one of many kings of the world. Moreover, the United States was rapidly losing its status as the world's greatest nation. Another thought, quite ugly, intruded into his pleasure: part of this loss was his own fault. But the two problems were intricately connected and thus were amenable to a common solution.

Continue to bring the United States into conformity with the European nations. Once that is accomplished, become the head of it all.

Cathy

His self-satisfaction changed course, to be replaced by thoughts of necessary actions. His mental musings returned to a frequently-visited topic, that of developing the plans by which he might bring this vision into reality. He refocused on his awareness that he had one very powerful tool at his disposal: he had just won reelection. It was no longer necessary to please his party, his base, or, as a matter of fact, anyone. Given that reality, the world was at his disposal with implications of power beyond anything available to a ruler since the beginning of civilization.

The knock on his door, timidly discreet as it was, interrupted his pleasant reverie. "What do you want?" he spat out meanly. He'd made it clear to his staff that under no circumstances was he to be disturbed while in this room.

The door parted fractionally, just enough to frame a peeping eye. "Get in here, you insignificant little jerk," he commanded his head of press liaison. "You've already interrupted me, so what good is it going to be for you to go all tippy-toes on me?" The president hated this miserable little cretin, but he'd personally selected him for his naïve, dweebish appearance, knowing that his innocent look would help mask the obvious nature of the egregious lies he would spew out to the White House press corps. Beyond that, despite the fact that his pronouncements were laughably false to all but the lowest percentile of Washington's rodent population, which equated to the highest percentile of the press corps, the little wimp never dared to question the veracity of the fictions he was told to perpetrate.

The red-faced kid stood before him, nervous eyes darting from side to side, partially-developed little Adam's apple bobbing up and down. He began to open his mouth to speak, but the president cut him off.

"Out with it!" he commanded in a near shout. "I don't have all day." He looked down to the kid's crotch to see if he was wetting his pants.

"I – I thought you'd want to know that—"

"Sir! You address me as 'sir' when you speak. How many times do I have to tell you—"

"Yessir!" the boy screamed. It sounded like a woman in distress. "What I wanted to say is that, is that, uh, sir, the reporter from Fox News is doing it to me again. He's giving me a hard time, sir, like he doesn't believe me. Sir."

"So? If your testicles ever descend to where they belong, you'll manage to put him in his place. Do I need to tell you again how stupid those press people are? They're no better than the general population, so you shouldn't have trouble telling them off." Lately the president had begun to wonder whether he didn't go overboard on the appearance of honest innocence by picking this guy for the job. Maybe he'd have to replace him with someone more assertive. The notion set him to daydreaming of the underling's removal. Perhaps get him into a situation, maybe a bar, a conservative one frequented by lots of meaty blue-collar types where he'd naturally piss off the regulars, get himself into a world of hurt. The president pictured the ensuing slaughter, grinning with delight. It would be better than a football game. He narrowed his eyes, boring them into the kid's face. "Borrow yourself a decent set of balls tonight," he said. "Go out there tomorrow and use them. If you can't do that, I don't need you. Understand?"

Defeated, the little assistant began to salute, but then turned and removed himself from the room, his shoulders registering his utter humiliation. The president grinned more broadly, thinking that perhaps he'd detected a spot of moisture in the kit's pants. *Now, where was I —*

CHAPTER THREE

Earl and Joyce arrived back at the nursing home early the next Saturday morning, where they observed Cathy's waking, dressing, eating breakfast, and attending a class of modest objectives where she was taught the basics of self-sufficiency and a somewhat superficial level of reading. Handwriting was out of the question, of course, but a variety of new communications devices had come onto the market in the last decade, and Cathy had access to one that had buttons she could press to spell letters, words and even some phrases that would appear on a screen. Earl watched her at work with the device, and soon was going beyond observation to active participation, showing her pictures of objects and helping her spell out the representations in English. He backed off when it came time for the bathroom functions, letting Joyce do the observing there as they had agreed earlier.

The day passed quickly and Earl was relieved at the end to note that Laurie had returned to a full acceptance of Joyce and him. Beyond that, Joyce had not been put off by her observation of the less desirable chores associated with maintaining Cathy's well-being. Despite the encouragement this offered, Earl reserved his congratulations to her for when she would actually perform the tasks herself.

That evening at home Joyce had a surprise phone call. "Hi, Joyce," the feminine voice said. "It's me."

"Mom!" Joyce replied happily. "It's been weeks since we've talked. How are you, and why haven't you called?"

"I've been busy," she said cryptically. "But we – I – will see you in Church tomorrow morning. I have something to show you."

"Tell me now."

"No. I want it to be a surprise. See you tomorrow, and let's have lunch together downtown."

"Sure." When they hung up, Joyce called to Earl. "Earl, that was mom on the phone. She's going to Church tomorrow. She sounded strange, like she has a secret."

"Oh?" he replied. "Well, it'll be good to see her again. It's been a while."

The next morning Earl and Joyce arrived at Church early and waited in the parking lot for Janet. They both laughed to see her tool up in her bright green Mazda Miata convertible, sporting shades. There was a large gap between her age and the appropriate age for the car, but it also was good to see her enjoying life so thoroughly in her sunset years. What was more surprising was that she wasn't alone. A very tall male sat in the passenger seat of the tiny vehicle, giving the appearance that he was playing with a toy. When they parked he struggled like a long-legged spider to extricate himself from the car, and finally stood up to his full height of 6 feet 6 inches. Janet was all smiles as she came up to Earl and Joyce and presented Henry to them.

"Henry's my insurance agent," she said after they'd introduced themselves. "His wife died three years ago. Now he's my friend, too. My good friend."

"Nothing like getting right to the point, mom," Joyce said, but she was grinning along with Janet. She took an instant liking to Henry. Perhaps it was the kindness in his eyes, but she was very happy for her mother. They went into the Church together and sat toward the front in deference to Henry's deteriorating hearing.

In his sermon, Pastor George presented a brief overview of the Book of Revelation before beginning to read the Scripture. "The Book of Revelation has some definite arrangements of topics," he began. "The first three chapters deal with the Church throughout its history. The Church is mentioned only peripherally in the remaining chapters of the book, which has led many to believe that the Rapture and consequent end of the Church age on earth takes place in Chapter 4. In the first chapter Jesus approaches John and demonstrates the intimacy of His connection to His Church. He commands him to write the things that he has seen, the things that are, and the things yet to happen. The 'things he has seen' are Jesus as He shall appear in His second coming, the seven representative Churches to whom He has messages and His commandment to write His messages to seven churches. The 'things which are' are the messages to the seven Churches, which occupy Chapters 2 and 3. The 'things yet to happen' are the events that take place beginning in Chapter 4 and continue through the remainder of the book.

"Chapters 4 and 5 are visions of heaven and Jesus' taking of the scrolls to unseal them to begin the judgment of God upon the earth. This judgment is a woeful series of plagues upon the earth and mankind that runs from Chapter 6 through Chapter 20. These devastating miseries are arranged into three groups of seven: seven seals, seven trumpets and seven bowls. There's a wide range of opinions about the time periods each of these three sets occupy. To some, they all occur within a final seven-year period called the Tribulation or the Time of Jacob's Trouble spoken of in Chapter 30 of Jeremiah.

Why do we think in terms of a final seven-year period? According to many Bible scholars, the vision in Chapter 9 of Daniel foretold to the exact day when Jesus would make His triumphal entry into Jerusalem. Indeed, Jesus did make that very entry exactly 69 weeks after the foretold beginning point – to the very day. But this prophecy of Daniel's spoke, along with a 69-week period to Jesus, of a total of 70 weeks when Israel takes center stage in God's timing.

Again, Bible scholars understand this seventieth week not to be contiguous with the other 69, but to have been interrupted by the Church Age, or the Time of the Gentiles. When the fullness of the Gentiles is come in, then the seventieth week of Daniel is to begin. To many others, only the final seven bowl judgments occur within the Tribulation period, the other two having taken place earlier. At least one well-known Bible scholar considers most of the seal judgments to have begun shortly after the beginning of the twentieth century. Regardless of that, the judgments get more intense as time progresses; the last three and a half years, or the midpoint of the Tribulation period, are called by many the Great Tribulation, which sees the awesome violence of God's wrath. It's an awful time that I, for one, would prefer not to go through. There will be Christians throughout this time, but many are hoping that the Rapture will take us up before we get to that point. As for me, I haven't yet reached an opinion either way.

"Chapters 20 through 22 are occupied by the judgment of God on those who rejected Jesus, the thousand-year reign of Christ on earth, otherwise known as either the Millennium or the Seventh Day of God, the new heaven and earth, and the new paradise. But before we get there, and even before we get into Chapter 6, we'll have to cover some prerequisites. The Book of Revelation, you see, is closely connected to the imagery in the Book of Daniel and in Jesus' Olivet and Temple Discourses, in Matthew 24, Mark 13 and Luke 17 and 21. But for today we'll start with a reading of Revelation Chapter 1." He read the chapter to them and the service closed with a hymn.

"Let's go to lunch, Janet said when they emerged into the parking lot. "We're buying. You can follow us."

"Mom, this place is pretty spendy," Joyce said as they were seated. "Let us at least pay our own way."

"No. I'm celebrating." She waved her left hand in front of her daughter, who gasped in surprise.

"Oh!" Joyce cried. "What a beautiful ring!"

"Henry gave it to me yesterday. We're planning our honeymoon in two months."

"Congratulations to you both!" Earl said.

"Thanks, and now we'll have some wine." She signaled a waiter and ordered a carafe of shiraz. On the verge of declining because of his upcoming Bible study at the nursing home that evening, Earl decided to take a sip in fellowship.

When the wine arrived and they'd placed their orders Henry did the honor with the pouring and stood up beaming to make a toast. He decided to go formal and raised a spoon for mock attention. "Ahem," he intoned with a silly grin on his face and tapped his wine glass.

He must have been nervous, for his tap was somewhat on the hard side. "Oh!" he exclaimed as his wine glass disintegrated into shards. "Oh!" Janet exclaimed as the unrestrained liquid made a beeline over the tablecloth into her lap. "Oh No!"

Poor Henry was beside himself at what he'd done to ruin the lunch and Janet's dress. He just couldn't understand why Janet wasn't crying. He was shocked, in fact, to see the three of them holding their sides laughing.

"Welcome to the family, Henry," Earl said after he caught his breath. "You're not the first." Joyce told him about Earl's first time meeting Janet and how she'd returned from the bathroom finding Earl on top of her mother after tripping on the door sill. "He's a keeper, mom," Joyce told her mother. "Anyone who can maintain a tradition like that can't be all bad." Earl grinned at prospect of passing the torch to Henry.

Sheepish at first, Henry was finally convinced to join in on the fun. Lunch wasn't ruined at all. It was the best time they'd had together since Earl's disaster with Janet in her foyer.

That evening at the nursing home Earl continued in Luke's Book of Acts from where he'd left off last time. "So Peter, emboldened by the Holy Spirit inside him, did exactly what Jesus foretold in John 21: he fed Jesus' sheep with the word of God in three very important events, first saving three thousand souls, then five thousand, and after that the Gentile world through Cornelius the devout Italian. But preaching wasn't his only gift. I'll read to you beginning at the first verse of Acts Chapter 3:

> *Now Peter and John went up together into the temple at the hour of prayer, being the ninth hour [or 3 o'clock in the afternoon]. And a certain man, lame from his birth, was carried, whom they laid daily at the gate of the temple, which is called Beautiful, to ask alms of them that entered into the temple; Who, seeing Peter and John about to go into the temple, asked an alms.*

"In other words," Earl interrupted the narrative, "the man was lame like us," he said, waving the stump of his right arm, "and he was begging for money to live on." He returned to the narrative:

> *And Peter, fastening his eyes upon him, with John, said, Look on us. And [the beggar] gave heed unto them, expecting to receive something from them. Then Peter said, Silver and gold have I none, but, such as I have, give I thee. In the name of Jesus Christ of Nazareth, rise up and walk. And [Peter] took him by the right hand, and lifted him up; and immediately his feet and ankle bones received strength. And he, leaping up, stood and walked, and entered with them into the temple, walking, and leaping, and praising God. And all the people saw him walking and praising God; and they knew that it was he who sat for alms at the Beautiful Gate of the temple; and they were filled with wonder and amazement at that which had happened unto him. And as the lame man who was healed held Peter and John, all the people ran together unto them in the porch that is called Solomon's, greatly wondering. And when Peter saw it, he answered the people, Ye men of Israel, why marvel ye at this? Or why look ye so earnestly on us, as though by our own power of holiness we had made this man walk? The God of Abraham, and of Isaac, and of Jacob, the God of our fathers, hath glorified his Son, Jesus, whom ye delivered up and denied in the presence of Pilate, when he*

was determined to let him go. But ye denied the Holy One and the Just, and desired [the murderer Barabbas] to be granted unto you; and killed the Prince of life, whom God hath raised from the dead, of which we are witnesses. And his name, through faith in his name, hath made this man strong, whom ye see and know; yea, the faith which is by him hath given him this perfect soundness in the presence of you all.

And now, brethren, I know that through ignorance ye did it, as did also your rulers. But those things, which God before had shown by the mouth of all his prophets, that Christ should suffer, he hath so fulfilled. Repent, therefore, and be converted, that your sins may be blotted out, when the times of refreshing shall come from the presence of the Lord; and he shall send Jesus Christ, who before was preached unto you, whom the heaven must receive until the times of restitution of all things, which God hath spoken by the mouth of all his holy prophets since the world began. For Moses truly said unto the fathers, A prophet shall the Lord, your God, raise up unto you of your brethren, like unto me; him shall ye hear in all things, whatever he shall say unto you. And it shall come to pass that every soul, who will not hear that prophet, shall be destroyed from among the people. Yea, and all the prophets from Samuel and those who follow after, as many as have spoken, have likewise foretold of these days. Ye are the children of the prophets, and of the covenant which God made with our fathers, saying unto Abraham, And in thy seed shall all the kindreds of the earth be blessed. Unto you first God, having raised up his Son, Jesus, sent him to bless you, in turning away every one of you from his iniquities.

"This passage gives us something to think about," Earl told his audience. "The Holy Spirit not only gave Peter the power to preach the Word of God to the saving of many souls, but also the power to heal, just like Jesus did. Do we have that kind of power today? And if we do, why doesn't every one of us get healed like that lame man? The answer is this: we don't live for ourselves. Every one of us lives for the glory of God in one way or another. It doesn't matter whether the Holy Spirit operates the same today as then, even though I think that the Holy Spirit doesn't change. Even Jesus didn't heal everyone, nor did Peter, but only those whose healing glorified God. Some people get healed for this glory; others do not, and they don't for the same glory that others do get healed. A couple of weeks ago, the pastor of the Church that Joyce and I attend gave us a Scripture lesson out of John 18:36. I'll read what Jesus said there to you:

> *My kingdom is not of this world; if my kingdom were of this world, then would my servants fight, that I should not be delivered to the Jews; but now is my kingdom not from here.*

"You see," Earl continued, "God's universe is much bigger than this little earth that we live on now. Eventually all of us will be whole, without any missing or lame parts. But for the short time that we are on the earth, God is able to show the world the love of Christ through the compassion that Christians show toward the infirm. If Joyce still had her legs, how could Jesus show His love through my compassion toward her difficulties and my loving support of her? If I still had both arms, how could Jesus show His love through Joyce's support of my infirmity? It's the same with you: you are the means by which God shows His love through the compassionate care that Laurie and the other staff here show you. At the same time God is developing in you the patience and endurance of saints, the strength of character to love God in the face of your difficulties. The caregivers and the caregiven complement each other in a beautiful way to develop the selfless nobility of both, a trait that He will cherish in His Bride, the Church. The bottom line is that it's not about being better than others. It's all about representing God as best you can with what He gave you to work with. May it always be that way," Earl continued under his breath, suspecting that hard times lay ahead for those dependent on bureaucratic systems.

"Next time we'll see that Peter and John are given supernatural power along with plenty of trouble to go with it. It has always been that way with the Church. The Church is at her very best when she faces danger and persecution. She's at her very worst when times are good. We'll see that while some like us are stuck with bodies that don't work like they should, other Christians are stuck with suffering and tests of faith. Remember this word from Paul in Romans 8:28:

And we know that all things work together for them that love God, to them who are the called according to his purpose.

"Good job," Joyce told Earl as he gently deposited her in the car.

"It wasn't me, as you know. Just like the beauty of your voice and piano playing. We know where that came from."

"Thanks for that. It's great being a team at work in the fields of the Lord, isn't it? I love you."

Chapter Four

The president sat in his overstuffed chair, as was his invariable custom while he was in his special room. But tonight he was not entirely alone. Not yet. Arrayed within easy chatting distance from him were several chairs, none of which were occupied. Nor would they be. The presence of the other man who stood before him was a necessary annoyance, one that he would correct in the shortest possible time consistent with the task he had in mind. Despite the necessity of his presence, the man's intrusion into his pleasurable self-contemplations enflamed his temper to the verge of verbal abuse. The importance of the man's mission was the only thing that kept his urges in check.

"Are they assembled here?" he asked his chief of staff.

"Yes, sir," replied Milton Anderson. "They're downstairs in the daily conference room."

"Do you fully understand your instructions?"

"Yes, sir." By a series of vague, innuendo-filled conversations with Mr. Anderson that supplemented his numerous and more openly-stated public speeches, the president had managed to convey, with full deniability, his sociopathic wishes with regard to two large but politically insignificant minorities of the nation's population, the non-productive members of society and the Judeo-Christian community. The deniability actually was almost a don't-care, but with the preservation of some outward semblance of decency he would have fewer nuisances to contend with in the attainment of his ultimate objective. The misfits and elderly were simply disgusting, but the 'people of the Book' were as repulsive to him as the Book itself. Emboldened by the public timidity that accompanied his early, more tenuous acts of suppressing the depiction of Jesus Christ at the various venues in which he spoke, he proceeded to accelerate the eradication of Christ in America, all the while claiming his own "Christianity" when pressed by the few members of the press who dared to speak out on the topic. Despite his own rather indifferent protestations to the contrary, his preference for the more violent, self-serving and anti-Christian religion of Islam soon became public knowledge. Through the progressive vindictiveness of his speeches and the less overt companion events he had promulgated he had so marginalized the Christian community in the intellectually and morally indolent public mind that he had no doubt of his present ability to handle 'that situation' with impunity. Throughout government, including the military, the removal of Christ was overtly institutionalized in policy, much to the consternation of those few chaplains who still cared. Having created a number of negative financial situations, he had been spectacularly successful in transferring the blame onto the Jews and Christians. In all these moves he'd had a lot of help. Much of the American populace, having become complacent and apathetic in their enjoyment of America's great wealth, were quite willing to support this agenda. They as well as he didn't particularly want the Judeo-Christian God hovering around telling them what to do.

"I've exercised patience long enough," he told the vassal who stood before him, observing with pleasure the fear in his eyes. He could see the twitching of his mouth and the tremors in his hands, and speculated on how he might cause the hapless man to wet his pants. But that was for another time. The man had an important mission to execute, and now wasn't the time to toy with him. His use of the word 'patience' was a code fully understood by Mr. Anderson as an order to commence immediate action on the issue at hand.

"Yes, sir," Milton responded. "I'll get on it right now." He bowed slightly, backing out toward the door.

The transformation of Mr. Milton Anderson as he addressed the members of the very small, extremely elite group of the country's inner circle of movers and shakers was nothing short of spectacular. He seemed to grow several inches and his voice dropped a full octave as he exercised his authority as the president's proxy. Those whom he addressed accepted this authority without question, being so slavishly dependent on their own self-interest that their complete corruption had taken place in the distant past. For all except one individual with a tiny remnant of conscience, moral considerations were simply not relevant to their conduct.

"Now that the president has been reelected, the opportunity presents itself to pursue a number of programs that he's been patiently waiting to start work on," Milton said to the people seated around the oblong conference table. "Projects that, as you well know, will significantly strengthen our efficiency and productivity while greatly enhancing our economic position. And, at the same time make the world a greener place."

The pontification was entirely unnecessary. Every person there knew precisely what the speaker was getting at, and what his own particular role in the plans amounted to. Now that the time had come to act, however, Fred Jamison was getting cold feet. It showed in his eyes, and, as Milton scanned the assembled faces to ensure that he was being understood, his eyes stopped and locked on Fred. Milton said nothing, simply stared. As he did so, the wisdom of including Fred in his trusted inner circle had ceased to be questionable. He had harbored suspicions before as to whether Fred was suitable for work at this level of government; now he was certain. As he reached this conclusion, Fred became so unnerved by the stare that he felt the need to talk. Unfortunately, what he spoke was the very essence of what was dominating his thoughts, the source of his newfound squeamishness. "Golly," he began in a tentative attempt at ingratiating humor, "maybe we'll be able to accomplish what Hitler tried to do." With a meaningless grin he tried to create a semblance of lighthearted indifference to the task set for him. Then, horrified with what he'd just said, he clasped a trembling hand to his offending mouth.

There was but one way to proceed from here. Milton continued to communicate silently with Fred until the man understood. Dropping his head, Fred rose from his chair and made a silent but awkward exit from the room. Once out of the room he chastised himself for his awful mistake, perfectly aware that it had sealed his doom. He vowed to get his wife safely out of the city before his own end came.

Having settled the issue with Fred, Milton addressed Jake West. "You ready to go, Jake?" he asked in a more jovial tone. Jake, whose area of responsibility focused on the facilities end of things, nodded. "We've been looking into the desert southwest, Milt," he said easily. There's a lot of open space down there, plenty of scorpions and snakes to share the ecosystem with the newbies." The remark drew a few chuckles. "We've also thoroughly vetted the contractors as to our intentions there. Not just at the top, but with the workers, too, at every level. Told our companies to take their time in hiring, we'll pick up the tab for time lost."

Milton next turned his attention to Michael Zweig. "How about you, Mike?" Michael was the garbage man, but he didn't mind at all. In fact, of all the available tasks, he preferred his own. The nature of the garbage gave him a most seductive sense of godhood. Before he could respond, Milton continued. "You're going to need a large area as well as Jake. I can place some crack troops at your disposal, no pun intended." The offer wasn't trivial. The troopers of whom he spoke were part of an elite core of combat-hardened veterans who, to the man, had displayed character traits useful for homeland service. These qualities included an apparent fondness for self, a pronounced lack of nobility, and a proclivity toward sadistic violence. Their promised rewards for faithful obedience didn't include medals for valor, which were irrelevant to them. Instead, they were told that they could look forward to the spoils of war, particularly rape. To whet their appetites in this regard, they regularly were offered pornography of the most base, disgusting and sadistic kind for their viewing pleasure.

"That would help a great deal, and thanks. I'll count on them."

"And you?" Milton asked as he turned to Ace Smith. Ace was responsible for managing the shakers, as they called the destabilization committee. Again, Milt continued before his subject could respond. "As we've talked about before, you'll need coverage for every city over a hundred thousand population, say three to five hundred men for each city."

"I know that, Milt," Ace replied rather testily at the clumsy attempt to micromanage. "They're already in place, just waiting for the green light to stir up the pot. The media has been taken care of too, as well as the scheduling of each phase of the information transfer process." Milt glared at the man as he spoke, pruning back his tendency toward rebellion. When he was satisfied that Ace understood his displeasure, he moved on to consider Will Franklin, the regulatory guru who was responsible for the formulation of executive orders and other bureaucratic processes to legitimize things until the time when it would no longer be necessary to work in the dark. Of all the department heads gathered at the table, Will had been busily productive well before this momentous occasion, having successfully stymied the attempts of the House and Senate, working together, to regain control over the legislative process. Milt merely nodded at the man, who acknowledged with a nod of his own. He turned back to Ace, who was most adept at organization.

"In the absence of a man to permanently replace Fred," he ordered, "you'll be handling his job too, for the time being, dealing with the prioritizing and scheduling of the other, ah, projects, and working out the hitches as they come up." Ace acknowledge with a curt nod. "For planning purposes," Milton continued, "consider the most important of the undertakings to be the elderly, handicapped and Christian. All three of these are worthless. They're just dragging us down. You'll focus first on those in nursing homes and assisted-living facilities. If anyone from the Christian or Jewish communities bothers you in any way, take care of them immediately. We've already marginalized as probable terrorists those who are most likely to protest. Besides, we have agencies to protect you. Your cover story for that will start with the need for consolidation, for purposes of bulk cost savings. Make sure the taxpayers perceive an advantage in going along with this effort. A final note: I want the infrastructure for this to be complete before the end of the next year. Okay. Make it happen. We'll meet again next month to see how you're getting along."

As Ace left the room his usual arrogant demeanor hid a growing concern. Contrary to the impression he gave Milt, there remained some loose ends that needed to be taken care of. The biggest was the situation at the *Seattle Reporter-Journal*, a trendy newsmagazine with a large local readership. Only the mag wasn't trendy. Anything but. Despite his subtle warnings to editor Jim Forrester, a Christian slant still hung around. It was time to end the pussy-footing and start cracking the whip.

Ace wasn't alone with troubling thoughts. Will Franklin's brow maintained a frown as he followed Ace out the door. He had a big problem, and, like Ace, had chosen to conceal that fact to Milton, of whom he was deathly afraid. His big, no, huge problem was the lawsuit that Congress had initiated against the president. It claimed that the flurry of executive orders promulgated by the White House amounted to a usurpation of the Executive Branch over the Legislature. Worse, anyone with a dollop of common sense could see that the lawsuit had the weight of logic going for it. The president was making a blatant end-run around congress to perform nothing less than a change in the form of the United States government from a constitutional republic to a socialist state, over which the president, with the help of the United Nations, would assume dictatorial powers.

This lawsuit problem couldn't be fixed with reason. Only muscle could do the job, which wasn't usually a problem with Will. The big problem was the person to whom the muscle had to be applied: Gerald Robbins, Chief Justice of the Supreme Court.

The thought of who he had to intimidate was scary, but not scary enough. He knew what was going to happen to Fred Jamison. Its inevitability gave him the willies. Worse, he knew that the pain would be unthinkably cruel, violent and prolonged, and he knew he had to do something quick about his own problem before he joined Fred in making an extremely unpleasant exit from this life.

As he watched Ace and Will leave the room, obviously focused on problems engendered by the finality of his call to action, Milt reflected on Fred Jamison's inappropriate commentary on Hitler. *Actually, he wasn't all that far off-base*, Milt noted with a smirk. A number of parallels did indeed exist, all of which emphasized the malleability of the public in the hands of a determined leader. In the face of economic depression throughout Europe, many people in the occupied countries supported Hitler's takeover, believing that their own welfare might improve thereby despite their loss of freedom. *And their religious beliefs. It was almost nothing for Hitler to wicker their faith from Christ to himself and the Nazi Party. It's the same now with the president, particularly with his master stroke of equating Christian fundamentalism with hate in the face of the church's stance on gays.* He laughed to himself on the way the mainstream churches were falling all over themselves to welcome practicing gays into their community, even to the extent of accepting actively gay pastors. With the disintegration of their moral sense, they would be willing to go along with whatever the president wanted to do, just like the Germans were quick to ignore the atrocities being committed in their very own neighborhoods. *Peace and safety. Well, we'll give them peace and safety. Some of them.*

Chapter Five

That Saturday Earl and Joyce pursued their work with Cathy, this time getting hands-on familiarity with the tasks related to her daily life. This intimate participation was exhausting. When they arrived back home they had a dinner of Cheerios and went directly to bed, where they slept so deeply that they had difficulty responding in the morning to the alarm clock. Nevertheless, they had decided the day before that they'd take Cathy to Church with them, a task that required them to arrive quite early at the nursing home and once there to dress Cathy and feed her. Earl groused to Joyce on the way over. "I wonder if we aren't a little old to be taking on a job like this, even for a day or a weekend," he told her.

"Patience, Earl," she replied. "Give it your best today. You'll have all week to recuperate. If you feel the same way by Friday, well maybe we can talk about it then."

But something unexpected happened that Sunday morning. Even through their exhaustion, or perhaps in a large way related to it, they both acquired new feelings toward Cathy that they hadn't realized they were capable of. Had they had a child of their own, they would have appreciated that this was part of the natural process of parent-to-child bonding. It came from the effort involved in caring for another, and represented that special quality of nobility that is associated with a closely-knit family. Neither Earl nor Joyce felt tired as they drove to Church with Cathy.

"We've already learned a great deal about the Book of Revelation," George told his congregation, "and we've only gotten through the first chapter. What have we learned so far? That Jesus is the author, John being the scribe; that Jesus addresses seven Churches in the second and third chapters, which we'll get into today; that these seven Churches represent all the Churches on earth in time and space; that Jesus has assigned seven angels to support these seven Churches; that when Jesus returns to earth He will have a different role and appearance – He came the first time to suffer on our behalf, and will come the second time to rule and judge." He turned on a computer at his podium to illuminate a large screen behind him.

"Now we'll move on past Chapter 1 to Chapters 2 and 3, which, taken together, are the messages to the seven churches. Chapter 2 carries the messages for the first four, and Chapter 3 for the last three. The messages are structured around a common organization that can be presented quite simply and easily remembered in a two-dimensional format." George signaled to the ushers, who went down the aisles distributing copies of a chart. At the same time the screen displayed a Powerpoint graphic, the same chart that consisted of seven columns, one for each Church, and nine rows. A note on the chart stated that the Churches are listed in their historical order throughout the Church Age. The rows were labeled: row 1 was the Church name; row 2 the name that Jesus chose for Himself; row 3 His commendation to the Church; row 4 His concern for that Church; row 5 His exhortation; row 6 His promise to the overcomer; row 7 the closing comment; row 8 the time period, and row 9 the functional identification of the Church.

George let the congregation become familiar with the chart before speaking. After a lengthy pause, he said "Some explanations are necessary. First, the closing comment is the same for all seven Churches. It is 'He that has an ear, listen'. For the first three Churches, the closing is delivered before the promise to the overcomer; the order is reversed from that for the last four Churches. Then, there are two Churches, Sardis and Laodicea, for which there is no commendation; Jesus had nothing good to say to them; there also are two Churches, Smyrna and Philadelphia for which there is no concern; Jesus had nothing bad to say to them. Finally, the Churches are representative in three ways; first, there were indeed these seven Churches in the region of Turkey when John wrote, and together they comprise the characteristics of all the Churches throughout the world and in time; second, each of the seven Churches is representative of one of seven Church ages throughout its history; and third, the message for each Church applies as well to each Christian. With that brief introduction, I'll walk you through the chart.

"The first Church that Jesus spoke to through John is the Church at Ephesus. For this Church, Jesus chose His name to be 'He who holds the seven stars in His right hand and walks in the midst of seven candlesticks.' As we were told in Chapter 1, the candlesticks represent the seven Churches, and the seven stars represent the angels in charge of the Churches. Jesus commended this church for its labors, patience and hatred of evil; His concern for it was that it had lost its first love. To me this indicates that the Ephesian Church had become reactionary in the firmness of her stance against the evils of her day, and in the process had hardened herself against her primary duty: her love of God. Remember, it was to the Ephesian Church that Paul had written much of the material dealing with the role of the Church as the Bride of Christ. To me, Paul's letter to the Ephesians reads like a prenuptial counseling session, and I cherish that association. Jesus reinforces the issue of His troubled heart over the Church's missing love in His exhortation to remember the first works of love and faith and repent. His promise to the overcomer is the Tree of Life in Paradise. The time period of this first Church began with the beginning of the Church Age at Pentecost following Jesus' resurrection and continued through the first to fourth centuries A.D. It is identified as the Apostolic Church.

"The second church is Smyrna. For this Church Jesus chose His name to be 'The First and the Last, which was dead and is alive'. He commended this Church for enduring tribulation and physical poverty and promised that it was spiritually wealthy. He had nothing bad to say about her. Jesus was filled with compassion and love for this Church. Instead of reprimanding her, He exhorted her not to fear suffering and physical death and warned that she will be severely tried for ten days or periods and asked her to be faithful unto death. These ten periods represented a prophecy that was fulfilled with precision. This is where theologian John Foxe enters into the picture. Born in England in 1516 and living until 1587, Foxe was a contemporary of Church greats Martin Luther and John Calvin. His book *Foxe's Book of Martyrs,* a recent translation being entitled *Foxe's Christian Martyrs of the World* is considered by many to be one of the three greatest Christian books outside the Bible itself ever printed, the other two being Calvin's *Institutes of the Christian Religion* and Bunyan's *Pilgrim's Progress.*

"In his book of martyrs, Foxe identifies ten periods of persecution of Christians before the Roman Emporer Constantine made it a state religion, most probably in the year A.D. 313. The first persecution noted by Foxe began in A.D. 64 by Nero and included the beheading of Paul and the crucifixion of Peter; the second was directed by Domitian around A.D. 90 and included John's exile to the island of Patmos; the third occurred in the early second century under Trajan; the fourth under Marcus Aurelius in A.D. 161. Polycarp, bishop of Smyrna, was murdered in this persecution. The fifth persecution took place under Severus in A.D. 200 and was noted for the courage of the young lady Perpetua; the sixth occurred in A.D. 235 under Emporer Maximinus; the seventh came not long after that, in A.D. 249 under Decius; following that the eighth took place in A.D. 257 during the reign of Valerian; the ninth occurred in A.D. 270 under Aurelian, and the tenth in A.D. 303 during the joint reign of Diocletian and Maximian. These ten persecutions shared an interesting trait in common: during them the Church thrived.

"I'd like to dwell a bit on the sixth persecution, since it so vividly describes the kind of hatred that we ourselves are beginning to face. It also strikingly brings out the nobility that Jesus is looking for in His Church, and also the involvement of both women and men in suffering for their Savior. I'll read Foxe's entry for that persecution:

"'This persecution was begun by the emperor Maximinus, who ordered all Christians hunted down and killed. A Roman soldier who refused to wear a laurel crown bestowed on him by the emperor and confessed he was a Christian was scourged, imprisoned, and put to death.

"'Pontianus, Bishop of Rome, was banished to Sardinia for preaching against idolatry and murdered. Anteros, a Grecian who succeeded Pontianus as Bishop of Rome, collected a history of the martyrs and suffered martyrdom himself after only forty days in office.

"'Pammachius, a Roman senator, and forty-two other Christians were all beheaded in one day and their heads set on the city gates. Calepodius, a Christian minister, after being dragged through the streets, was thrown into the Tiber River with a millstone fastened around his neck. Quiritus, a Roman nobleman, and his family and servants, was barbarously tortured and put to death. Martina, a noble young lady, was beheaded, and Hippolitus, a Christian prelate, was tied to a wild horse and dragged through fields until he died.

"'Maximinus was succeeded by Gordian, during whose reign and that of his successor, Philip, the Church was free from persecution for more than six years. But in 249, a violent persecution broke out in Alexandria without the emperor's knowledge.

"'Metrus, an old Christian of Alexandria, refused to worship idols. He was beaten with clubs, pricked with sharp reeds, and Apollonia, an old woman nearly seventy, confessed that she was a Christian, and the mob fastened her to a stake, preparing to burn her. She begged to be let loose and the mob untied her, thinking she was ready to recant, but to their astonishment, she immediately threw herself back into the flames and died.'

"Returning to the Book of Revelation after this rather lengthy side trip and continuing with the Church at Smyrna, Jesus promised the overcomer the Crown of Life and immunity from the second death. In the face of the member's likelihood of meeting with physical death, it promises spiritual life. Like the Church at Ephesus, the Church at Smyrna represented the time period between the first through the fourth centuries. Her identification, of course, is 'The persecuted Church'.

"The next Church is Pergamos. The name for Himself that Jesus associated with this Church is 'He who has the sharp sword with two edges'. His commendation for her was to hold fast in the midst of evil, not denying the name of Jesus. He noted His concern for her promiscuity and heresies, probably for tolerating Gnosticism and Arianism. Jesus also noted His hatred of the doctrines of the Nicolaitans, which involved fornication and idolatry. Some theologians also speculate that the Nicolaitans attempted to insert mediators between Christian laypeople and Christ, a practice that Scripture makes plain is unnecessary but which was adopted by the Roman Catholic Church. Jesus exhorted this Church to repent of her errors, and promised the overcomer hidden manna and a white stone with his name inscribed, which only the overcomer shall know. Like the Churches at Ephesus and Smyrna, the Church at Pergamos represented the first through fourth centuries. Its identification was the heretical church.

"The fourth Church is Thyratira, for which Jesus gave Himself the name 'Son of God who has eyes like fire and feet like brass'. He commended this Church for her charity, service, faith and patience, but He was also concerned over her promiscuity, worldliness including fornication and false teaching, and politicization. In His exhortation, Jesus warned her that He will punish the false Christians within her, but added that He will put no other burden on those who remained faithful. He promised the overcomer power over the nations and the gift of the morning star. This Church represented the period from the fifth through the ninth centuries, which was identified as the post-Constantine politically-accepted era of the Church.

"We have now covered the Churches addressed in Revelation Chapter 2, and I'm sure that your minds are ready for a breather. We'll tackle Revelation Chapter 3 next week."

As Bob Smith walked down the steps of the Church with his wife Evelyn on his arm, his boss James Forrester at the *Seattle Reporter-Journal* was at home picking up his phone. "Hello, Jim," Ace said.

Cathy 51

"Can we talk?"

"Yeah, sure, Jim replied, looking about the room and down the hallway to ensure that he was alone. "What's up?" he asked as he went over to the door and closed it.

"I've warned you before about the content and flavor of your articles. The Christianity has to go, no negotiating. And start getting busy on getting the word out on the problem of the elderly in America, how they're dragging down the economy." He emphasized his intractability with a hard glare. "Get with the program, Jim, or your ass is on the line. And I'm not talking about your job. I'm talking about your health, understand?"

"I hear you five-by-five, Ace," Jim said. He noticed that his hand was shaking when he put down the phone.

Earl and Joyce headed back to the nursing home after Church to drop off Cathy and allow Earl to prepare his evening talk at home without interruption. Their eyes met as he glanced in the rearview mirror to observe how she was doing. She had a look of pure joy and trust that melted his heart. Seeing that, he moved over to the curb and parked. "Call the nursing home," he told Joyce. "Ask Laurie if we can wait till evening to bring Cathy back." He heard a joyful sound from the back seat as Joyce called Laurie.

"She gave her okay," Joyce told Earl. Another whoop came from the back seat as Cathy twisted in happiness.

That evening Earl continued to read from the Book of Acts. "We've covered how the Holy Spirit came like a mighty wind upon those who were waiting on God as Jesus had instructed them," he told the assembled people. Their lives were changed forever and they would be known by those who came later as the first Christians. Peter was instantly changed into a powerful preacher and also a healer. We know from Acts Chapter 2 that he saved three thousand souls with the Word of God; we also know from Acts Chapter 3 that he healed a man who was lame from birth. We'll go tonight to Acts Chapter 4, where we find Peter preaching to another large crowd.

And as they spoke unto the people, the priests, and the captain

> *of the temple, and the Sadducees, came upon them, being grieved that they taught the people, and preached through Jesus the resurrection of the dead.*

"In other words," Earl said, "the officials of the Jewish faith came down upon Peter and others as they preached. They preached the hope of the resurrection of the dead in Christ, using Jesus as an example. But the religious officials didn't like that one bit, especially the Sadducees, who didn't believe in the resurrection. I'll continue in the Scripture:

> *And they laid hands on them, and put them in hold unto the next day; for it was now eventide. But many of them who heard the word believed; and the number of the men was about five thousand.*

"Translating that into modern language, the religious officials arrested them and tossed them into the slammer. Despite all that, a huge crowd, including five thousand men, were saved by the Word of God.

"Here we come to a most interesting fact that I'll draw out with a question: how effective were these religious officials in stopping the spread of the Gospel?" Seeing no answers, Earl continued. "The answer is that these people who went about trying to stop the preaching actually helped to spread the Gospel throughout the world. The persecutions became so bad that many Christians fled from the slaughter, and they spoke the Gospel to others wherever they went, spreading the Word abroad. Those who refused to flee, on the other hand, became mighty in their faith.

"So here's a pattern, first revealed by that first Church: the Christian Church always does well in the midst of persecution. On the other hand, when life is comfortable for Christians, the Church doesn't do so well. That's the way it's been throughout the history of the Church, going on two thousand years now. The movement of God and the persecution of God's people go hand-in-hand, but it's something that God uses to His advantage. He wins two ways: first, in tribulations false Christians are quickly weeded out; second, those times toughen the true Christians and work to take their selfishness away, endowing them with nobility. That is what it means to go through a refining process. In refining silver, for example, when the metal is heated the impurities separate out. The same thing happens to us: when the heat comes, what's left of us is purified. But we aren't left alone in the process. We have the very great help of the indwelling Holy Spirit to get us through the rough spots." A strong memory of how the Holy Spirit gave him the peace to jump off the cliff with Buddy came flooding in. On the heels of that image came a second, sharper one, that of the Holy Spirit getting him out of a tight spot with Buddy in the air. The image shifted to the incident where Buddy's jaw scooped up a cow pie on their landing. He chuckled and winked at Cathy.

"At the point in the history of the Church that we are reading about," Earl continued, "the hand of God is strong on His people, and persecution is rampant. We read about that very thing next as we continue in Chapter 4.

> *And it came to pass, on the morrow, that their rulers, and elders, and scribes, and Annas, the high priest, and Caiphas, and John, and Alexander, and as many as were of the kindred of the high priest, were gathered together at Jerusalem. And when they had set [Peter and the others] in the midst, they asked, By what power, or by what name, have ye done this? Then Peter, filled with the Holy Spirit, said unto them, Ye rulers of the people, and elders of Israel, if we this day be examined of the good deed done to the crippled man, by what means he is made well; be it known unto you all, and to all the people of Israel, that by the name of Jesus Christ of Nazareth, whom ye crucified, whom God raised from the dead, even by him doth this man stand before you [as a well man]. This is the stone which was [rejected] of you builders, which is become the head of the corner. Neither is there salvation in any other; for there is no other name under heaven given among men, whereby we must be saved.*

"After being harassed for a while, they were freed, as the religious leaders, jealous as they were for having people of such strength outside their tight circle of control, really had nothing they could say against Peter and the rest for the healing of the lame man. If they had continued to hold them at that point, they would have faced an angry crowd. Continuing in the Scripture narrative,

> *So when they had further threatened them, they let them go, finding nothing how they might punish them, because of the people; for all men glorified God for that which was done. For the man was above forty years old, on whom this miracle of healing was shown.*
>
> *And being let go, they went to their own company, and reported all that the chief priests and elders had said unto them. And when [the other Christians] heard that, they lifted up their voice to God with one accord, and said, Lord, thou art God, who hast made heaven, and earth, and the sea, and all that in them is; who, by the mouth of thy servant, David, hast said, Why did the heathens rage, and the peoples imagine vain things? The kings of the earth stood up, and the rulers were gathered together against the Lord, and against his Christ. For of a truth against thy holy child, Jesus, whom thou hast anointed, both Herod, and Pontius Pilate, with the heathen, and the people of Israel were gathered together, to do whatever thy hand and thy counsel determined before to be done. And now, Lord, behold their threatenings; and grant unto thy servants, that with all boldness they may speak thy word, by stretching forth thine hand to heal; and that signs and wonders may be done by the name of thy holy child, Jesus. And when they had prayed, the place was shaken where they were assembled together; and they were all filled with the Holy Spirit, and they spoke the word of God with boldness.*

"I'll end my talk tonight with this thought: in their prayers, these early Christians spoke about something that David had said a thousand years before. David had asked why the heathens rage, and the peoples imagine vain things. The Christians were speaking about David's Second Psalm, which applies just as much to our own generation as it did to them. Psalm 2 says:

Why do the heathen rage, and the peoples imagine a vain thing? The kings of the earth set themselves, and the rulers take counsel together, against the Lord, and against his anointed, saying, Let us break their bands asunder, and cast away their cords from us. He who sitteth in the heavens shall laugh; the Lord shall have them in derision. Then shall he speak unto them in his wrath, and vex them in his great displeasure. Yet have I set my king upon my holy hill of Zion. I will declare the decree: The Lord hath said unto me, Thou art my Son; this day have I begotten thee. Ask of me, and I shall give thee the heathen for thine inheritance, and the uttermost parts of the earth for thy possession. Thou shalt break them with a rod of iron; thou shalt dash them in pieces like a potter's vessel. Be wise now, therefore, O ye kings; be instructed, ye judges of the earth. Serve the Lord with fear, and rejoice with trembling. Kiss the Son, lest he be angry, and ye perish from the way, when his wrath is kindled but a little. Blessed are all they who put their trust in him.

"Hmmm. A thousand years before Jesus came in the flesh, David was speaking of Him. That was just one of many Psalms that David wrote about Jesus. But this Psalm is particularly important for the times that we are in now, where the Church is coming into persecution again around the world. We'll bid you goodnight with that thought. Next week we'll continue in the book of Acts, and we're going to read about some amazing things. See you then." He gave Cathy a hug before going over to Joyce. "Thanks, Cathy, for gracing our day. I hope there'll be many more like it." She responded with a squeal.

Chapter Six

With a smirk on his face, James Forrester thrust his way self-importantly into Bob Smith's office and positioned himself on the edge of his desk. He looked down aggressively at the face of his subordinate. The smile remained but it wasn't friendly. "Come into my office, Bob," he announced. "There's something I want to go over with you." Warily, Bob rose from his chair and followed James. They'd worked together for over eleven years but weren't close. In fact, their personalities clashed. While James was an easy-going gladhander who was gifted in interpersonal relationships, his people skills curdled when it came to interfacing with Bob. Unlike James, Bob was an earnest sort who rarely smiled. Rumor had it that he was a Christian, which explained everything to James. Bob, in fact, would have been kicked out the door long ago if he hadn't been so good at his job on the staff of the *Seattle Reporter-Journal*, a newsmagazine with a West-Coast flavor that increasingly catered to the liberal mindset. Bob implemented the editorial policy initiated by James, and frequently became irritated over the necessity of carrying out orders from James that went against the grain of his convictions.

The situation came to a head this morning in James' office. Pastor

Cathy

George's sermon on the martyrdom of Christians had firmed up his backbone, and now that the expected confrontation had arrived he was prepared to deal with it as his conscience required. "Sorry, James," he told his boss in response to the latest policy directive, "no can do. I will not be a part of a deliberate plan to demonize the elderly."

"Are you quite certain that you wish to disobey me?" James asked him, his voice ominously quiet. "Your job might depend on it."

"No it won't. Not this time. Your last several policy directives amount to propaganda of the most blatant, disgusting sort. What's more, they beg the lie. Our poor writers are getting disgruntled and I haven't lifted a finger to stop their complaining. In fact, I've let them know where these directives came from. If I go, you'll be left without a staff."

"Okay," James said in a voice that was softer yet. "We'll treat this conversation as if it never happened. Now I'd like to leave you with this thought to ponder deeply on: maybe you'd best watch your back."

Bob watched him depart, relieved and elated with this minor victory. *That was too easy*, he thought. *No, James, my soul belongs to God and there is nothing you can do about that.*

Chapter Seven

Earl and Joyce began to settle into a routine with Cathy. They picked her up on Saturday, telling the staff to expect her back with them Sunday evening at the Bible study.

Their next weekend with Cathy was joyful. Joyce was developing senses she didn't know she possessed to communicate with the girl, and she put them to use before they left the nursing home with her. At the nursing home Joyce dressed Cathy and they shared a leisurely breakfast with Earl in the dining room. With voice and an ear for Cathy's movements Joyce made certain that she knew where they wanted to take her and that it was something that she herself wanted to do. The result of this exchange was an enthusiastic assent. Her desire to go to their home was obvious to Laurie and Earl as well.

Instead of heading straight for their home, Earl drove them to the zoo. Cathy had never been to a zoo, and was entranced with the strange animals and their behavior. She laughed at the chimpanzees and was awed by the large cats. After they'd seen the elk, giraffes and other grazing animals they parked themselves on a little lawn surrounded by trees and shared the picnic lunch that Joyce had packed in the morning. There was still much to see afterward, and Cathy made the most of it. At her insistence they went twice around the windows in the reptile house, interrupted by the hot-dog stand where she devoured one. She obviously had never seen a snake before and was entranced by their colorful designs and amazed at their ability to move without limbs. It was with great reluctance that they finally left the zoo, but the emotional stimulation had left Cathy so tired that she fell asleep immediately after they had placed her into the car.

Cathy awoke, turned her head to see that they had arrived at Earl and Joyce's house and let out a screech of delight as Earl parked the car in the driveway and another as he brought her into the house with Joyce following. He set a fire in the fireplace while Joyce made them cups of hot cocoa. After their companionable drink he turned on the television and set the channel for cartoons. He and Joyce sat together in their double recliner and simply watched Cathy's happy expression. Cathy soon lost interest in the cartoon she was watching. She had been drowsy when they woke her up to go back into the house, and she fell asleep again when they tucked her into a cozy little bed in the guest room after Joyce had helped her with her bathroom needs. She remained asleep while Earl and Joyce had a light supper. Apparently the lunch, hot dog and ice cream were sufficient for her.

They took Cathy to Church with them on Sunday morning. With her extra-long sleep the night before, she remained attentive throughout the sermon, although the topic was somewhat on the adult side. Apparently the past week the Church building was broken into and the sound equipment was stolen. The thieves had thanked the Church for their acquisition by spraying graffiti on two walls. The pastor dealt with the situation generously, interrupting his series of sermons on the Book of Revelation to address this unexpected development.

"Here in the United States," he began, "our expectations of normal, even rather mundane lives, are high. We've been blessed by many years of relative prosperity. Oh, we hear about thefts, and vandalisms, even murders, on the news regularly. But we tend to see these things as aberrations, things that don't happen to you and me.

We just don't expect that such things can happen to us. But we live in an increasingly violent world, even here in the States. It's sad to say, but we can no longer live with the expectation that we won't be caught up in the turmoil. I'm not really surprised at what happened to the Church building this week. In fact, I've been expecting it for some time, although I've kept it to myself. Why am I not surprised? Perhaps I'm wrong, but I see us entering that time spoken of by Daniel and the Apostles Peter and Paul and Jesus Himself. That's precisely why I had decided to share the Book of Revelation with you. Listen to what Paul said in Second Timothy Chapter 3 about the nature of people as this age draws to a close, and ask yourself whether it doesn't seem distressingly familiar." He opened his Bible and started to read as Earl jotted down the reference.

This know also, that in the last days perilous times shall come. For men shall be lovers of their own selves, covetous, boasters, proud, blasphemers, disobedient to parents, unthankful, unholy, without natural affection, trucebreakers, false accusers, incontinent, fierce, despisers of those that are good, traitors, heady, high-minded, lovers of pleasures more than lovers of God, having a form of godliness, but denying the power of it; from such turn away. For of this sort are they who creep into houses, and lead captive silly women laden with sins, led away with diverse lusts, ever learning, and never able to come to the knowledge of the truth. Now as Jannes and Jambres withstood Moses, so do these also resist the truth, men of corrupt minds, reprobate concerning the faith.

"What bothers me the most," Pastor George continued, "is that the rejection of God and the evil that goes with it begins with selfishness. The upcoming generation, those who will eventually be running the world, seem to be infected with self-absorption to such a degree that selfless nobility, what the Bible fosters and what Jesus presented to us in Himself, is an alien concept. I'll go next to Romans 1, where Paul pinpoints the cause of the rejection of Jesus as plain selfishness:

For the wrath of God is revealed from heaven against all ungodliness and unrighteousness of men, who hold the truth in unrighteousness, because that which may be known of God is manifest in them; for God hath shown it unto them. For the invisible things of him from the creation of the world are clearly seen, being understood by the things that are made, even his eternal power and Godhead, so that they are without excuse; because, when they knew God, they glorified him not as God, neither were thankful, but became vain in their imaginations, and their foolish heart was darkened. Professing themselves to be wise, they became fools, and changed the glory of the incorruptible God into an image made like corruptible man, and birds, and four-footed beasts, and creeping things. Wherefore, God also gave them up to uncleanness through the lusts of their own hearts, to dishonor their own bodies between themselves, who exchanged the truth of God for a lie, and worshiped and served the creature more than the Creator, who is blessed forever. Amen.

For this cause God gave them up unto vile affections; for even their women did exchange the natural use for that which is against nature; and likewise also the men, leaving the natural use of the woman, burned in their lust one toward another, men with men working that which is unseemly, and receiving in themselves that recompense of their error which was fitting. And even as they did not like to retain God in their knowledge, God gave them over to a reprobate mind, to do those things which are not seemly, being filled with all unrighteousness, fornication, wickedness, covetousness, maliciousness; full of envy, murder, strife, deceit, malignity; whisperers, backbiters, haters of God, insolent, proud, boasters, inventors of evil things, disobedient to parents; without understanding, covenant breakers, without natural affection, implacable, unmerciful; who, knowing the judgment of God, that they who commit such things are worthy of death, not only do the same but have pleasure in them that do them.

"Wow," Joyce whispered in Earl's ear as George paused to take a sip of water, "there's that same list again. Paul seems to be saying that people of that sort don't believe in God for the reason that they simply don't want to believe in God. They want to be able to do their own thing. If doing their own thing cuts in on someone else's happiness, it's a don't-care."

"Yeah," he whispered back. "You see them all around us. I'm particularly concerned about our young folk. They are supposed to be our future. But I'm afraid that with them at the helm, our future is going to be bleak indeed. And with that mentality, it doesn't seem a reach at all to think of them wanting to rid themselves of expensive inconveniences like Cathy." He looked up to George, who was waiting for their whispering to stop. "Sorry," he mouthed.

"Peter, in Chapter 3 of his second letter," George continued with a smiling nod to Earl, "made the same kind of assessment as Paul of what people would be like as the end of the age approached." He turned to 2 Peter 3:8 as Earl scribbled down this latest reference.

This second epistle, beloved, I now write unto you, in both of which I stir up your pure minds by way of remembrance, that ye may be mindful of the words which were spoken before by the holy prophets, and of the commandment of us, the apostles of the Lord and Savior; knowing this first, that there shall come in the last days scoffers, walking after their own lusts, and saying, Where is the promise of his coming? For since the fathers fell asleep, all things continue as they were from the beginning of the creation. For this they willingly are ignorant of, that by the word of God the heavens were of old, and the earth standing out of the water and in the water, by which the world that then was, being overflowed with water, perished. But the heavens and the earth which are now, by the same word are kept in store, reserved unto fire against the day of judgment and perdition of ungodly men. But, beloved, be not ignorant of this one thing, that one day is with the Lord as a thousand years, and a thousand years as one day. The Lord is not slack concerning his promise, as some men count slackness, but is longsuffering toward us, not willing that any should perish, but that all should come to repentance.

"I've certainly seen my share of scoffers," Pastor groused. "I can't understand why they're so dedicated to the belief that God doesn't really exist. Well, yes I can. Selfishness, as I said before. But I guess evolution is another big reason. I even wonder if evolution is the great deception that God has given the human race. In Second Thessalonians Chapter 2, Paul spoke of a strong delusion:

> *And now ye know what restraineth, that he might be revealed in his time. For the mystery of iniquity doth already work; only he who now hindreth will continue to hinder until he be taken out of the way. And then shall that wicked one be revealed, whom the Lord shall consume with the spirit of his mouth, and shall destroy with the brightness of his coming, even him whose coming is after the working of Satan with all power and signs and lying wonders, and with all deceivableness of unrighteousness in them that perish, because they received not the love of the truth, that they might be saved. And for this cause God shall send them strong delusion, that they should believe the lie, that they all might be judged who believed not the truth, but had pleasure in unrighteousness.*

"In another reference, Paul seems to associate deception with falsehood commonly passed off as science. I'm turning to First Timothy 6:

> *O Timothy, keep that which is committed to thy trust, avoiding profane and vain babblings, and oppositions of science falsely so called, which some, professing, have erred concerning the faith. Grace be with thee. Amen.*

"That sure sounds like the frantic way some supposedly very respectable organizations are attempting to peddle the theory of evolution," George said. "I'm sure glad that brother Bob—or was it God through him?—led me to read some of the books written by cutting-edge biologists," pastor said, referring to deacon Bob Smith. "They leave us with no doubt about the amazing things they're just beginning to find that totally refute the Darwinian notion. God willing, some time in the not-too-distant future I'll be sharing with you what I've found out so far about how the theory of evolution has fared in the face of some of the latest – and spectacular – discoveries in the field of molecular biology. But don't let my backlog of sermon topics slow you down. If you want to jump the gun and find out for yourselves what I've been learning I'd welcome the company. No, I'd truly appreciate it. Let me refer you to a few of the works that have been real eye-openers. If you read just one or two of them, you'll be well-equipped to refute that pseudoscience that is falsely called science. You'll be far more advanced in your insight into the lie that evolution represents than those shallow thinkers who inhabit the desks of Time and Newsweek magazines and National Geographic as well."

"If you're ready to jot down this information, one book is called *The Edge of Evolution*, written by Michael Behe. He was the same scientist who wrote *Darwin's Black Box* and formulated the concept of irreducible complexity. Another two are William Dembski's *Intelligent Design* and Stephen Meyer's *Signature in the Cell*. And, of course, there are the several works of Phillip Johnson. While these are intended to bring the harsh light of reason and logic to bear on the arguments of the evolutionists, they're very readable and often humorous. As a matter of fact, the priority of what they have to say is high enough within the category of necessary Christian education that blowing the whistle on evolution has become a hot-button issue with me.

"I'll close with this caution: having heard these things, don't go home and break out the guns and ammo." This comment evoked laughter from the congregation. "What you must keep in mind, and perhaps this is the most difficult thing for Christians to do, is that as Christians you are not to hate. Instead, you are to love your enemies. Your job is not to pull a Bronson and try to clean the world of the criminal element. Your job is to show the light of Christ to a fallen world. That's something that will take far more guts than brandishing a weapon, but it's also something that God holds dear in those who can master it. We'll learn more about that in the coming weeks. Join me now, please, in hymn 174, 'Rise up, O Men of God'."

"It's good to have a pastor who is committed enough to the inerrancy of the Bible to take the time to study microbiology," Joyce commented to Earl as they left the Church. "I may want to look up a book or two and read it myself. As a matter of fact, why don't we invite Bob and Evelyn Smith over sometime and let him give us a rundown on what he's found out about evolution?" She looked down at Cathy as Earl wheeled her toward their car. "I just saw a show on National Geographic that made it sound like evolution was an established fact. I'll bet I can teach you why you shouldn't believe in such junk, Cathy. I wonder why people nowadays are so bent on treating God as either non-existent or unnecessary?"

"As George said, it's nothing more or less than basic selfishness," Earl spoke up. "People just don't want any outside interference in the way they want to run their lives. And that's what makes the problem worse. Once they decide that they are the masters of their own fate, the notion of a God becomes linked with an alien presence. They completely throw out the thought that God was their Creator in the first place." He thought for a second, and looked at Joyce. "That wouldn't be a bad idea – to have the Smiths over, I mean. We seem to have something in common with them. I'd like to get to know him better."

Joyce made lunch for them when they reached home. Afterwards, she brought Cathy into the den and read to her out of a Dr. Seuss book she'd gotten while shopping the past Wednesday. The gurgles of delight coming from her mouth were infectious, causing Joyce to giggle along as she read. In the meantime, Earl went into the study to prepare for his talk.

"Last week we saw the power of the Holy Spirit in the lives of Peter and John," Earl spoke to the assembled residents that evening. "We also saw in a small way that with the power of God comes persecution. The persecution gets much worse, but at the same time the Church is growing by leaps and bounds. Tonight I'll start at verse 12 of Acts Chapter 5:

And by the hands of the apostles were many signs and wonders wrought among the people (and they were all with one accord in Solomon's porch. And of the rest dared no man to join himself to them; but the people magnified them. And believers were the more added to the Lord, multitudes both of men and women), insomuch that they brought forth the sick into the streets, and laid them on beds and couches, that at the least the shadow of Peter passing by might overshadow some of them. There came also a multitude out of the cities round about unto Jerusalem, bringing sick folks, and them who were vexed with unclean spirits; and they were healed every one.

"Here we see the great power of God being manifest in the Apostles," Earl interrupted the narrative. "But with it came – guess what.

Then the high priest rose up, and all they that were with him (which is the sect of the Sadducees), and were filled with indignation, and laid their hands on the apostles, and put them in the common prison. But an angel of the Lord by night opened the prison doors, and brought them forth, and said, Go, stand and speak in the temple all the words of this life. And when they heard, that, they entered into the temple early in the morning, and taught. But the high priest came, and they that were with him, and called the council together, and all the senate of the children of Israel, and sent to the prison to have them brought.

Earl interrupted the narrative again. "These religious leaders were very angry with the Apostles for the power of God in them. The leaders thought that this power should belong only to themselves because they were, after all, the leaders. Who was God to take away their position?" Earl made a face and several in the audience giggled. "So they tossed the Apostles into jail. But God, being stronger than any prison, released them through an angel and they continued to teach. When the religious leaders heard about this, they were confused. They knew that the Apostles were in jail, and yet they heard otherwise from some who'd seen them. Not believing in the power of God, they rejected the reports that the Apostles were out and about and ordered the guards to fetch the prisoners from their cell. I'll continue from here:"

> *But when the officers came, and found them not in the prison, they returned, and told, saying, The prison truly found we shut with all safety, and the keepers standing outside before the doors; but when we had opened, we found no man within. Now when the high priest and the captain of the temple and the chief priests heard these things, they were concerned about them, how this would grow. Then came one and told them, saying, Behold, the men whom ye put in prison are standing in the temple, and teaching the people.*

"In other words," Earl said, putting the Bible down momentarily and scratching his head theatrically, "they didn't know what to make of this odd event. But even then, with this open proof of the power of God, they refused to repent. Instead, they tried to figure out how to cover this incident up, lest more people come to salvation in Jesus. You see, the religious leaders didn't care about the souls of the people they were supposed to serve. They were only thinking of maintaining their own positions. And they refused to consider the possibility that God just might be in charge of everything. Selfish. Extremely." Earl shook his head in disgust. "To continue:

> *Then went the captain with the officers, and brought them without violence; for they feared the people, lest they should have been stoned. And when they had brought them, they set them before the council; and the high priest asked them, saying, Did not we strictly command you that ye should not teach in this name? And, behold, ye have filled Jerusalem with your doctrine, and intend to bring this man's blood upon us. Then Peter and the other apostles answered, and said, We ought to obey God rather than men. The God of our fathers raised up Jesus, whom ye slew and hanged on a tree. Him hath God exalted with his right hand to be a Prince and a Savior, to give repentance to Israel, and forgiveness of sins. And we are his witnesses of these things; and so is also the Holy Spirit, whom God hath given to them that obey him. When they heard that, they were cut to the heart and took counsel to slay them.*

"Here the Apostles are saying that they intend to obey God whatever it takes, even if it means that they must disobey their religious leaders. Faced with the loss of their authority over the people, the leaders discussed among themselves how they might murder the Apostles. Their selfishness was so bad that they'd rather murder than let God take over. But one of them, a brilliant rabbi named Gamaliel, cautioned them about their plans to harm the Apostles, saying that if God really does exist, they would do themselves more harm than the Apostles would get from them. So the leaders beat up the Apostles and told them not to preach any more about Jesus. Nevertheless, the name of Jesus was spoken in a good many households. I'll leave these adventures of the Apostles for now and resume next week with the testimony of Stephen." As before, he hugged Cathy as he and Joyce prepared to leave the room. "We had a wonderful weekend with you," he told the girl. And we'll come back for you next weekend."

"Maybe you should have been an actor, Earl," Joyce told him on the way home. "You can make a pretty funny face."

He laughed. "As long as they enjoy it, Joyce." He started to put his arm around her shoulder but remembered that he didn't have one. She had to struggle to do it, but she made up for it by putting an arm around his shoulder.

There was a message on the phone when they arrived back home. It was Janet, who asked Joyce to call her back as soon as she was able.

"What's up, mom?" Joyce asked.

"Absolutely nothing, dear," she replied. "I got my Social Security check today. Now they've withheld a tax from it that I knew nothing about. What gets me is the size of it. It's comparable to the value of the benefit itself. Now I'm not sure that I'll be able to make ends meet. Oh, I shouldn't have said that. Under no circumstances will I accept anything from you, let's make that plain. I was thinking of selling my home anyway. I won't need it when I marry Henry, who, by the way, also received a very reduced Social Security check. We were going to go on a honeymoon cruise, but that's out of the picture now."

"Oh, mom," Joyce said in shared disappointment. "I'm so sorry. How can the government act so unilaterally? After all, you did earn it. They took it out of your paycheck for years."

"I guess that the government can do anything it pleases. If a gorilla can do anything it wants to, King Kong has *carte blanche*."

"Well, you and Henry are going to go on your cruise. You can't stop me from buying tickets. If you don't use them, the money will just be wasted."

"Thank you, dear. But only if you promise that that will be the end of it."

"Deal." *For now,* she added to herself.

Chapter Eight

Jake looked out on the vast expanse of virtually uninhabited Arizona land situated thirty miles south of Willcox. The tiny community of Pearce was located a few miles to the west, but it was of no significance. More than a decade ago a local developer had great hopes of helping to offload the congestion of Tucson and Phoenix and had even created a golf course as an incentive to buyers. The valley in which he stood actually was quite beautiful, being enclosed to the west by the Dragoon Mountains that contained the spectacular, historically interesting Cochise Stronghold and to the east by the equally historic Chiricahua Mountains with their strange and rare rock formations. At an elevation of over four thousand feet, the valley was somewhat cooler than the two great Arizona cities to the west, and the snakes and scorpions were hidden by grassland.

Jake saw none of that, except that this planned "community" would be hidden by distance from the main roads connecting Douglas and Bisbee to the South with Willcox to the north and Sierra Vista to the west. What he did see was a land that, with the liberal application of barbed wire, could enclose a very large transient population out of the sight and minds of the rest of America. Transient because it would be temporary quarters for people with a more permanent destiny elsewhere. There was room enough here, in fact, for the co-location of that "elsewhere", which meant that the transportation issues would be minimal and support a very green solution to the entire endeavor.

The north-south road passing through the town of Pearce was of little concern. Once the construction roughnecks invaded the town, the very few people who insisted upon continuing to live in this godforsaken place after the "border situation" continued to heat up would move out soon enough. He chuckled at the thought of how the illegals-and-drugs traffic had done such a fine job of getting rid of the natives. *What a master stroke that was!* he thought to himself. With that little depopulation bomb having done such a good job, they hardly needed the cover of another prison community to explain the presence of what they really had in mind.

He extracted his phone from a jacket pocket and called a well-used number. When the connection was established, he greeted his friend and associate. "Come on out, Michael," he said. I'm looking at an ideal place for both of our projects." When they had firmed up the details, he rang off. Extracting a handkerchief from another pocket, he wiped his dripping forehead. It was extremely hot here, but that wasn't going to be his problem for long. In three steps he'd be in the luxury SUV with the air conditioning on high. In half an hour, he'd be poolside with a double scotch in his hand.

"After last week's unexpected interruption," Pastor George said to his congregation, "we'll return to the Book of Revelation, where we'll delve into the final three Churches of the seven that Jesus addressed to John. The fifth Church, then, is Sardis, for which Jesus had this to say:

> *And unto the angel of the Church in Sardis write: These things saith he that hath the seven spirits of God, and the seven stars. I know thy works, that thou hast a name that thou livest, and art dead. Be watchful, and strengthen the things which remain, that are ready to die; for I have not found thy works perfect before God. Remember, therefore, how thou hast received and heard, and hold fast, and repent. If, therefore,*

thou shalt not watch, I will come on thee as a thief, and thou shalt not know what hour I will come upon thee. Thou hast a few names even in Sardis that have not defiled their garments, and they shall walk with me in white; for they are worthy. He that overcometh, the same shall be clothed in white raiment; and I will not blot his name out of the book of life, but I will confess his name before my Father, and before his angels. He that hath an ear, let him hear what the Spirit saith unto the churches.

George let the congregation chew on these words of Jesus to the Church in Sardis as he turned on the overhead projector and displayed the chart of the churches that he had used during his sermon on Revelation Chapter 2. He pointed to the "commendation" block for Sardis. "What do you see there?" he asked his congregation. "I don't see anything but a fat "X" in that block," he said, answering his own question. "That's right – nothing. Jesus had nothing good to say about the Church. We'll find out presently that Sardis was one of just two of the seven Churches to have that distinction. Jesus called them 'dead'. His concern was," George said, pointing to the "concern" block, "that although they claim to be alive, they are dying and dead from their corruption. In the grand scheme of things regarding the sequential period when that Church existed, it is known as the medieval Church. As such, it represented exactly what Jesus said it did. It was this Church that was given over to idols, the collection of vast material wealth, the denial of Scripture to the common folk, the sale and purchase of Church positions – all the way up to the Pope himself, and a multitude of other felonious acts. I could give a month's worth of sermons on how this Church so thoroughly misrepresented Christianity, but now we have to move on. By the way, if you're thinking of condemning Catholicism because of this Church's sins, don't, at least not yet. There are some good things about the present Catholic Church that many Protestant Churches lack; at the same time, a distressingly large number of modern Protestant Churches have fallen into similar errors. We'll get back to the end time Roman Church—nominally Catholic, but probably integrated with 'mainstream' Protestant Churches, and some non-Christian religions—when we come to Revelation 17. Hold your judgments until then. But notice another trait of Sardis —bad as Jesus labeled it, He noted that even this Church had a few good Christians. I expect that this is the case with any number of fallen Churches—they'll still have some committed Christians.

"The sixth church on Jesus' list in the Church in Philadelphia. Notice," he said, pointing to the 'Philadelphia' column on the chart, that this Church is the opposite from the previous one. Here there's only a commendation from Jesus, but no concern, just like the only other Church with that quality, Smyrna. Here, I'll read the Scriptural text regarding Philadelphia:

> *And to the angel of the Church in Philadelphia, write: These things saith he that is holy, he that is true, he that hath the key of David, he that openeth, and no man shutteth; and shutteth, and no man openeth. I know thy works; behold, I have set before thee an open door, and no man can shut it; for thou hast a little strength, and hast kept my word, and hast not denied my name. Behold, I will make them of the synagogue of Satan, who say they are Jews, and are not, but do lie; behold, I will make them to come and worship before thy feet, and to know that I have loved thee. Because thou hast kept the word of my patience, I also will keep thee from the hour of temptation, which will come upon all the world, to try them that dwell upon the earth. Behold, I come quickly; hold that fast that thou hast, that no man take thy crown. Him that overcometh will I make a pillar in the temple of my God, and he shall go no more out; and I will write upon him the name of my God, and the name of the city of my God, the new Jerusalem, which cometh down out of heaven from my God; and I will write upon him my new name. He that hath an ear, let him hear what the Spirit saith unto the churches.*

"What a beautiful report!" exclaimed George. "Notice that Jesus vowed His love toward this Church. Notice also that they will be shielded from the dreadful Tribulation that Daniel spoke of and that will be fleshed out in this book very shortly. Insofar as the sequence of Churches is concerned, this Church was the missionary Church comprised of the 'mainstream' churches up to the beginning of the twentieth century, whose representatives went out through the world proclaiming our beloved Gospel in obedience to His commandment. During that time, the lack of technology had prevented warfare from being the global affairs that they now are, so that Church did indeed escape the horrors and massive slaughters of the twentieth and twenty-first centuries. However, if Jesus is referring to the Great Tribulation as the time of temptation that will come over the world, perhaps He is saying that the Missionary Church, which blossomed so close to our own time, will not exist at the end. This confuses me to some extent, because I was taught in seminary that all the Churches that Jesus addressed have components throughout all of the Church history as well. The demise of the Missionary Church, if that's what it is, may well be confirmation that the Tribulation begins at the end of the Church age, when Israel again comes to the forefront of human history. I still cling to the hope that Jesus would favor our particular Church as 'Philadelphian' in spirit, and for that I'd willingly give up my life along with that of our Church.

"The last of the seven Churches addressed by Jesus is the Laodicean Church, the thought of which makes me fervently pray that we have no part of. Listen to what Jesus says about it:

> *And unto the angel of the Church of the Laodiceans, write: These things saith the Amen, the faithful and true witness, the beginning of the creation of God. I know thy works, that thou art neither cold nor hot; I would thou wert cold or hot. So, then, because thou art lukewarm, and neither cold nor hot, I will spew thee out of my mouth. Because thou sayest, I am rich, and increased with goods, and have need of nothing, and knowest not that thou art wretched, and miserable, and poor, and blind, and naked, I counsel thee to buy of me gold tried in the fire, that thou mayest be rich; and white raiment, that thou mayest be clothed, and that the shame of thy nakedness do not appear; and anoint thine eyes with salve, that thou mayest see. As many as I love, I rebuke and chasten; be zealous, therefore, and repent. Behold, I stand at the door and knock;*

if any man hear my voice, and open the door, I will come in to him, and will sup with him, and he with me. To him that overcometh will I grant to sit with me in my throne, even as I also overcame, and am set down with my Father in his throne. He that hath an ear, let him hear what the Spirit saith unto the churches.

"Here we have the second of the two Churches for which Jesus had nothing good to say, just bad. And 'bad' isn't strong enough. Jesus' words were harsh, to say the least. As you have probably guessed, the Laodicean Church is designated the 'end-time' Church. You don't have to look far to see how so many supposedly 'mainstream' Churches have fallen completely away from God: they don't consider Scripture to represent truth; they often don't even respect Jesus as God; they claim, against Scripture, that there are many ways to heaven; they place as much weight on their own efforts as the grace of God in attaining to heaven; they practice things that, despite their political correctness, are openly disobedient to God's commands; and they have turned the places of their worship into social clubs. All this makes many of us think that the end times are very close. Well, that's a subject for another time. We'll sing a closing hymn, after which I invite you to spend some of this next week reading Scripture on your own. May God richly bless you."

Earl and Joyce left the Church with Cathy, greatly subdued by the gravity of George's sermon. Earl purposed in himself to re-read the first three chapters of Revelation at the first opportunity. So did Joyce.

Chapter Nine

"How about a movie?" Earl said to Joyce on Friday as he walked into the den. He stepped over to the fireplace and spread out his left hand to collect the warmth. Their furnace worked fine, but they both preferred the cheerfulness of a log fire and usually had one going well into spring, until the summer warmth finally arrived in the Northwest.

"Okey-dokie," she replied. She'd been reading a romance novel, but happily put it down and rose from their double recliner to make popcorn. She could return to the book later, but for now she looked forward to sharing the rest of the evening with Earl. He watched her, marveling at the ease with which she handled her prosthetic legs. It was like they were an integral part of her body. He remembered the pain involved with her adjustment to their use and thanked God for her grit.

"I thought you'd be working later than this," she called from the kitchen.

"I got done sooner than I expected. I had a lot to say and it came out pretty fast." He tossed a log onto the fire, sat down on his side of the recliner and flicked the TV on with his remote. He declined to make a posting tonight, considering his time with Joyce to be every bit as important.

He went into the guide and after a few minutes of searching found a movie that looked good. It was coming on shortly, so he turned to the channel and waited patiently for the latest run of incessant commercials to end. Another one followed and he continued to wait quietly as Joyce returned with a bowl of popcorn and two cans of pop. A third commercial appeared, which angered him until Joyce put a calming hand on his wrist. But his interest picked up when he saw that it was a recruitment commercial for the Marine Corps. "I was a Marine," he commented to her, the pride obvious in his tone.

"Oh, wow!" she replied, batting her eyes. A grin betrayed her thoughts.

"No need to mock," he said, offended. "There's a reason for the pride."

"Come here, big boy," she said, wrapping an arm around his neck and drawing him to her for a wet kiss. "I am proud of you. But for a lot more than that."

Mollified, he turned to the movie, which was just beginning. They enjoyed the film together and turned into bed.

Startled, Earl awoke to the diffuse light and sat up in bed. As always when he first saw Her, he was shocked at the beauty of the face before him, fully appreciating that Her appearance was but a pale representation of Her magnificent soul.

"Wisdom!" he cried joyfully. "You're back!"

"Shhhh," She replied, raising a finger to her lips. "I don't want to wake your lovely bride. It's you I want to talk to this time."

"I'm sorry. It's just that I'm so glad to see You again. I've missed You so much."

She gave him a sympathetic laugh. "I've been here all the time, Earl, but I know what you mean. I'm also glad to be sharing with you face-to-face." She stared at him lovingly. "So how's My big jarhead?" She asked coyly, fluttering Her huge lashes theatrically. A grin lit up Her face.

"Not You too!" he shot back. "What's so wrong with me telling Joyce that I was a Marine? After all, I was."

"No need to be petulant," She said, laughing at his pout. "You neglected to tell her that you never saw combat."

"Was that my fault?" he asked defensively. "I would have if there was a war on. I was ready to go and you know it. It just so happened that there wasn't a war during my time in the Corps."

"As I recall, you didn't call it the Corps. You called it the Crotch."

"Do You have to know everything? Of course we did. We all did. But it was said with affection. You also may recall that I had a very hard time deciding whether to re-up or not when my enlistment ended. It was just that I wanted to go to college."

"Oh, is that why you were so merciless with the poor guy who went to see Battle Cry at the movies and re-upped for six? You were brutal. And laughing inside. I know."

"Yeah, well, I had mixed feelings about it. And I don't care what You say, I was ready to go. Remember Lebanon?"

"All right. Enough joking around. There's a reason why I've returned so directly to you. I have a job for you as a Christian. It's a battle to make a Marine weep. Are you ready to go to war now?"

"Are You serious? You know I'll do anything for You."

"Oh, now you sound like Peter. You can't do anything without My help. But are you ready to accept a really unpleasant mission?"

"Would it be with Joyce?"

"I'll ask her, but that'll just be a formality. Yes, she'll agree. Her love for you is very strong. But then you know that."

"Yes, I'm very blessed, thanks to you. And yes, I'll accept, although You already know that, too. And I understand that I'll be needing you every step of the way."

"Good. Because, Earl, We're looking for a few good people too, just like the Marines. And this is a good chance for you to get the combat experience you missed before."

"So what's the mission?"

"You're maturing as a Christian, so you've figured out by now that being a Christian isn't all fun and games."

Earl looked at Her with a growing concern, attempting to get from Her eyes a hint at what was coming next. "I'm not sure that I like the sound of this. Where's it all heading?"

"What do you think about the Rapture?"

"We're ready. Joyce and I are really looking forward to it."

"Oh. So you think it's imminent."

"Well, yes I do. We do. Isn't it?" He said this last with a squeak of apprehension, which made Her laugh.

"What's happening to my big Marine? Is that what you're waiting for? The Rapture for an easy out?"

"Well—kind of," he admitted in a small voice.

"Not going to happen. Not that way. You and a whole bunch of other very fine Christians have misled themselves and been misled by others with this misplaced hope. I'm afraid when the flag goes up you're going to be stuck right here in the thick of things, Earl. You and Joyce both. What do you say to that?"

"Not much that I can say, is there? I'm disappointed, sure, but You're the boss. Not only that," he said, reassembling his backbone, "but I love You. All of You. Me and Joyce both. We'll do everything we can for Jesus' sake. With Your help, of course."

"Of course. I'll still be around, because you'll really be needing Me. Things are going to be heading south ever faster, and to many people it will seem like the Rapture actually happened. Chaos will become a normal state of affairs. Communications will be disrupted, and in the general turmoil it will seem like Christianity has departed from the face of the earth. To compound that general impression, many Christians are being persecuted as we speak. Many more will be following them, such that your ranks will be systematically decimated. Above and beyond that little item, a good many so-called Christians are falling away into open apostasy, further thinning out the ranks as they depart from the faith. But others—particularly Jews, beloved people of the Book, will get right with Us through their trials, and it'll be part of your job to help them get there."

"Will there be others like us?"

"Yes, but that's not your concern. As for you, you're going to be doing a whole lot more than you can imagine at this point. You're going to know—intimately—just how the Tribulation will impact the Jews, who remain the apple of God's eye, and how your life, as well as Joyce's, will be inextricably tied in with them. You and Joyce are going to learn some things that'll put you on fire for your Jewish brothers and sisters. For starters, we're going to visit some highlights of Israel's history, which involves some unfinished business between you and Me. Remember what I told you about Hebron, that it was very important to God? It was a long time ago when I told you that, just about when you first met Me."

Earl thought back to when Wisdom first directly visited him. It was before Joyce, when he was grieving over Alicia. What an awful time, but then Wisdom came into his life... "Yes! I do remember! You said it was important, but then the subject didn't come up again."

"There's a time for everything. Up till now it wasn't important for you to be particularly aware of Israel, or Hebron either. Now it is. Hebron's a town on the west bank of the Jordan River, Earl. It's part of the territory occupied by the Israelis after the 1967 war but which is now of course, thanks to pressure applied to Israel by the United States under several administrations up to and including the present one, by your continuously unwise State Department, an integral part of territory claimed by Palestinian militants. Hebron and the surrounding West Bank territory are frequently in your news as elements of animosity between Palestinians and Israelis. America continues to join the world in siding with Palestinian claims on this sacred territory, as if the region will finally be blessed with peace if only Israel will have the good sense to acquiesce to the demand for a two-state solution, under the terms of which Hebron will be offered to the Islamic militants who clamor for it as their rightful due.

"Sadly, Earl, the world forgets Hebron and its rich Biblical history. That was in the region, according to Genesis 12 and 13, where, as far back in time as when the nation of Israel was still but a thought in Our mind, Abraham stood as We first gave him the promise:

> *Now the Lord had said unto Abram, Get thee out of thy country, and from thy kindred, and from thy father's house, unto a land that I will show thee: And I will make of thee a great nation, and I will bless thee, and make thy name great; and thou shalt be a blessing: And I will bless them that bless thee, and curse him that curseth thee: and in thee shall all families of the earth be blessed...*
>
> *And the Lord said unto Abram, after that Lot was separated from him, Lift up now thine eyes, and look from the place where thou art northward, and southward, and eastward, and westward: For all the land which thou seest, to thee will I give it, and to thy seed for ever. And I will make thy seed as the dust of the earth: so that if a man can number the dust of the earth, then shall thy seed also be numbered. Arise, walk through the land in the length of it and in the breadth of it; for I will give it unto thee. Then Abram removed his tent, and came and dwelt in the plain of Mamre, which is in Hebron, and built there an altar unto the Lord.*

"We later formalized this promise by a unilateral, everlasting covenant which also established specific boundaries for the land of Israel, the borders of which extended far beyond both the region of Hebron and the present-day borders established by modern statesmen." She looked at Earl and decided that at this point a mere introduction to the topic was about all his mind was capable of receiving. "Go back to sleep, my darling," She said, accepting his *de facto* lack of focus, and left.

Chapter Ten

"It is so good to see you this evening, your honor," the maitre'd beamed at Gerald Robbins, turning next to his extravagantly pretty wife. "And how absolutely stunning you look tonight, madame. Our modest establishment has been languishing in drab sorrow until you came to illuminate it with your beauty. Please follow me." Gerald and Mary followed him to an empty table, which he designated as theirs with a flourish. He helped her with her chair and clapped loudly for the attention of the wait staff, who rushed over with frosted glasses, an iced water pitcher, the waiter and the sommelier.

His clap for attention was superfluous. All eyes were riveted on the Chief Justice's wife. Younger than her husband by fifteen years, she carried herself with regal grace. Her elegant beauty radiated throughout the busy dining room, bringing conversation to a halt. The attention on Mary wasn't lost on Gerald, who welcomed it as the capstone of a lengthy, enormously successful career. Despite the large difference in their ages, their twelve-year marriage had been uncommonly happy for both of them. She respected his intellect and the forcefulness of his personality in dealing with other men; he, of course, appreciated her beauty, but he was grateful that along with it came a generous heart capable of an astonishingly earthy passion. She was one in a million and he knew it; despite his own successes, he had been extremely lucky in finding her and persuading her to be his life partner.

Mary put a gentle hand over his. "I have to use the lady's room," she said. "I'll just be a minute. Why don't you order for both of us?"

Gerald turned to the sommelier as she arose from the table and walked off. "I'll take your own recommendation for tonight, Ted," he told him. Make it a dark wine, and rare. I have a big case coming up and I don't know when I'll be able to relax again."

"Absolutely, sir," the sommelier said, and departed, leaving him with the waiter. "Hi, George," he began. "Is fresh lobster on the menu tonight?"

"Of course, sir. Not only are the creatures still alive, but they were in the ocean yesterday. May I suggest a rare chateaubriand on the side?"

"Splendid." He folded the menu and returned it to George as the sommelier hurried toward them with the wine.

Gerald mused on the upcoming trial as he sipped at the wine. He was on his second glass before he became aware that Mary was taking an unusual length of time in the bathroom. He looked at his watch. After ten more minutes his concern morphed into alarm. He got the attention of the waiter, and asked him if he would be so kind as to ask a female member of the staff to inquire as to her presence in the bathroom. The waiter returned a few minutes later. His hands were empty and he was wearing a frown. "I'm afraid the bathroom is empty, sir," he told Gerald, who began to rise from his chair in distress.

He returned to his chair under the command of a gentle but firm hand on his shoulder. "Mary's just fine, Mr. Robbins," he said. "She's outside talking to an unexpected friend." The large, cheerful man dismissed the greatly relieved waiter and sat down in Mary's chair. The matching relief on Gerald's face quickly fled. "Who are you?" he asked the stranger. "How do you know Mary?"

"The first thing you must do, sir, is to remain calm," the man replied. Mary will indeed be all right, after a fashion, but only if you stay calm and don't make a fuss. No police, no 9-1-1. We're past that. If you do everything exactly as I say, I might not get to know Mary in a way that you'd find quite appalling. Tell me you understand. Quietly, and smile."

Gerald forced himself to comply. "Okay. I'll be leaving now, but other people are watching. You don't know them, but they know you, and if you do anything out of the ordinary, well, Mary will know about it."

Heart racing, Gerald called the waiter over and paid the bill with the excuse that an emergency meeting had intruded on their dinner. As he left the restaurant, the friendly face returned and grasped him by the arm. "What do you want from me?" he asked the man, his heart racing in panic. "If it's money you want, just tell me and I'll be glad to hand it over." The man remained silent. Presently they came up to a blue Bentley, and the man ushered Gerald into the back seat. When they were alone, the man told him that Mary would be held in custody for a period of time. His stomach dropped with the news and his inability to do anything about it. "You'll have to explain her absence," the man told Gerald. "Say what you want, but make it convincing."

"But for how long?" Gerald was almost weeping.

"Until your case is over. The lawsuit against the White House."

"Why?"

"The Supreme Court has, in addition to you, four liberals and four conservatives. They'll be certain to vote in a predictable fashion. You're the wild card. You figure it out."

"Will you promise to return Mary if the vote goes your way?"

"No. But I'll promise you this: if the vote doesn't go our way, Mary won't be coming back. And don't think that you can cry foul once she is returned to you, if that ever happens. Or if you never see Mary again. You're up against some people who are infinitely more successful than you. And infinitely more powerful besides. You and Mary take your next breaths at the pleasure of these people. You'd just be going through this all over again, only for a very short period of time."

At the other end of the country and several days later, the Cooks' weekend was filled with Cathy and Church. "Chapters 1 through 3 of Revelation, you will recall," Pastor George told his congregants, "dealt exclusively with the Church. Now we come to Revelation 4, where the scene shifts to heaven as John is taken there in the Spirit. This abrupt change in scenario and topic has led many Christians, both laypeople and theologians alike, to think that the Rapture occurs at this juncture, with the Church leaving earth behind to be in heaven. I tend to agree with this view, although I want you to know that there are good arguments in support of a Rapture that occurs toward or at the end of the Tribulation. At this point I feel obligated to insert a few words of caution regarding the notion of the Rapture being delayed until after the Millennium. Note that I said the Millennium, not the Tribulation." His emphasis on the word "Millennium" brought a chuckle to those who knew that some Christians tended to confuse the very widely-separated ends of these two different events. "Although I have just acknowledged the real possibility that the Rapture will not occur until the end of the Great Tribulation, I can't think of any good argument for a delay of the Rapture until after the thousand-year reign of Christ on earth called the Millennium. To some, that mindset involves the notion that we're in the millennium age even now, or what variously is called "preterism", "replacement theology" or "dominion theology", which asserts that the Church has replaced Israel as the apple of God's eye, and that the Church will hand over a perfect world to a passive Jesus at the end of the Millennium. This very false teaching has led to untold misery for both the Church and the Jews. The truth is that the world will continue to get worse until Jesus Himself comes back to set things straight during the Millennium. Oh, yes, the Church will be involved during that time, but only with the active Lordship of Jesus Christ." George ran a hand through his hair. "Sorry. I guess I got sidetracked. At any event, getting back to Revelation 4, John finds himself in heaven seeing things that are difficult to put into words:

> *After this I looked, and, behold, a door was opened in heaven; and the first voice that I heard was, as it were, of a trumpet talking with me; which said, Come up here, and I will show thee things which must be hereafter. And immediately I was in the Spirit and, behold, a throne was set in heaven, and one sat on the throne. And he that sat was to look upon like a jasper and a sardius stone; and there was a rainbow round about the throne, in sight like an emerald. And round about the throne were twenty four thrones, and upon the thrones I saw twenty four elders sitting, clothed in white garments; and they had on their heads crowns of gold. And out of the throne proceeded lightnings and thunderclaps, and voices; and there were seven lamps of fire burning before the throne, which are the seven spirits of God. And before the throne there was a sea of glass like crystal and in the midst of the throne, and round about the throne, were four living creatures full of eyes in front and behind. And the first living creature was like a lion, and the second living creature like a calf, and the third living creature had a face like a man, and the fourth living creature was like a flying eagle. And the four living creatures had each of them six wings about him, and they were full of eyes within; and they rest not day and night, saying, Holy, holy, holy, Lord God Almighty, who was, and is, and is to come. And when those living creatures give glory and honor and thanks to him that is seated on the throne, and worship him that liveth forever and ever, the twenty four elders fall down before him that is seated on the throne, and worship him that liveth forever and ever, and cast their crowns before the throne, saying, Thou art worthy, O Lord, to achieve glory and honor and power; for thou hast created all things, and for thy pleasure they are and were created.*

"Think, my friends, of the glory that John must have seen! I happen to be one of the very many knowledgeable Christians who are convinced that John's visions included a panoramic view of modern civilization, complete with cars and trucks, freeways, trains, airports, airplanes, skyscrapers, factories, smog, and what-have-you. Beyond that, of course, is the spiritual realm which John was also gifted to see. Our earthy vocabulary simply isn't sufficient to describe the things that belong to the heavenly domain. But he soon encounters an unexpected situation that troubles him greatly.

> *And I saw in the right hand of him that sat on the throne a scroll written within and on the back, sealed with seven seals.*

"I'll briefly interrupt the narrative to tell you that in the days of John the backside of a document was used to write any legal conditions that applied to the document, including its terms of unsealing and use. Continuing, then, we see that there are indeed legal conditions that are attached to this sealed document.

> *And I saw a strong angel proclaiming with a loud voice, Who is worthy to open the scroll, and to loose the seals? And no man in heaven, nor in earth, neither under the earth, was able to open the scroll, neither to look on it. And I wept much, because no man was found worthy to open and to read the scroll, neither to look on it. And one of the elders saith to me, Weep not; behold, the Lion of the tribe of Judah, the Root of David, hath prevailed to open the scroll, and to loose its seven seals. And I beheld and, lo, in the midst of the throne and of the four living creatures, and in the midst of the elders, stood a Lamb as though it had been slain, having seven horns and seven eyes, which are the seven spirits of God sent forth into all the earth. And he came and took the scroll out of the right hand of him that sat on the throne.*

"I'll interrupt the narrative again to explain two things. First, as to the identity of the Lion of Judah: all the way back in Genesis 49, the Patriarch Jacob, or Israel, pronounces his prophetic blessings on his twelve sons, the patriarchs themselves of the twelve tribes of Israel as he nears the end of his life. Among these is Judah, over which he says

> *Judah, thou art he whom thy brethren shall praise: thy hand shall be in the neck of thine enemies; thy father's children*

shall bow down before thee. Judah is a lion's whelp: from the prey, my son, thou art gone up: he stooped down, he crouched as a lion, and as an old lion. Who shall rouse him up? The scepter shall not depart from Judah, nor a lawgiver from between his feet, until Shiloh come; and unto him shall the gathering of the people be. Binding his foal unto the vine, and his ass's colt unto the choice vine, he washed his garments in wine, and his clothes in the blood of grapes. His eyes shall be red with wine, and his teeth white with milk.

"This prophecy is generally interpreted as Messianic, for reasons that would take me too long to go into here. Perhaps I'll deliver a later sermon on the subject. In other words, it is thought to be a direct reference to Jesus Christ, whose bloodline indeed was of the tribe of Judah.

Glancing over at Cathy, Joyce noted something unexpected as Pastor George presented this interpretation of Revelation. She was surprised to see her nod and move appropriately to the words that George spoke. *Can she really understand what he is saying?* she asked herself.

"The second item that wants interpretation is the identity of the Lamb. Recall in Exodus 12 the institution of the Passover ceremony on the eve of the exodus of Israel from Egypt. As a preliminary to that ceremony, each family was to take into their house a yearling lamb without blemish and keep it for four days, just long enough to become attached to it. Then they were to kill it and sprinkle its blood on the lintel and doorposts. Those families who obeyed this instruction were passed over by God on His way to execute the tenth plague, which was the death of the firstborn of every family in Egypt. This ritual obviously also was Messianic: it was a direct reference to Jesus, whom John the Baptist named the Lamb of God as He came to him to be baptized. Jesus, it must be noted, was crucified on the day of preparation for the Passover, fulfilling the ceremony in Himself. It is to His blood that we look for our own salvation from spiritual death."

Again, Joyce looked at Cathy and was surprised at her apparent grasp of what George was saying. She resolved to ask Laurie about Cathy's intellectual capabilities.

George concluded his sermon by saying that the opening of the first four seals would unleash the four horsemen of the apocalypse. "We'll go into that next week, God willing. It will be an interesting sermon," he said, "especially since there are two very different ways that we can view these horsemen and their colors. So stay tuned and have a good week. Let's turn to that stirring hymn, "Am I a Soldier of the Cross, number 239."

After the hymn, George held up his hand for a final announcement. "As most of you know, the Supreme Court has just ruled in favor of the White House in the matter of the rash of executive orders the president has issued. It came as a big surprise to most of us conservatives, who thought that the Chief Justice was one of us. I expect this betrayal to have a very large impact on the future of America. We seem to be following in lockstep the process that enthroned Hitler in Nazi Germany. What concerns me most is the complete government takeover of care for the elderly and handicapped, really for health care in general. I can almost hear them calling the infirm "useless eaters", as they did in Hitler's Germany. But no matter. Remember that God is on the throne and everything will work out according to His loving will. Go in peace. I look forward to seeing you back here next Sunday. Oh, and for those who want to pursue the subject at a little deeper level, you're welcome to come to our Bible study on Wednesday night at six thirty."

Chapter Eleven

At their own Bible study that Sunday evening at the nursing home, Earl thought to himself about how appropriate was the Book of Acts to the information that came out of his latest encounter with Wisdom. The power of God that was so abundant in the people whom God had chosen to represent Him to the world gave Earl joy in the midst of the bad news that permeated the world about him. He also noted the martial flavor of the hymns that Joyce had selected to play: *Onward Christian Soldiers* topped the list. He suspected that sometime during the past two days Wisdom had had a chat with Joyce too.

"Today we're going to continue with the exploits of the Apostles," Earl told the assembled residents. "We're at the point, in Acts Chapter 7, where the evil religious leaders are attempting to bring Christianity to a screeching halt. Here they pick on a devout Christian named Stephen, finding people who will bear false witness against him, claiming that he is saying blasphemous things against God. The leaders confront him and restrain him, demanding that he answer the charges against him. His reply, in which he gave the leaders a lesson in their own history, is a famous defense of the faith:

And he said, Men, brethren and fathers, hearken: The God

of glory appeared unto our father, Abraham, when he was in Mesopotamia, before he dwelt in Haran, and said unto him, Get thee out of thy country, and from thy kindred, and come into the land which I shall show thee. Then came he out of the land of the Chaldeans, and dwelt in Haran; and from there, when his father was dead, he removed him into this land, in which ye now dwell. And he gave him no inheritance in it, no, not so much as to set his foot on it; yet he promised him that he would give it to him for a possession, and to his seed after him, when as yet he had no child. And God spoke in this way, that his seed should sojourn in a strange land; and that they should bring them into bondage and entreat them evil four hundred years. And the nation to whom they shall be in bondage will I judge, said God; and after that shall they come forth, and serve me in this place. And he gave him the covenant of circumcision; and so Abraham begot Isaac, and circumcised him the eighth day; and Isaac begot Jacob; and Jacob begot the twelve patriarchs. And the patriarchs, moved with envy, sold Joseph into Egypt; but God was with him, and delivered him out of all his afflictions, and gave him favor and wisdom in the sight of Pharaoh, king of Egypt; and he made him governor over Egypt and all his house.

Now there came a famine over all the land of Egypt and Canaan, and great affliction; and our fathers found no sustenance. But when Jacob heard that there was grain in Egypt, he sent out our fathers first. And at the second time Joseph was made known to his brethren; and Joseph's kindred was made known to Pharaoh. Then sent Joseph, and called his father, Jacob, to him, and all his kindred, [seventy five] souls. So Jacob went down into Egypt, and died, he and our fathers, and were carried over into Shechem, and laid in the sepulcher that Abraham bought for a sum of money of the sons of Hamor, the father of Sechem.

But when the time of the promise drew near, which God had sworn to Abraham, the people grew and multiplied in Egypt, till another king arose, who knew not Joseph. The same dealt craftily with our kindred, and evil entreated our fathers, so that they cast out their young children, to the end they might not live. In which time Moses was born, and was exceedingly fair, and nourished up in his father's house three months; and when he was cast out, Pharaoh's daughter took him up, and nourished him as her own son. And Moses was learned in all the wisdom of the Egyptians, and was mighty in words and in deeds. And when he was full forty years old, it came into his heart to visit his brethren, the children of Israel. And seeing one of them suffer wrong, he defended him, and avenged him that was oppressed, and smote the Egyptian. For he supposed his brethren would have understood how that God by his hand would deliver them; but they understood not. And the next day he showed himself to them as they strove, and would have set them at one again, saying, Sirs, ye are brethren; why do ye wrong one to another? But he that did his neighbor wrong thrust him away, saying, Who made thee a ruler and a judge over us? Wilt thou kill me, as thou diddest the Egyptian yesterday?

Then fled Moses at this saying, and was a sojourner in the land of Midian, where he begot two sons. And when forty years were expired, there appeared to him in the wilderness of Mount Sinai an angel of the Lord in a flame of fire in a bush. When Moses saw it, he wondered at the sight; and as he drew near to behold it, the voice of the Lord came unto him, saying, I am the God of thy fathers, the God of Abraham, and the God of Isaac, and the God of Jacob. Then Moses trembled, and dared not behold. Then said the Lord to him, Put off thy shoes from thy feet; for the place where thou standest is holy ground. I have seen, I have seen the affliction of my people who are in Egypt, and I have heard their groaning, and am come down to deliver them. And now come, I will send thee into Egypt.

This Moses whom they refused, saying Who made thee a ruler and a judge? The same did God send to be a ruler and a deliverer by the hand of the angel who appeared to him in the bush. He brought them out, after he had shown wonders and signs in the land of Egypt, and in the red Sea, and in the wilderness forty years. This is that Moses who said unto the children of Israel, A Prophet shall the Lord, your God, raise up unto you of your brethren, like me; him shall ye hear. This is he that was in the church in the wilderness with the angel who spoke to him in Mount Sinai, and with our fathers, who received the living oracles to give unto us. Whom our fathers would not obey, but thrust him from them, and in their hearts turned back again into Egypt. Saying unto Aaron, Make us gods to go before us; for, as for this Moses who brought us out of the land of Egypt, we know not what is become of him. And they made a calf in those days, and offered sacrifice unto the idol, and rejoiced in the works of their own hands. Then God turned, and gave them up to worship the host of heaven; as it is written in the book of the prophets, O ye house of Israel, have ye offered to me slain beasts and sacrifices by the space of forty years in the wilderness? Yea, ye took up the tabernacle of Molech, and the star of your god, Remphan, figures which ye made to worship; and I will carry you away beyond Babylon.

Our fathers had the tabernacle of witness in the wilderness, as he had appointed, speaking unto Moses, that he should make it according to the fashion that he had seen; which also our fathers that came after brought in with Joshua into the possession of the heathen, whom God drove out before the face of our fathers, unto the days of David, who found favor before God, and desired to find a tabernacle for the God of Jacob. But Solomon built him an house. Nevertheless, the Most High dwelleth not in temples made with hands, as saith the prophet, Heaven is my throne, and earth is my footstool. What house will ye build me, saith the Lord. Or what is the place of my rest? Hath not my hand made all of these things? Ye stiffnecked and uncircumcised in heart and ears, ye do always resist the Holy Spirit; as your fathers did, so do ye. Which of the prophets have not your fathers persecuted? And they have slain them who showed before of the coming of the Just One, of whom ye have been now the betrayers and murderers; who have received the law by the disposition of angels, and have not kept it.

When they had heard these things, they were cut to the heart, and gnashed on him with their teeth. But [Stephen], being full of the Holy Spirit, looked up steadfastly into heaven, and saw the glory of God, and Jesus standing on the right hand of God, and said, Behold, I see the heavens opened, and the Son of man standing on the right hand of God. Then they cried out with a loud voice, and stopped their ears, and ran upon him with one accord, and cast him out of the city, and stoned him; and the witnesses laid down their clothes at a young man's feet, whose name was Saul. And they stoned Stephen, calling upon God, and saying Lord Jesus, receive my spirit. And he kneeled down, and cried with a loud voice, Lord, lay not this sin to their charge. And when he had said this, he fell asleep.

"Thus ended the life of Stephen, the first of a long and illustrious line of Christian martyrs who died for their faith in Jesus Christ," Earl told them. "It's a sad story, but then again, it's not. How did Jesus tell us to deal with persecution? Did He tell us to get our own back in spades? To seek revenge? No, He told us to leap for joy, because we, in our persecution, are closest to Him, who was persecuted for our sakes. Stephen has all eternity to recall his deed of love, faith and courage with great happiness. I'll leave you with that thought for tonight with a promise that the next story in the Book of Acts ends up as a wonderful tale with lots of hope and happiness."

"Laurie, I noticed something about Cathy in Church today," Joyce said as they prepared to leave and were out of earshot of the residents.

"Oh?" she asked. "What was that?"

"Our pastor gives us the Word in rather deep sermons. We like him for that among other things, because he's so Scripturally-oriented. But he certainly speaks at the adult level. I watched Cathy a couple of times during his sermon today, and I was taken aback, because she seemed to be following him perfectly."

"Oh boy," she laughed. "What you have, Joyce, is the standard prejudice of normal people regarding the handicapped. If they look odd, their minds are odd too."

"But..." she began.

"No. Wait. It's a very normal reaction. It takes a long time to get over it. Actually, some handicaps justify that feeling, but cerebral palsy isn't one of them. You have an excellent example in one of the world's foremost physicists, Stephen Hawking. He's afflicted with cerebral palsy too, but the scientific community generally considers him to have an unusually gifted mind, something on the order of Einstein's. From what I've observed, Cathy's mind is as sharp as a normal person's, and probably considerably sharper."

"What a wonderful surprise!" was all that Joyce could say. She shared her conversation about Cathy with Earl on the drive home. She was surprised at his reaction, for he laughed too.

"Yeah, Joyce, I got to know Buddy pretty well, and I ended up thinking that he was smarter than me. I wouldn't be shocked if Cathy had that same quick intelligence."

That Tuesday evening they received a phone call from Pastor George. The news he gave them was both terrifying and depressing. "You know Bob and Evelyn Smith, don't you?" He asked Joyce. "I hate to tell you this," he continued after she answered in the affirmative, "but they're both dead. Murdered. They haven't caught a suspect yet, but apparently intruders came into their home in the middle of the night and slaughtered them as they slept. From the graffiti that they left behind, the police think that the creeps who did this were Christian-haters. Now I'm trying to pass the word around our Church, and it's not a pleasant task."

"I should say not," Joyce replied. "It there anything that Earl and

I can do?"

"Not really," the pastor said. "We'll have a funeral service for them this Saturday, and it would be good if you could show up for that. Otherwise, they didn't have any family to speak of, at least that I or the police know about."

"Hi, Earl," She said at his bedside that night.

"Hello, Wisdom," he managed to think. As always, Earl's emotions overcame him at the sight of the love that flowed from Her gorgeous eyes.

"Bob and Evelyn are doing just fine," She told him. "They were real warriors for Us," She continued. "Their murder wasn't a random event. It was motivated by politics and involved some political heavyweights, enough to let every conspiracy theorist in the world say 'I told you so'. But they refused to compromise for the sake of happiness in the material world, and, most happily, they kept their souls intact." She looked deeply into Earl's eyes and went on. "Last time I came to you I had brought up the subject of Hebron and gave you some background involving Our promise to Abraham. Now for the details. I had told you that out of our love for Abraham we had promised to make him the father of many nations, out of which we would particularly favor his seed Isaac, and after him, Jacob, whom We named Israel. We made a covenant with Abraham regarding land. That covenant, Earl, was an everlasting one, and it included Hebron. Abraham's wife Sarah died at the age of 127, in Hebron. Abraham purchased a grave for her there, in the cave in Machpelah near Mamre, from Ephron the Hittite. He paid four hundred shekels of silver for it. When he died at the age of 175 he was also buried there, as were his son Isaac and his wife Rebekah, and his grandson Jacob and his primary wife Leah, the mother of Judah. To sum it up, all the patriarchs of Israel are buried in Hebron, along with their primary wives.

"Hebron was conquered later by the Israelites under Joshua during the conquest of the Promised Land. Although it was given to them as a gift from God—Us, if you will—they still had to fight for possession of it. The particular band of men who actually took the city were of the tribe of Judah. Caleb, their leader, was eighty years old at the time and, as he reminded Joshua, he took it by virtue of the fact that it belonged to him. Hebron belonged to Caleb because it was promised to him as a reward by Us for his courageous faith. Two years into Israel's Exodus sojourn the nation was encamped at the wilderness of Paran, where, as recorded in Chapter 13 of the book of Numbers, We told Moses to send twelve men, one representative from each of the tribes, to spy out the land of Canaan:

> *And the Lord spake unto Moses, saying, Send thou men, that they may search the land of Canaan, which I give unto the children of Israel: of every trive of their fathers shall ye send a man, every one a ruler among them. And Moses by the commandment of the Lord sent them from the wilderness of Paran: all those men were heads of the children of Israel...*
>
> *And Moses sent them to spy out the land of Canaan, and said unto them, Get you up this way southward, and go up into the mountain: And see the land, what it is; and the people that dwelleth therein, whether they be stong or weak, few or many; And what the land is that they dwell in, whether it be good or bad; and what cities they be that they dwell in, whether in tents, or in strongholds; And what the land is, whether it be fat or lean, whether there be wood therein, or not. And be ye of good courage, and bring of the fruit of the land. Now the time was the time of the first ripe grapes. So they went up, and searched the land from the wilderness of Zin unto Rehob, as men come to Hamath. And they ascended by the south, and came unto Hebron; where Ahiman, Sheshai, and Talmai, the children of Anak, were. (Now Hebron was built seven years before Zoan in Egypt.) And they came unto the brook of Eshcol, and cut down from thence a branch with one cluster of grapes, and they bare it between two upon a staff; and they brought of the pomegranates, and of the figs. The place was called the brook Eshcol, because of the cluster of grapes which the children of Israel cut down from thence. And they returned from searching of the land after forty days.*

"Caleb was among these twelve. Of the spies, ten returned in fear and recommended a hasty retreat because of the massive size of the men who dwelt in the land:

> *And they told [Moses], and said, We came unto the land whither thou sentest us, and surely it floweth with milk and honey; and this is the fruit of it. Nevertheless the people be strong that dwell in the land, and the cities are walled, and very great: and moreover we saw the children of Anak there...*

> *And Caleb stilled the people before Moses, and said, Let us go up at once, and possess it; for we are well able to overcome it. But the men that went up with him said, We be not able to go up against the people; for they are stronger than we. And they brought up an evil report of the land which they had searched unto the children of Israel, saying, The land, through which we have gone to search it, is a land that eateth up the inhabitants thereof; and all the people that we saw in it are men of a great stature. And there we saw the giants, the sons of Anak, which come of the giants: and we were in our own sight as grasshoppers, and so we were in their sight.*

"Only two men held fast. They claimed the land in faith, because it had been promised by Us. One of these heroes was Joshua of the tribe of Ephraim, a son of Joseph. His reward was the reign of leadership which was handed down to him by Moses. The other hero was Caleb of the tribe of Judah. Within the seed of Judah is the bloodline of David and Solomon, and ultimately of Jesus Christ. Caleb's reward, as noted, was the city of Hebron. The gift was specifically unbound by time: it was to belong to the tribe of Judah forever. Caleb's discourse to Joshua in the matter at the time that Israel was conquering the land of Canaan and his subsequent action is recorded in Joshua 14, verses 6 through 15:

> *Then the children of Judah came unto Joshua in Gilgal: and Caleb the son of Jephunneh the Kenezite said unto him, Thou knowest the thing that the Lord said unto Moses the man of God concerning me and thee in Kadeshbarnea. Forty years old was I when Moses the servant of the Lord sent me from*

Kadeshbarnea to espy out the land; and I brought him word again as it was in mine heart. Nevertheless my brethren that went up with me made the heart of the people melt; but I wholly followed the Lord my God. And Moses sware on that day, saying Surely the land whereon thy feet have trodden whall be thine inheritance, and thy children's for ever, because thou hast wholly followed the Lord my God. And now, behold, the Lord hath kept me alive, as he said, these forty and five years, even since the Lord spake this word unto Moses, while the children of Israel wandered in the wilderness: and now, lo, I am this day fourscore and five years old. As yet I am as strong this day as I was in the day that Moses sent me: as my strength was then, even so is my strength now, for war, both to go out, and to come in. Now therefore give me this mountain, whereof the Lord spake in that day; for thou heardest in that day how the Anakim were there, and that the cities were great and fenced: if so be the Lord will be with me, then I shall be able to drive them out, as the Lord said.

And Joshua blessed him, and gave unto Caleb the son of Jephunneh Hebron for an inheritance. Hebron therefore became the inheritance of the son of Jephunneh the Kenezite unto this day; because that he wholly followed the Lord God of Israel. And the name of Hebron before was Kirjatharba; which Arba was a great man among the Anakim. And the land had rest from war.

"This promise from Us as a reward to Judah links Hebron with Israel in a tie so strong that to ignore it amounts to blasphemy; but there is yet more to the association. Several hundred years after Caleb's victorious battle for Hebron, David was anointed by the prophet Samuel for kingship over Israel while its first king Saul still reigned. He was blessed for the office in Saul's place because Saul fell into disobedience against Us. Yet this anointing was for a future time, as Saul continued to reign as king over Israel, just as he continued to seek after David's death, until his iniquity came to the fullness appointed by Us. Eventually he arrived at that state where, being overwhelmed by Philistines in battle and sensing that We would not come to his rescue, Saul committed suicide by falling on his sword. Upon the death of Saul, the tribe of Judah made David their king, and he reigned over them. At that time, the seat of his government was Hebron. As for the rest of Israel, Abner, the captain of Saul's army, took it upon himself to appoint Ishbosheth, a son of Saul, as their replacement king. As Ishbosheth's commission represented a usurpation of Our will, events brought Abner and Ishbosheth into conflict. They became alienated from each other, leading Israel into decline as Judah accumulated strength under David's rule. Soon the other tribes began to seek after David's kingship. Within seven and a half years, they willingly submitted themselves to David and he acquired the kingship of Israel. In claiming his rule over the entire twelve tribes of Israel, David removed the Jebusites from Jerusalem and moved there from Hebron. He reigned for a total of forty years, first for seven years over Judah in Hebron, followed by thirty-three years over Israel in Jerusalem. But note that David's first kingdom had Hebron as its capital.

"So here we have at least three heavy-duty bands that tie Hebron with Israel: the location of the Patriarchs' graves; the gift of Hebron to Caleb of the tribe of Judah directly by Us; and Hebron as the location of the initial capital of David's reign. Yet not one mention of these links has been made by those who are attempting to bring order to the Middle East. Their efforts completely ignore Us. We have explained to you and countless others that We had promised the land to Abraham. We also haven't forgotten that Abraham's sons included Ishmael as well as Isaac. But We clearly defined the inheritor of the land as Isaac and his seed, not Ishmael, for the covenant which We established with Abraham was repeated for Isaac and Jacob, but not Ishmael. The account in Genesis 17 should make this clear to all:

> *And God said unto Abraham, As for Sarai thy wife, thou shalt not call her name Sarai, but Sarah shall her name be. And I will bless her, and give thee a son also of her: yea, I will bless her, and she shall be a mother of nations; kings of people shall be of her. Then Abraham fell upon his face and laughed, and said in his heart, Shall a child be born unto him that is a*

hundred years old? and shall Sarah, that is ninety years old, bear? And Abraham said unto God, O that Ishmael might live before thee!

And God said, Sarah thy wife shall bear thee a son indeed; and thou shalt call his name Isaac: and I will establish my covenant with him for an everlasting covenant, and with his seed after him. And as for Ishmael, I have heard thee: Behold, I have blessed him, and will make him fruitful, and will multiply him exceedingly; twelve princes shall he beget, and I will make him a great nation. But my covenant will I establish with Isaac, which Sarah shall bear unto thee at this set time in the next year.

"Along with their ungrateful grasp upon of the autonomy which has been granted them in Hebron, the Palestinians are ever more loudly demanding the removal of all Jewish influence over this historic city. Yet this disdain for the Scriptural history of Hebron is only one instance of many by which the world spits in Our face. Nevertheless, Earl, We'll turn this into a blessing for mankind. It's what We do, and We're very good at it."

"I have no doubt," he said with a laugh. "And I'm very glad that Joyce and me are a part of your plan. After your lecture, I'm pumped about Hebron. And Israel, of course."

She laughed with him. "There's more to the story. But for now have a good rest." He was already asleep as She kissed his forehead.

Chapter Twelve

On Saturday they went to the funeral of the Smiths. They took Cathy with them, as they felt that it was important for her to understand such an important event in one's life as its physical end, given the comfort that spiritual resurrection awaits all Christians after they come to this milestone in their lives. Being aware of the sadness of death to those left behind, they also were comforted with George's words:

"Bob and Evelyn were Christians," George said in his brief service in their honor. "For them, death has no sting, for even now they await a resurrection into the arms of Jesus. Remember what Jesus said in Matthew 10:28:

And fear not them who kill the body, but are not able to kill the soul; but rather fear him who is able to destroy both soul and body in hell.

"Perhaps they met an untimely death; and perhaps also they have left behind the grief of their passing. But thank our God that they left this world with their souls intact. For those who are grieving, permit me to give you a hope-filled message from Paul. It's in 1 Corinthians 15:

Behold, I show you a mystery: we shall not all sleep, but we shall all be changed. In a moment, in the twinkling of an eye, at the last trump; for the trumpet shall sound, and the dead shall be raised incorruptible, and we shall be changed. For this corruptible must put on incorruption, and this mortal must put on immortality. So, when this corruptible shall have put on incorruption, and this mortal shall have put on immortality, then shall be brought to pass the saying that is written, Death is swallowed up in victory. O death, where is thy sting? O grave, where is thy victory? The sting of death is sin; and the strength of sin is the law. But thanks be to God, who giveth us victory through our Lord Jesus Christ.

"One further word is in order," George told them. "It's in Revelation 21:

And I heard a great voice out of heaven saying, Behold, the tabernacle of God is with men, and he will dwell with them, and they shall be his people, and God himself shall be with them, and be their God. And God shall wipe away all tears from their eyes; and there shall be no more death, neither sorrow, nor crying, neither shall there be anymore pain; for the former things are passed away. And he that sat upon the throne said, Behold, I make all things new. And he said unto me, Write; for these words are faithful and true.

"So we shall grieve for a season for the fellowship we shall no longer have with Bob and Evelyn. But they are in a better place, and we, too, have the same blessed hope. Let us pray together, upon Psalm 23..."

The culprits still had not been found.

The next day at Church George continued with his preaching out of the Book of Revelation. As he had promised, he went directly to Revelation 6, out of which came the four horsemen of the Apocalypse. "In Revelation Chapter 6, like in the previous two chapters," George began, "The Apostle John writes the vision that Jesus shows him.

And I saw when the Lamb opened one of the seals, and I heard, as it were, the noise of thunder, on of the four living creatures saying, Come and see. And I saw and, behold, a white horse; and he that sat on him had a bow; and a crown was given unto him, and he went forth conquering, and to conquer.

"I'll interrupt the narrative here to talk about this first horse, the white one that emerges with the opening of the first seal on the scroll by none other than Jesus Christ. For over a hundred years the horseman on the white horse has been interpreted as the Antichrist. Notice that he had a bow, but no arrows were mentioned. This has been interpreted as the Antichrist conquering with a deceptive peace, but always with the threat of violence. To continue with the narrative,

And when he had opened the second seal, I heard the second living creature say, Come and see. And there went out another horse that was red; and power was given to him that sat on it to take peace from the earth, and that they should kill one another; and there was given unto him a great sword.

"The red horse always has been interpreted as suggestive of open warfare. This interpretation is validated by the passage itself in which peace was taken from the earth. Right now we Christians are expecting two great wars in the future. The first is the war described by the prophet Ezekiel in Chapters 38 and 39 in his book; the second is the final war of Armageddon, which apparently enmeshes the entire world in warfare. The great sword given to the horseman on the red horse is suggestive of mass slaughter. I'll return to the narrative:

And when he had opened the third seal, I heard the third living creature say, Come and see. And I beheld and, lo, a black horse; and he that sat on him had a pair of balances in his hand. And I heard a voice in the midst of the four living creatures say, A measure of wheat for a denarius, and three measures of barley for a denarius, and see thou hurt not the oil and the wine.

"The black horse has universally been interpreted as signifying famine. A denarius was the equivalent of a day's wage, which means that when the black horseman comes into history, a day's wage will be required to purchase just enough to survive on. Notice, too, that the oil and wine are not to be touched. This is usually interpreted as meaning that great wealth will remain in the hands of a few privileged people in the midst of the famine. Back to Scripture:

> *And when he had opened the fourth seal, I heard the voice of the fourth living creature say, Come and see. And I looked, and, behold, a pale horse, and his name that sat on him was Death, and Hell followed with him. And power was given unto them over the fourth part of the earth, to kill with sword, and with hunger, and with death, and with the beasts of the field.*

"In some ways, this fourth horseman is the most terrifying. Historically, the pale horse has been interpreted as pestilence, disease. But there's a problem with that interpretation. Note that the killing includes death by sword and hunger, the method of the red and black horsemen. There's an even bigger problem with that interpretation, in that the translators got it wrong because they had trouble believing what Scripture said. In the original Greek, this fourth horse was described by the word *chloros*. *Chloros* doesn't mean pale, but green. The translators decided that this didn't make sense, as green horses just don't exist. So they changed the meaning of the word from 'green' to 'pale'." George chuckled at the irony. "After all the improper allegorization of passages that should have been taken literally, they chose this rare instance where allegorization is appropriate to insist on a literal interpretation. What they didn't understand was the allegorical nature of these horses. In that context, green would be perfectly permissible. Not only that, but God can do anything He wants. If He wants to make a green horse, who's to stop Him? But back to the point. A green horse can suggest disease as well or better than a pale horse, so it doesn't change the dynamics of the interpretation. But the other matter does, that of the inclusion of sword and hunger in the method of killing. That application of other modes of killing in addition to disease opens the door to another interpretation entirely of all four horsemen. Sometimes I enjoy watching some prophetic teachers on television. They give me fresh perspectives on the Word of God. At times they obviously aren't correct in what they say, but in this case the viewpoint of Irvin Baxter on the four horsemen gave me pause. It doesn't necessarily contradict the standard interpretations – either or both may be correct. But since it does make sense, I'll share it with you.

"Under this interpretation," George continued, "the four horses represent socio-political systems of man as the end of the age approaches. Under this regime, the white horse represents the Catholic Church, which indeed has exercised much control over the peoples of the earth. The Catholic Pope wears white in his public ceremonies; also, the Popemobile and the Pope's personal airplane are white. Has the Catholic Church indulged in corruption in its past? Yes indeed, but before I present some details, you must remember that any organization of man, even if it starts out in service to God, is susceptible to corruption. This is particularly true when it becomes enmeshed in politics and other worldly issues in contrast to Jesus' clear claim that His kingdom is not of this world. How can I have any doubt that the Protestent Churches aren't susceptible to the same failures when I see it happening before my very eyes? But in the early 1500s, Martin Luther certainly had a case against the established and deeply politicized Church. The arrogance of her leaders, even at the intermediate level of the bureaucracy, was both astonishing and disgusting. Her idolatry, heresy, moral filth, unbelievable cruelty, indifference to human suffering and many other human failings were rampant. Her rejection of the true God in favor of pomp and wealth was virtually complete. I'll present just one example, taken from Foxe's *Book of Christian Martyrs:*

"John Browne ran into trouble with the Church by sitting too close to a priest on a public barge in 1517.

"'Do you know who I am?' the priest demanded. 'You're sitting on my clothing!'

"'No sir,' replied Browne, 'I don't know who you are.'

"'I'm a priest.'

"'Oh. Are you a parson? A vicar? Or a lady's chaplain?'

"'No. I'm a soul priest,' the man replied. 'I sing for a soul.'

"'Do you? That's wonderful!' Browne exclaimed. 'But where do you find this soul when you go to mass?'

"'I don't know.'

"'Ah. And when the mass is done, where do you leave this soul?' continued Browne.

"'I don't know.' Pastor George made a theatrical face with this.

"'But if you don't know where to find or leave this soul, how can you save it?'

"'Get out of here! The priest yelled. 'You're a heretic, and I'll get even with you!'

"As soon as he left the barge, this priest went directly to Archbishop Warham. Three days later John Browne was taken from his house and imprisoned in Canterbury, where he remained from Low Sunday until the Friday before Whit-Sunday, without his family knowing where he was.

"The night before he was to be burned as a heretic, Browne was locked in the stocks at Ashford, Kent, where he lived, and found by his wife, who stayed by his side all night listening to his story. Browne showed her his feet, which had been burned to the bones with hot coals by bishops Warham and Fisher, 'to make me deny my Lord, which I will never do. Please, Elizabeth,' Browne continued, 'do as you have done in the past and bring the children up virtuously in the fear of God.'

"The next day Browne was burned at the stake, saying, 'Into thy hands I commend my spirit. You have redeemed me, O Lord of Truth.'"

"But to return to the subject at hand," George continued, "the association of the white horse with a corrupted end-time version of Catholicism, possibly having merged with the fallen Protestant Churches and the Islamic religion, seems to be strengthened by the narrative of Revelation 17, in which a harlot representing a false end-time church sits atop a vicious beast representing the end-time political-economic system. The harlotry of the end-time false religion is symbolic of this church's infidelity to the true God. A foretaste of such harlotry is presented in the Book of Hosea. The association of a fallen-away Catholic Church with this harlot is the inclusion of some key identifiers in Revelation 17, including the color white, which is traditionally worn by the pope, the color scarlet in which cardinals deck themselves out, the color purple, the traditional color of bishops, and the great material wealth of this false church.

"The red horse in this new interpretation in the context of the most powerful of the systems of man represents communism, to which the color red is strongly associated. It has certainly engaged in much warfare and bloodshed, often against its own people. The latest estimates for the number of deaths that Stalin was responsible for are around forty million, far more than the number associated with Hitler. And then we are still waiting for the Ezekiel 38 war, in which Ezekiel specifically named Russia. Now, as to the color black, the association here is to capitalism, which is not exempt from the charges of suffering and death. There is the thought that the Antichrist's one-world government will have elements of socialism and capitalism. Black is an apt color for capitalism. When things are going well economically, the numbers are said to be 'in the black'.

"But the most ominous horseman in the systems interpretation, at least for the near future, is the green one. Green is associated with Islam, which is currently on the move. This religious system actually is attempting to take over the entire world, and is rather far more advanced in that objective than most westerners realize. In Europe, it's well on the way toward executing a bloodless coup. At the same time, the historically Islam nations of the Middle East are becoming more fundamentalist and religious in their outlook as well as more militant. I'll finish up today's sermon with a warning: make no mistake; at its core, Islam is not a religion of peace, nor does it have anything in common with the Judeo-Christian understanding of God. It is monotheistic to be sure, but that monotheism is so simplistic that in its insistence on a single God, Allah the father, it denies the deity of both Jesus and the Holy Spirit. It is a religion of hatred. But don't fall into the trap of hating its adherents. They are to be understood as misguided, and must be loved, even when they hate you."

Earl and Joyce followed their routine of taking Cathy home with them and bringing her back with them to the nursing home in time for the Bible study. Joyce was troubled when they left the Church.

"Earl, did you notice that the attendance has dropped significantly since George began the Book of Revelation?" she asked. "Not only that, but this is the second week in a month that someone has walked out on his sermon."

"Yeah. But the guy who left was creepy. He looked mean. I don't know if there's a connection, but he ducked out when George linked the fourth horseman with Islam. And boy, was he mad!"

They had forgotten their concern over the Church by the start of the Bible study at the nursing home. "The Book of Acts has been pretty exciting so far," Earl told the residents in his Sunday evening talk. "People, filled with the Holy Spirit, became bold in talking about Jesus, in healing others, in being fearless in the face of evil. Wonderful things were happening. Powerful things. Some were set free from the bonds of jail while others were willing to die for their faith. But if there's anything important, even magnificent that came from, no, *comes* from the indwelling Holy Spirit, it's the love for God that the Spirit offers those who accept the price that Jesus paid for them on the cross.

"I'm going to tell you such a love story tonight, one of the most moving in the entire Bible. It starts in the Book of Acts, pretty near where we left off last week. On one level, it's the story of two men. They had nearly the same name. One was named Saul, and the other Paul.

"Saul was not a Christian. In fact, he hated Christians. He was a Pharisee, one of the religious leaders. He was an Israelite, being from the tribe of Benjamin, which historically was the closest to Judah of the other tribes. He was proud of his Hebrew heritage, and, like the other Pharisees, he rejected the deity of Jesus. He rejected Jesus altogether, as a matter of fact, and he tried to stamp out this new Christianity through jail and even murder. We read about Stephen last week, which ended with his death by stoning. Was Saul lurking around that event, getting involved in mischief? You bet he was. We already read in Acts Chapter 7 how the Jewish religious leaders ran upon Stephen after his speech, and cast him out of the city, and stoned him to death. Listen to this:

> *Then they cried out with a loud voice, and stopped their ears, and ran upon him with one accord, and cast him out of the city, and stoned him; and the witnesses laid down their clothes at a young man's feet, whose name was Saul. And they stoned Stephen, calling upon God, and saying, Lord Jesus, receive my spirit. And he kneeled down, and cried with a loud voice, Lord, lay not this sin to their charge. And when he said this, he fell asleep.*

Earl looked up from his Bible. "When the Bible said that Stephen fell asleep," he said, "it was a soft way of saying that he died. From that passage we immediately enter Chapter 8 of Acts, where we find that Saul not only consented to Stephen's death, but actively willed it. Here I'll read that terrible first sentence to you:

> *And Saul was consenting unto his death.*

"The Bible's condemnation of Saul goes yet further. In the first two verses of Acts Chapter 9, we read:

> *And Saul, yet breathing out threatenings and slaughter against the disciples of the Lord, went unto the high priest, and [asked him for letters] to Damascus to the synagogues, that if he found any of this way, whether they were men or women, he might [arrest them and] bring them bound unto Jerusalem.*

"Okay. Enough of Saul for now and his evil deeds against Christians." Earl again looked out from his reading to his audience. His eyes settled on Laurie, and what he saw surprised him. Expecting to see her usual jovial, compassion-filled expression, he saw instead a tight-lipped frown on her face, one that spoke of bitterness. He resolved to talk to her after the session, but for now he wished to continue with his subject. His glance moved over to Joyce at the piano. He was relieved to see her smiling face.

"Now," he continued, "we'll talk about quite a different man whose name was Paul. Paul was a religious leader, but he discarded that to follow in the footsteps of Jesus Christ. If there's anything that can be said about Paul, it's his love for Jesus, and with that love, his love for the Church. Paul, in fact, made several dangerous missionary journeys throughout the shores of the Mediterranean Sea to plant and nurture Churches. He suffered snake bite, shipwreck and the venom of Christian-haters like Saul on his journeys, and pressed on despite the many hardships. Here's what he himself said about his tribulations in 2 Corinthians 11:23-30:

> *Are they ministers of Christ? (I speak as a fool) I am more; in labors more abundant, in stripes above measure, in prisons more frequently, in deaths often. Of the Jews five times received I forty stripes save one. Thrice was I beaten with rods, once was I stoned, thrice I suffered shipwreck, a night and a day I have been in the deep; in journeyings often, in perils of waters, in perils of robbers, in perils by mine own countrymen, in perils by the Gentiles, in perils of the city, in perils in the wilderness, in perils among false brethren; in weariness and painfulness, in watchings often, in hunger and thirst, in fastings often, in cold and nakedness. Besides those things that are without, that which cometh upon me daily, the care of all the churches. Who is weak, and I am not weak? Who is offended, and I am not indignant? If I must needs glory, I will glory of the things which concern mine infirmities. The God and Father of our Lord Jesus Christ, who is blessed for evermore, knoweth that I lie not.*

"This beloved man," Earl said, "this most holy man of God, this humble giant of a Christian, wrote most of the books of the New Testament. He established numerous Churches and cared for them and wept over them like a mother. Listen, from Ephesians 1:1-3, to a typical way that he would address the Churches in the beginning of a letter:

> *Paul, an apostle of Jesus Christ by the will of God, to the saints who are at Ephesus, and to the faithful in Christ Jesus: grace be to you, and peace, from God, our Father, and from the Lord Jesus Christ. Blessed by the God and Father of our Lord Jesus Christ, who hath blessed us with all spiritual blessings in heavenly places in Christ,...*

"Paul was, perhaps, the greatest Christian who ever lived. Now I have a question to ask you: did this man of God ever meet the evil Saul?" Earl looked around for a response. He didn't expect any. He knew that Joyce and possibly Laurie knew the answer, but they held back to maintain the suspense.

"Actually they did. Do you want to hear about it?" The response was rather loud in the affirmative. "Well, then. I'll turn to Acts 13:9. It's all in that one little verse:

> *Then Saul...*

"After this there is a comment in parenthesis that lets the cat out of the bag:

> *...(who also is called Paul)...*

"What!" Earl exclaimed theatrically. "Did you hear that? According to my Bible, Saul and Paul are the same man! Now what on earth could have happened to Saul to turn him into Paul? The answer to that is in Acts Chapter 9. I'll start from the beginning, repeating just a little:

> *And Saul, yet breathing out threatenings and slaughter against the disciples of the Lord, went unto the high priest, and [asked him for] letters to Damascus to the synagogues, that if he found any of this way, whether they were men or women, he might [arrest them and] bring them bound unto Jerusalem. And as he journeyed, he came near Damascus, and suddenly there shone round about him a light from heaven; and he fell*

to the earth, and heard a voice saying unto him, Saul, Saul, why persecutest thou me? And [Saul] said, Who art thou, Lord? And the Lord said, I am Jesus, whom thou persecutest; it is hard for thee to kick against the goads. And [Saul], trembling and astonished, said, Lord, what wilt thou have me to do? And the Lord said unto him, Arise, and go into the city, and it shall be told thee what thou must do. And the men who journeyed with him stood speechless, hearing a voice, but seeing no man. And Saul arose from the earth, and when his eyes were opened, he saw no man; but they led him by the hand, and brought him into Damascus. And he was three days without sight, and neither did eat nor drink. And there was a certain disciple at Damascus, named Ananias; and to him said the Lord in a vision, Ananias. And he said, Behold, I am here, Lord. And the Lord said unto him, Arise, and go into the street which is called Straight, and inquire in the house of Judas for one called Saul of Tarsus; for, behold, he prayeth, and hath seen in a vision a man, named Ananias, coming in and putting his hand on him, that he might receive his sight. Then Ananias answered, Lord, I have heard by many of this man, how much evil he hath done to thy saints at Jerusalem; and here he hath authority from the chief priests to [arrest] all that call on thy name. But the Lord said unto him, Go thy way; for he is a chosen vessel unto me, to bear my name before the Gentiles, and kings, and the children of Israel. For I will show him what great things he must suffer for my name's sake.

And Ananias went his way, and entered into the house; and putting his hands on him said, Brother Saul, the Lord, even Jesus, that appeared unto thee in the way as thou camest, hath sent me, that thou mightest receive thy sight, and be filled with the Holy Spirit. And immediately there fell from [Saul's] eyes as it had been scales; and he received sight, and arose, and was baptized. And when he had received food, he was strengthened. Then was Saul certain days with the disciples who were at Damascus. And immediately he preached Christ in the synagogues, that he is the Son of God. But all that heard him were amazed, and said: Is not this he that destroyed them who called on this name in Jerusalem, and came here for that intent, that he might bring them bound unto the chief priests?'

"I'll close this talk by naming two lessons that we can learn from Paul's life-changing encounter with Jesus. First, never underestimate the power of God. Sometimes He is polite enough to stay in the background so that we don't think that He's around. But He is around, 24-7, and He is in control over everything that happens on earth. Second, we must heed what Jesus commanded, to love our enemies and not to judge them. For who knows whether this enemy might not change in the Hands of God into the best friend you ever knew?"

Earl had forgotten about Laurie's consternation, but she accosted him before he reached his wife. "Earl," she said, placing a hand softly on his arm, "can I speak to you and Joyce in my office?"

"Of course," he replied. Let me collect Joyce and we'll follow you."

When they were seated in her office, Earl asked whether he had said something that she didn't approve of. He was ready to apologize and do whatever she wanted to set things straight.

"It's not about you at all," Laurie responded. She came right to the point. "It's about Catherine," she began. "The Department of Health and Human Services came here this afternoon. Cathy doesn't have any close relatives, just a cousin who could care less about what happens to her. The cousin, as a matter of fact, signed her over to the government last week, to do what they want with her. They want to move her to their main facility in Seattle in the name of cost savings. We can't do anything about it, because the state is going to cut off their funding to us for her upkeep. Have you ever been to their main facility?"

"No," they said in unison.

"Well, let me tell you," she continued, "it's a nightmare. Hell on earth. What gets me is that it's already way overcrowded. The thought's almost unbearable, but I can't help wondering whether she eventually will be euthanized."

Joyce put a hand up to her mouth in shock. "That's hard to believe. Surely you're being too cynical."

"Look at what we've been doing to the unborn for years," Laurie countered. "And society's just getting more selfish each year. The more recent crop of graduating high-schoolers have been brought up to think of focus on self as natural, and those who go on to college get a huge dose of survival-of-the-fittest training. You think God is no longer in public life? Well, He got kicked out of college years ago. We are very far along in creating a brave new world where there's no room for defects. And now just think about the way the president has gotten around saner heads in congress by misusing the power of executive orders. Think what the government takeover of health care is going to do for kids like Cathy. You know yourselves that doctors have the means to detect Mongolism in fetuses, and already give the choice to the parents as to whether to terminate the pregnancy, which is just another euphemism for infanticide."

With that troubling thought in mind, Earl and Joyce left the nursing home. Joyce remained silent for much of the ride back to their house, but before they arrived, she turned to Earl. "What about adopting Cathy?" she asked. "It's just one person out of so many, but we should do whatever we can to show the light of Christ to a rapidly darkening world. And we could give her a decent life."

Earl stared straight ahead. She knew he was thinking about what she'd just said, but his lack of response began to bother her. Before she could say anything, he abruptly turned to her. "What a good idea!" he replied.

They both remained quiet for the rest of the ride home, each absorbed in the implications of that new idea. Later in bed they returned to the subject.

"Are you still thinking about it?" Joyce asked.

"Yes. Do you have any idea what we'd be getting into?" Before she could respond, he continued. "It would be plenty hard for an intact couple to deal with, and neither of us has a full set of limbs. You already know that Cathy has special potty needs – demanding ones. I've seen what it takes out of you. Could you handle that on a daily basis? And then there's the bathing. And eating. And communicating. And the teaching, although that would be a privilege."

"It all would be a privilege, Earl. I know it would be difficult, but didn't you tell me about the amazing way that God helped you take Buddy hang gliding? I even saw it for myself. With God all things are possible, at least when we're within His will. I have a distinct feeling that this definitely would be in His will."

"You are so right. Thanks for setting me straight. I'll call Laurie in the morning, and maybe you can work out the details."

"Done," she said. In the dark he didn't see the broad smile on her face.

They had no idea what lay ahead.

In Washington, D.C., Ace made three phone calls to the West Coast, one each to Los Angeles, San Francisco and Seattle. They were all directed to the local destabilization leaders and they consisted of the same message: the time is now- saddle up and prepare to move.

Chapter Thirteen

"We've decided to commit to an adoption," Earl told Laurie over the phone Monday. "We have an inkling now of what is involved and we know it won't be easy. But it's what we both want. We've had our doubts too. But then we remembered what you said about what might happen to Cathy if we don't do this thing. So I'm asking you to start the paperwork."

At first Laurie was excited with the offer, but before Earl got off the phone with her, she began to have second thoughts. "Gee, Earl, I don't know. I have a feeling that you and Joyce could handle her needs – they're pretty demanding as you know – but that's not the only problem. It's a bureaucratic jungle out there. You'd have to convince the powers that be that your own handicaps don't make the job insurmountable. If you think that taking care of Cathy would be hard, just wait 'til you have to deal with the government."

"Well, we're very sure that we want to do this thing, Laurie. "Let's just do what we can and play it by ear. We're of the opinion that with God, all things are possible."

"Let's pray that God wants this to happen, Earl. And thanks to both of you from the bottom of my heart. I'm very proud of you.

You don't know what a load this takes off my mind about Cathy, even with the bureaucracy looming ahead of us. I'll get busy on the process right away."

It wasn't a friend who crept into Pastor George's study Wednesday as he prepared for his next sermon and knifed him in the gut with the intent to kill him. His attacker fled the scene of the crime when he was satisfied that the man writhing in agony on the floor by his feet was bleeding out so profusely that there wasn't a hope of aid arriving in time to save his life.

God had other plans. With all the strength he could muster, and a helping hand from the Holy Spirit, George picked himself off the floor long enough to grab the phone on the desk and call 911. He was unconscious when the aid car arrived, but he wasn't dead. The rescuers immediately rigged up a plasma transfusion, and by the time they arrived at the hospital George had returned to consciousness. "I'd like you to call my deacon," George gasped. "I have his number. Tell him to tell our regular members and let them know what happened. They'll have to bring in a substitute for next Sunday.'

A representative of the hospital followed George's wishes, and Joyce took the call from Jim Preston, who had replaced the murdered Bob Smith as the Church's deacon. "Hello, Joyce," Jim said. "I'm afraid I have a bit of bad news. Pastor George is in the hospital."

"Oh, no!" she exclaimed. "A heart attack?" George was somewhat elderly. His wife had died of cancer several years ago, and he lived alone.

"No. It's worse than that. Someone tried to take his life, like what happened to Bob. He was stabbed in the stomach and he's hanging on by a thread. I'm going down now to see him.

"Can Earl and I come too?"

"I don't know whether I'll get in or not, it's pretty late and George is probably sleeping. Why don't you call the hospital in the morning and find out what the visiting hours are?"

Joyce thanked him for the call. By the time she got off the phone, Earl was all ears from her side of the conversation. "What happened?" he asked.

"George is in the hospital with stab wounds. Somebody tried to kill him."

"What a terrible thing," he said, shaking his head. First Bob and Evelyn. Now this."

Joyce wasn't listening to him. The events of the last few days had unnerved her. Depressed, she left the den for their bedroom.

"Earl," She said sweetly.

"Hi, Wisdom," he responded.

"I'm going to be filling you with understanding of the Rapture tonight. I want you to use this knowledge first to comfort your poor wife. As you know, she isn't coping too well with the outside world. You are going to get her faith back on track with the promise of the Rapture."

"But You told me before that we were going to have to brave the Tribulation. What kind of faith builder is that to give Joyce an empty hope?"

"Oh, just that you'll see the power of God like you never have before, especially inside of you. You may not be going immediately, but the Rapture itself is very real, and you'll have that prospect before you always. Nevertheless, the Rapture is a good introduction to the heavenly realm, which is infinitely more important than your material world. Despite your continuing presence here on earth, you'll be direct participants in that realm when you and Joyce will be working regularly on the behalf of others. Okay with that?"

"You bet."

"For your reference, Scripture has plenty to say about the Rapture. Paul supplies you with much of that information, as he does with many of the deeper things about Us. His first major reference to it is in First Corinthians 15:

Behold, I show you a mystery: we shall not all sleep, but we shall all be changed, in a moment, in the twinkling of an eye, at the last trump; for the trumpet shall sound, and the dead shall be raised incorruptible, and we shall be changed. For this corruptible must put on incorruption, and this mortal must put on immortality. So, when this corruptible shall have put on incorruption, and this mortal shall have put on immortality, then shall be brought to pass the saying that is written, Death is swallowed up in victory. O death, where is thy sting? O grave, where is thy victory? The sting of death is sin; and the strength of sin is the law. But thanks be to God, who giveth us the victory through our Lord Jesus Christ.

"Next is Paul's mention of it in First Thessalonians 4:

But I would not have you to be ignorant, brethren, concerning them who are asleep, that ye sorrow not, even as others who have no hope. For if we believe that Jesus died and rose again, even so them also who sleep in Jesus will God bring with him. For this we say unto you by the word of the Lord, that we who are alive and remain unto the coming of the Lord shall not precede them who are asleep. For the Lord himself shall descend from heaven with a shout, with the voice of the archangel, and with the trump of God; and the dead in Christ will rise first; then we who are alive and remain shall be caught up together with them in the clouds, to meet the Lord in the air; and so shall we ever be with the Lord. Wherefore, comfort one another with these words.

"And, of course, Paul remarked about the eventual arrival of the fullness of time, which permits the antichrist to show his colors. That's in Second Thessalonians, as I said before:

And now ye know what restraineth that he might be revealed in his time. For the mystery of iniquity doth already work; only he who hindereth will continue to hinder until he be taken out of the way. And then shall that wicked be revealed, whom the Lord shall consume with the spirit of his mouth, and shall destroy with the brightness of his coming, even him whose coming is after the working of Satan with all power and lying wonders, and with all deceivableness of unrighteousness in them that perish, because they received not the love of the truth, that they might be saved. And for this cause God shall send them strong delusion, that they should believe the lie, that they all might be judged who believed not the truth, but had pleasure in unrighteousness.

"You," She continued, "like the 144 thousand Israelites, will be representing Us to the remnant who will become Christians in the Great Tribulation. It's really a great honor, Earl, but it's going to be tough being in your position and it's going to be lonely, especially when your supposedly fellow Christians fall away in disbelief. You'll remember just enough of this conversation to maintain your faith and pass it on to Joyce, but for the most part your knuckles will be white. Fortunately, you've already gone through enough that I know you'll be able to handle it."

"But that raises a problem, Wisdom. A big one. Pardon me for being selfish, but if events are that dire, what assurance will we have that we won't fall away too?"

"Do you really have to ask? What am I doing here now if I'd be wasting My time? Don't worry about being left out of Our relationship. If anything, you'll be a bigger part of it than otherwise. And when Jesus does come back to earth, We'll be having a special reward for you. And don't worry about the selfishness," she added with a smile. "We'll take care of that too."

"Will we live through it?"

"I'm not going to say. Knowing your fate either way wouldn't be helpful. I'll just tell you that it's highly doubtful. But recall what Jesus said about physical death in Matthew 10:

And fear not them who kill the body, but are not able to kill the soul; but rather fear him who is able to destroy both soul and body in hell.

"Actually," She continued, "when you see what's in store for the world during the Tribulation, I seriously doubt that either you or

Joyce would be particularly interested in continuing to live under those conditions."

"If that's the case, count me in."

"I already did." She gave him a loving look and faded away.

Earl lay back in bed and thought for a moment. Presently he turned on his side, wrapped an arm around Joyce's waist, and fell back into a deep sleep.

George healed slowly. The interim pastor was less than inspiring. Earl suspected that he harbored skepticism about the accuracy of the Bible, particularly with regard to the creation account at the beginning of Genesis. One of his sermons was devoted to the violence of mankind on earth at the time of Noah. Earl listened attentively, thinking that perhaps he was being too judgmental about Pastor Steve. But then Steve mentioned the flood, and the way he talked about it betrayed his misunderstanding that the flood had been purely local. From then on, Earl listened to Steve with extremely skeptical ears.

It took nine weeks for Earl and Joyce to get a response to the paperwork on Cathy's adoption. The manner in which it reached them blew their minds. Mildred Black was a state employee with credentials in social work. She came to their house on a Friday evening for the purpose of interviewing them to establish their suitability, in her eyes, for the proposed adoption. By the time she left two hours later, they had reason to question the fullness of her humanity.

Earl answered the doorbell to face a large, cadaverous middle-aged woman with sparse hair and prominent frown lines on her forehead and cheeks. From her attitude of cynical disappointment, either life had been unkind to her or she had been unkind to it. She stepped past him into the hallway without waiting for his welcome, and snapped out a hasty "I'm here about your desire to adopt. Is the missus in?"

Earl decided to be generous about his first impression of her. "Please come into the living room and make yourself comfortable on the couch. May I take your coat?"

She ignored his question and walked into the living room as if it was hers. She extended a hand in command for him to sit. He called Joyce in from the kitchen and she extended a hand in greeting. It was ignored. "Would you like a cup of coffee?" she asked. The woman pointed a commanding finger in response. She observed Joyce in the process of sitting. "Is there a problem with your legs?" she asked.

"I, uh, well, actually, not really," Joyce replied, flustered with the lack of tact. "I hardly notice it any more."

"Notice what? Are those prosthetics you're wearing?" The question was an accusation.

"Well, yes," Joyce answered, "but that doesn't mean. . ."

The woman raised the commanding arm once more, this time with palm outstretched for silence. She opened her binder and began to write. Presently she looked up and scowled at Joyce. "Why do you want to adopt?" Another accusation.

"We've been acquainted with Cathy for quite a while," Earl told the woman in a placating tone. "We don't have children of our own, and with the time we've spent with Cathy, we've established a bonding relationship with her."

The woman stared at Earl in an obvious attempt to assess his appetite for perversion. "Why were you visiting the nursing home? Why were you spending time with Catherine?" she accused.

"We have been conducting a weekly Bible study," he explained, to which she responded with another command for silence as she wrote in her binder.

"Christians, eh?" she accused. The interview had hardly begun, but apparently she'd heard enough. She closed the binder and stood up. "I'll put your request in with my comments, but I'll be honest with you. Taking care of an individual as severely handicapped as Catherine is not only difficult, but requires the kind of expertise that is possessed by professionals in the field. I wouldn't plan on the adoption taking place. You'll be hearing from us within the month." She opened the front door and walked out.

Stunned, Joyce sat unmoving on their double chair without saying a word. Eventually her eyes began watering. She got up and walked into their bedroom. Earl followed her in and attempted to comfort her, but she was inconsolable. She undressed in silence and slipped between the covers. "All I can say is this, Joyce," he said. "With God, all things are possible. If it is meant to be, it will be."

Her shoulders continued to shake. Sadly, he walked out to give her some privacy.

Eventually, he came back to bed and they both slept. It was still dark when Joyce awoke to a diffuse light. The beautiful face looked at her in earnest compassion. Her eyes glistened with moisture. Joyce turned to wake Earl, but a gentle hand restrained her. "It's you I want to talk to, Joyce," Wisdom told her softly. "Let him sleep. We gave him to you for love and comfort. You should listen to him and you wouldn't be as grieved as you are about Cathy. It's true, you know, what he said."

"W-what did he say?" She was taken aback by the apparition at her bedside. They'd communed like this before, but she still wasn't used to the intimacy of this exchange with God although she welcomed it with all her heart.

"He told you that with Us all things are possible. Mildred thinks she has you wrapped around her thumb. Know this for certain, Joyce: she doesn't have the control over matters that she thinks she does. By the time she comes to face Us, she'll have a better understanding of where she fits into the scheme of things. In the meantime, you need to have compassion for her, because her life is not very pleasant. Can you do that, in the face of her rudeness to you?"

"I-I guess so. I didn't look at life from her perspective, did I?"

"No. She's had her share of personal issues, but right now she's attending a slew of meetings about policy changes. Dark changes, and they're affecting her conscience. She's knuckling under to them because she fears for her financial survival, but she knows in her heart that they're evil. Dealing with darkness is part of your learning. You're coming along, so don't fret. Now about Cathy. Whatever happens, We do control the situation. Can you believe that?"

"Yes, of course." She spoke with more confidence. "But I have a question about that. Why are You so real to me when others never have a chance to see You? And it's not only about seeing You personally, but any sign of Your presence. A lot of people don't think You even exist."

"There's a reason for that. It's called faith. It's of the utmost importance to Us that those of you with whom We're going to have an everlasting relationship see Us through the lens of faith. For that faith to be anything but trivial, the question of Our actual existence must always hang in the air. Give yourself a helping hand. Go back and reread Hebrews Chapter 11. Burn it into your memory, so you'll be able to stand fast in opposition to attacks from the world." She smiled warmly to soften the lecture.

"Beyond the faith issue," She continued, "We generally leave it up to the individual as to whether or not that person sees Us or Our works. We're closest, Joyce, to those who wish Us to be. If some people don't want to see Us, and there are a lot of those people about, We usually oblige them. On the other hand, there are many others whom We cherish, who are simply plain, meat-and-potatoes Christians. For them, dear as they are to Us, life is more of a spectator sport. We'll be happy to welcome them into heaven, but We don't have any particular objectives for them to accomplish while they are on earth. But there are yet others, much fewer, whom We have selected for special tasks. We communicate far more directly with them. Jesus pretty much said it all as Luke recorded in Chapter 12, verses 47 and 48:

> *And that servant, who knew his lord's will, and prepared not himself, neither did according to his will, shall be beaten with many stripes. But he that knew not, and did commit things worthy of stripes, shall be beaten with few stripes. For unto whomsoever much is given, of his shall be much required; and to whom men have committed much, of him they will ask the more.*

Are you okay with that answer?"

"Yes, I understand."

"Good, because you'll be helping, from your own love toward them, to bring some of the more reluctant ones into the fold. I'll reinforce that understanding in your mind as to what We expect of you, maybe have Earl help out with that. Remember that we love you. Deeply. Whatever takes place in the future, everything will work out for your good."

"Oh. So we will get Cathy." She gave Wisdom a bright smile.

"Maybe. Maybe not. What happens may not be what you expect or even think should happen, but you must trust Us that everything will work out to the Glory of God in the long run. I'll repeat: as you've obviously guessed by now, you and Earl aren't of the meat-and-potatoes variety. We've given you much to hang your faith on, but We're also asking a greater faith from you in return. Have faith that what We do is done in love, even if things get dicey for you in the near term. Remember what Jesus told you in Luke 12: 'Are not five sparrows sold for two farthings, and not one of them is forgotten before God? But even the very hairs on your head are all numbered. Fear not, therefore; ye are of more value than many sparrows.' Also take to heart the Scriptures that Earl read to you and Laurie about the character of people as you approach the end of this age. You got a dose of that nature tonight, but it's for your good. You need to grow into the ability to handle that without breaking down, because you and Earl are going to be two of our front-line fighters. Your greatest battle is ahead of you, but you'll have plenty of joy to go with it. Do you know what your greatest strength is going to be?"

"No," Joyce replied in a subdued voice.

"It will be your ability to live outside of self. And to do so in love toward others, even your enemies. It will take lots of effort to get there, but you've come a long way since We brought Sam into heaven with Us. We're looking forward with great joy to seeing you and Earl continue to grow together. Tomorrow I want you to read Luke Chapter 6." Wisdom put a hand on her hair and stroked it gently. "Good night, my darling, and sleep tight," She whispered. With a kiss She faded from sight. Joyce turned to Earl and went back to sleep. She had a smile on her face.

Chapter Fourteen

The next day was Saturday. "I don't get it," Earl said as they drove to the nursing home. What's the deal with you? When you went to bed last night you couldn't stop crying. You've been happy as a lark ever since we got up this morning. I'm still feeling bleak. It might be a good idea if you'd share your good fortune with me."

"It's not something I can put into words," she replied. "It's just a feeling that everything will turn out okay in the end. Whatever happens."

"Ah." A light bulb went on in Earl's head. But he wished that he had been awake too. He deeply missed Her more frequent visits in the past.

Earl and Joyce spent that weekend with Cathy, as if the issue of the adoption was settled. When they told Laurie of the interview, she predictably expressed indignation.

"I know that woman," she said darkly. "She's a control freak. I'd like to..."

"Whoa," Joyce interrupted to their surprise. "How do you get rid of darkness, Laurie?"

She was taken aback by Joyce's assertiveness, but she managed to reply "Why, I guess with light."

"Exactly. And how do we Christians light up the world?"

"Well, I'd say with the light of Jesus."

"And what is the nature of that light?"

Laurie thought for a moment, unsure of the answer. "I guess it would be love. God is love, according to John."

"Right again. So we don't fight darkness with darkness. We fight it with the light of love, extended even to our enemies. Earl, give me your Bible."

When he handed it over to her, she opened it to Luke Chapter 6 and began to read at verse 26:

Woe unto you, when all men shall speak well of you! For so did their fathers to the false prophets. But I say unto you that hear, Love your enemies, do good to them who hate you. Bless them that curse you, and pray for them who despitefully use you. And to him that smiteth thee on the one cheek, offer also the other; and him that taketh away thy cloak, forbid not to take thy coat also. Give to every man that asketh of thee; and of him that taketh away thy goods ask them not again. And as ye would that men should do to you, do ye also to them. For if ye love them that love you, what thanks have ye? For sinners also love those who love them. And if ye do good to them who do good to you, what thanks have ye? For sinners do also even the same. And if ye lend to them of whom ye hope to receive, what thanks have ye? For sinners also lend to sinners, to receive as much again. But love ye your enemies, and do good, and lend, hoping for nothing again; and your reward shall be great, and ye shall be the children of the Highest; for he is kind to the unthankful and to the evil. Be ye, therefore, merciful, as your Father also is merciful. Judge not, and ye shall not be judged; condemn not, and ye shall not be condemned; forgive, and ye shall be forgiven; give, and it shall be given unto you; good measure, pressed down, and shaken together, and running over, shall men give unto your bosom. For with the same measure that ye measure, it shall be measured to you again.

Laurie stubbornly continued to frown. She started to speak, but Earl cut her off. "I wouldn't argue with that," he said. "It's the Word of God, and I also know where Joyce got the idea of where to turn."

"You mean that you didn't think of payback after Mildred got through with you?"

Earl laughed sheepishly. "You've got me there. I did. It was a very colorful sequence of images. To a large extent it was frustration on my part. The Bible is very definite about the callousness of the end-time society. The selfish, loveless indifference toward others. Already we can hear our younger generation grousing about how the elderly are cutting into what's left of Social Security. On top of that, wait 'til the full extent of the cost comes in for universal health care. Look how the Germans, among the most civilized people on earth, fell under the Nazi spell and went along with the labeling of some groups of targeted people among them as "useless eaters". As you surely know, that didn't end well."

"It looks like America is heading down that same bleak path," Laurie said.

"Yes, but there's one thing that we do have control over, which is our response to that evil. Thanks to God and Joyce, I have finally come to an understanding of how Christians are supposed to deal with that kind of thing. Sometimes, Laurie, it's not easy being a Christian. We really aren't supposed to think like society tells us to. As a matter of fact, we stand in opposition to the ways of the world. But always in love."

"Well, okay, if you say so." Laurie clearly remained dubious about loving those who try to stick it to others. But let me ask you something. Have you noticed any difference around the nursing home?

"Well, I..."

"Let me get to the point. It's a little quieter around here since some of our residents have been transferred to the main facility. Remember? The one I was worried that Cathy would be sent to? I wouldn't be surprised if we got shut down within a few more months."

It's starting, Earl though miserably. *Now more than ever we have to act like Christians in the face of evil.* Earl made a mental note to thoroughly cover that aspect of Christianity in the Bible study, as Laurie always attended. He thought of how the story of Joseph in Genesis 37 through 45 so perfectly demonstrated the selfless nature of Jesus in loving those who wished Him harm. His thoughts turned to Pastor George and his sermon on loving those who hated us. He wondered whether George still felt loving toward the guy who had tried to do him in.

Indeed he did. George had recovered enough to deliver the sermon in Church that Sunday. The congregation was greatly relieved to see him back. Earl felt somewhat guilty about Steve's going on to another congregation, there to mislead others, but this concern was quickly overshadowed by his joy at seeing George up and about.

"Remember my sermon about loving those who hate you?" George asked his congregation. "Well, it's time for me to practice what I preach." Laughter erupted from the aptness of the popular phrase. "They've caught the man who stabbed me. I went to visit him in jail last week. As a matter of fact, I plan to make that a weekly ritual. The man has some severe emotional problems, caused by a religion that's essentially hate-filled and godless. I won't go into specifics about it at that time, but just keep in mind that Christianity is the only religion on earth that isn't actually a religion but a relationship with God through Jesus Christ. There are a whole slew of religions that teach methods for storming the gates of heaven on the basis of our own merits. It can't be done, as you already know. I'd like you to pray for me in this new opportunity, as a matter of fact.

"Now I'll return to where I left off so many weeks ago. I presume that Steve didn't address the Book of Revelation?"

A resounding "no!" filled the Church. George ignored the

implication of the vehement response and went to his Bible. "We'll continue, then, in Revelation Chapter 6. We left off last, as you recall, with the four horsemen of the Apocalypse, where we found two possible interpretations. Moving on from there, we next encounter the opening of the fifth seal. I'll begin reading the Scripture:

> *And when he had opened the fifth seal, I saw under the altar the souls of them that were slain for the word of God, and for the testimony which they held. And they cried with a loud voice, saying, How long, O Lord, holy and true, dost thou not judge and avenge our blood on them that dwell on the earth? And white robes are given unto every one of them; and it was said unto them that they should rest yet for a little season, until their fellow servants also and their brethren, that should be killed as they were, should be fulfilled.*

"So here we find ourselves at a time when Christians are being killed for their faith. It's rather difficult to attempt to pinpoint the time that this represents, for persecution and martyrdom have been going on fairly continuously ever since the Church began after the first Pentecost following Jesus' resurrection. I really wish you'd all go out and get for yourselves a copy of Foxe's *Book of Christian Martyrs* to get a sense of how pervasive this persecution has been over the centuries. It certainly didn't stop after Foxe's day. More recently, Christians were martyred in droves in Cambodia and Thailand around the time of the Vietnam War. Then there's been the huge number of African Christians killed for their faith. More recently than that, we have been witnessing an ongoing persecution of Christians in Middle Eastern countries as the people there respond to their "Muslim Spring" by attempting to stamp out Christianity within the boundaries of their various countries. I want you remember this, however: Paul was trying to do the same to Christians in Israel and Syria when God turned him into the greatest Christian who ever lived. So again I say with Jesus, love your enemies; do good to those who try to hurt you.

"Returning to the Christians under the altar in Revelation 6, we can't be sure whether they represent those who die before or during the Tribulation. Personally, I tend to think that these are Christians who are martyred before the Tribulation. But you can be sure, from Revelation 14:13, that there will be Christians on earth during the Tribulation who will die for their faith, for the events of that chapter are definitely in the midst of the Tribulation. We'll eventually get to that chapter, God willing, but I'll read a verse to you now:

> *And I heard a voice from heaven saying unto me, Write, Blessed are the dead who die in the Lord from henceforth. Yea, saith the Spirit, that they may rest from their labors, and their works do follow them.*

"I'll end today's sermon with that. I'm happy to be back with you, and look forward to seeing you next week. Let's turn to our closing hymn, number 261: *What a Friend we have in Jesus*."

Chapter Fifteen

Even though he'd been forewarned by Wisdom about the near future, Earl wasn't prepared the next week for the rampant savagery that accompanied simultaneous terror attacks on multiple cities on the West Coast. In the San Francisco Bay Area, a BART train exploded inside the tunnel underneath the bay. The blast was so powerful that it compromised the integrity of the tunnel, which soon was filled with water. Experts estimated that it might take months, if not years, to get the BART system up and running again. Other experts were uncertain as to whether the bodies were recoverable.

In Los Angeles a fully-loaded 747 was blasted out of the sky by a heat-seeking missile launched from a boat in the vicinity of the airport. It had just taken off and was full of fuel. The explosion was spectacular. At the same time, another missile hit a 747 coming in for a landing. The hit affected the tail section; out of control, the plane plowed into a high-rise office complex near the airport. The destruction resembled the twin-tower catastrophe in New York. The two tragedies occupied the first-responders, a situation that had been anticipated by certain elements for months. Unrestrained by police, multiple mobs surged into shopping areas, looting and terrorizing store owners and employees. When the police finally reacted, they were a dollar short and a week late. Both the mayor of L.A. and the governor of California were too timid to call out the National Guard, fearing a greater backlash if they did. As a consequence, lawlessness reigned citywide for several weeks. Homeowners were too afraid to venture out to the stores. They were finally forced out by the threat of starvation. Many of them died at the hands of mobs, who had broken out of the slums and were overrunning the suburbs.

The Seattle area suffered the most. At several locations the high-voltage power lines were knocked to the ground by well-placed explosives. The outage was so extensive that Seattle, Everett, Tacoma, Bellevue and the cities in-between were without power for almost a month. The cities were trashed and there, too, the mobs headed out to the suburbs, where they wrought havoc and terrorized the innocent citizenry. There were so many crimes against humanity in the new suburban war zone that the hospitals were completely overwhelmed and had to install triage crews at the entrances. But then the big diesel backup generators that the hospitals relied on for emergency electricity were bombed out of existence at three of the hospitals, leaving them unable to care for the wounded. Untreated, thousands died in a number of agonizing ways. Rescue helicopters were deployed to transport patients outside the affected areas, but after they were riddled with bullets at one landing spot the practice was discontinued.

During this crisis period Earl and Joyce weren't at home. Early on, they had gone to the nursing home to volunteer their services. Fortunately, the nursing home had a backup generator that escaped the sabotage that had destroyed others, and power remained on for the entire duration of the siege. The lights served as beacons that attracted a large number of cold and hungry refugees. During the initial period of two weeks the neighborhood around the nursing home remained remarkably free of mobs. Earl used the time to canvass the neighborhoods, bringing in a large group of nearby residents along with their bedding and spares for those without. Satan worked against himself in that situation, as the timing couldn't have been more appropriate. Just before the chaos the government had removed a number of the former residents, leaving space for the accommodation of those who sought housing away from the violence that threatened them. Earl marveled that in the midst of the evil that had befallen them, God still maintained the upper hand.

Earl and Joyce continued their regular Bible study and found, to their delight, a strong interest on the part of the refugees. He continued in the Book of Acts; obviously many people took comfort from his reading and commentaries, for he was soon pressed into multiple services along with Joyce and her piano. They were surprised by the number of people who came to accept Jesus as their Lord. Although at first he was taken aback somewhat by his lack of pastoral credentials, he also knew that there need be no intermediary between an individual and Jesus, particularly if the guide was the Bible. At first he begged Pastor George to come over to the nursing home and take over the pastoral duties there. "No, Earl," the pastor said, declining the invitation.

"But it's safer here," Earl pleaded.

"Safer? Safer is up to God. You know that."

"You're right. But these people need a pastor. There are so many of them."

"I have a hunch that you're doing the job quite nicely. Just stick to Scripture and you'll be fine. God seems to want me here, Earl. I have a responsibility to this Church. I'll call you from time to time to see how you're doing. Keep the faith, Earl. Say hello to Joyce for me."

"Will do, George. Take care." Eventually he became comfortable in his new role.

A remarkable thing happened at the beginning of the third week of the outage. The mobs arrived, and, attracted by the light pouring out of the single building that could be seen many blocks away, headed for it bent on violence and destruction. Filled with an arrogant hatred, they pounded on the door and then shot the lock away with a bullet and began to surge into the opened doorway. Moved by a power beyond his own, Earl ran to the breach and stood fast in confrontation.

"Men!" he shouted to the mob. The boldness of his voice momentarily subdued them. "We have food. We have beds. We have warmth. You can have your share of all these comforts, but only if you put down your weapons, form a single file, and enter peacefully. This is God's house. If you want to come in by force, you will suffer the consequences."

The leader of the mob assessed Earl briefly. Then, with narrowed eyes he spat in Earl's face and waved an arm forward. But then he came up short, like he'd walked into a sliding glass door. Presently he fell backwards as if he'd been pushed by a giant. He looked up and his face was contorted with fear. He pushed himself to his feet and ran away. His companions followed suit, running down the street as if their lives depended on it. "Thank you, Lord," Earl breathed as he watched their retreating backs. An insight came to him: like the times recorded in Acts, and in the Exodus, times of great peril were when God chose to display His great power. This new understanding bolstered his faith.

Order and peace eventually were restored, for the time being at least. But the psychological wounds were long-lasting. The citizens in the affected cities now lived with the understanding that they shared a too-intimate closeness with people who didn't think like they did, who were unruly, ill-disciplined and ugly-natured cretins who thought only of their next score, whether it was booze, drugs, women or food; half-humans who were ready at the drop of a pin to satisfy their violent lusts.

"Why doesn't God stop those people?" Joyce complained to Earl one evening. In response, Earl went for his Bible and sat back down with her in their shared recliner.

"You must read the history of the Jews in Samuel, Chronicles and Kings, Joyce," he said. "It's most relevant to the times we're in."

"Please, just give me an overview for now," she said.

"Okay. During the latter years of Solomon's reign, sometime around the middle of the tenth century B.C., the nation started falling away from God, maybe like we were in the States around the beginning to middle of ou own past century. The process accelerated, and in the midst of the fall God raised up prophets to warn the people to turn back or suffer the consequences."

"What were the consequences?" Joyce interrupted.

"Oh, they were spelled out in great detail by Moses long before that. Chapter 28 of Deuteronomy is a particularly representative passage of that kind of thing. Want to hear it?"

"Sure. Then you can get back to your history lesson."

"I'm warning you. It doesn't make pleasant reading, but here goes:

> *And it shall come to pass, if thou shalt hearken diligently unto the voice of the Lord thy God, to observe and to do all his commandments which I command thee this day, that the Lord God will set thee on high above all nations of the earth; and all these blessings shall come on thee, and overtake thee, if thou shalt hearken to the voice of the Lord thy God.*
>
> *Blessed shalt thou be in the city, and blessed shalt thou be in the field. Blessed shall be the fruit of thy body, and the fruit of thy ground, and the fruit of thy cattle, the increase of thy kine, and the flocks of thy sheep. Blessed shall be thy basket and thy kneading-trough. Blessed shalt thou be when thou comest in, and blessed shalt thou be when thou goest out. The Lord shall cause thine enemies who rise up against thee to be smitten before thy face; they shall come out against thee one way, and flee before thee seven ways. The Lord shall command the blessing upon thee in thy storehouses, and in all that thou settest thine hand unto; and he shall bless thee in the land which the Lord thy God giveth thee. The Lord shall establish thee an holy people unto himself, as he hath sworn unto thee, if thou shalt keep the commandments of the Lord thy God, and walk in his ways. And all people of the earth shall see that thou art called by the name of the Lord, and they shall be afraid of thee. And the Lord shall make thee plenteous in goods, in the fruit of thy body, and in the fruit*

of thy cattle, and in the fruit of thy ground, in the land which the Lord swore unto thy fathers to give thee. The Lord shall open unto thee his good treasure, the heaven to give the rain unto thy land in its season, and to bless all the work of thine hand; and thou shalt lend unto many nations, and thou shalt not borrow. And the Lord shall make thee the head, and not the tail; and thou shalt be above only, and thou shalt not be beneath, if thou hearken unto the commandments of the Lord thy God, which I command thee this day, to observe and to do them. And thou shalt not go aside from any of the words which I command thee this day, to the right hand or to the left, to go after other gods to serve them.

"Gee, Earl," Joyce interrupted, "if Moses was talking about consequences, they don't sound all that bad to me."

"Ha ha. At first, after having fought for and succeeded in moving into their Promised Land, they were blessed beyond measure as a nation whose greatness and wealth culminated in the majesty of David's kingdom and that of his son Solomon. Again, there's an eerie parallel here with the United States before and shortly after our revolution. But hold on, now it starts to warm up." He continued from where he left off.

But it shall come to pass, if thou wilt not hearken unto the voice of the lord thy God, to observe to do all his commandments and his statutes which I command thee this day, that all these curses shall come upon thee, and overtake thee. Cursed shalt thou be in the city, and cursed shalt thou be in the field. Cursed shall be thy basket and thy kneading-trough. Cursed shall be the fruit of thy body, and the fruit of thy land, the increase of thy kine, and the flocks of thy sheep. Cursed shalt thou be when thou comest in, and cursed shalt thou be when thou goest out. The Lord shall send upon thee cursing, vexation, and rebuke, in all that thou settest thine hand to do, until thou be destroyed, and until thou perish quickly, because of the wickedness of thy doings, whereby thou hast forsaken me. The Lord shall make the pestilence cling unto thee, until he have consumed thee from off the land, to which thou goest to possess it. The Lord shall smite thee with a consumption, and with a fever, and with an inflammation, and with an extreme burning, and with the sword, and with blight, and with mildew; and they shall pursue thee until thou perish. And thy heaven that is over thy head shall be bronze, and the earth that is under thee shall be iron. The Lord shall make the rain of thy land powder and dust; from heaven shall it come down upon thee, until thou be destroyed. The Lord shall cause thee to be smitten before thine enemies; thou shalt go out one way against them, and flee seven ways before them, and shalt be removed into all the kingdoms of the earth. And thy carcass shall be food unto all fowls of the air, and unto the beasts of the earth, and no man shall drive them away. The Lord will smite thee with the boil of Egypt, and with tumors, and with the scab, and with the itch, whereof thou canst not be healed. The Lord shall smite thee with madness, and blindness, and astonishment of heart; and thou shalt grope at noonday as the blind gropeth in darkness, and thou shalt not prosper in thy ways; and thou shalt be only oppressed and spoiled evermore, and no man shall save thee. Thou shalt betroth a wife, and another man shall lie with her; thou shalt build an house, and thou shalt not dwell therein; thou shalt plant a vineyard, and shalt not gather the grapes thereof. Thine ox shall be slain before thine eyes, and thou shalt not eat thereof; thine ass shall be violently taken away from before thy face, and shall not be restored to thee; thy sheep shall be given unto thine enemies, and thou shalt have none to rescue them. Thy sons and thy daughters shall be given unto another people, and thine eyes shall look, and fail with longing for them all the day long; and there shall be no might in thine hand. The fruit of thy land, and all thy labors, shall a nation whom thou knowest not eat up, and thou shalt be only oppressed and crushed always. So that thou shalt be mad for the sight of thine eyes which thou shalt see. The Lord shall smite thee in the knees, and in the legs, with a sore boil that cannot be healed, from the sole of thy foot unto the top of thy head. The Lord shall bring thee, and thy king whom thou shalt set over thee, unto a nation whom neither thou nor thy fathers have known, and there shalt thou serve other gods, wood and stone. And thou shalt become an astonishment, a proverb, and a byword among all nations to which the Lord shall lead thee. Thou shalt carry much seed out into the field, and shalt gather but little in; for the locust shall consume it. Thou shalt plant vineyards, and dress them, but shalt neither drink of the wine, nor gather the grapes; for the worms shall eat them. Thou shalt have olive trees throughout all thy borders, but thou shalt not anoint thyself with the oil; for thine olive shall cast its fruit. Thou shalt beget sons and daughters, but thou shalt not enjoy them; for they shall go into captivity. All thy trees and fruit of thy land shall the locust consume. The stranger who is within thee shall get up above thee very high, and thou shalt come down very low. He shall lend to thee, and thou shalt not lend to him; he shall be the head, and thou shalt be the tail. Moreover, all these curses shall come upon thee, and shall pursue thee, and overtake thee, till thou be destroyed, because thou hearkenedst not unto the voice of the Lord thy God, to keep his commandments and his statutes which he commanded thee; and they shall be upon thee for a sign and for a wonder, and upon thy seed forever. Because thou servedst not the Lord thy God with joyfulness, and with gladness of heart, for the abundance of all things, therefore shalt thou serve thine enemies whom the Lord shall send against thee, in hunger, and in thirst, and in nakedness, and in want of all things; and he shall put a yoke of iron upon thy neck, until he have destroyed thee.

The Lord shall bring a nation against thee from far, from the end of the earth, as swift as the eagle flieth; a nation whose tongue thou shalt not understand; a nation of fierce countenance, who shall not regard the person of the old, nor show favor to the young. And he shall eat the fruit of thy cattle, and the fruit of thy land, until thou be destroyed; who also shall not leave thee either grain, wine, or oil, or the increase of thy kine, or flocks of thy sheep, until he have destroyed thee. And he shall besiege thee in all thy gates, until thy high and fortified walls come down, wherein thou trustedst, throughout all thy land; and he shall besiege thee in all thy gates throughout all thy land, which the Lord thy God hath given thee. And thou shalt eat the fruit of thine own body, the flesh of thy sons and of thy daughters whom the Lord thy God hath given thee, in the siege, and in the straitness, wherewith thine enemies shall distress thee; so that the man who is tender among you, and very delicate, his eye shall be evil toward his brother, and toward the wife of his bosom, and toward the remnant of his children whom he shall leave; so that he will not give to any of them of the flesh of his children, whom he shall eat, because he hath nothing left him in the siege, and in the straitness, wherewith thine enemies shall distress thee in all thy gates. The tender and delicate woman among you, who would not adventure to set the sole of her foot upon the ground for delicateness and tenderness, her eye shall be evil toward the husband of her bosom, and toward her son, and toward her daughter, and toward her young one who cometh out from between her feet, and toward her children whom she shall bear; for she shall eat them for want of all things secretly in the siege and straitness, wherewith thine enemy shall distress thee in thy gates. If thou wilt not observe to do all the words of this law that are written in this book, that thou mayest fear this glorious and fearful name, THE LORD THY GOD, then the Lord will make thy plagues wonderful, and the plagues of thy seed, even great plagues, and of long continuance, and severe sicknesses, and of long continuance. Moreover, he will bring upon thee all the diseases of Egypt, which thou wast afraid of, and they shall cling unto thee. Also every sickness, and every plague, which is not written in the book of this law, them will the Lord bring upon thee, until thou be destroyed. And ye shall be left few in number, whereas ye were as the stars of heaven for multitude; because thou wouldest not obey the voice of the Lord thy God. And it shall come to pass, that as the Lord rejoiced over you to do you good, and to multiply you, so the Lord will rejoice over you to destroy you, and to bring you to nought; and ye shall be plucked from off the land to which thou goest to possess it. And the Lord shall scatter thee among all people, from the one end of the earth even unto the other; and there thou shalt serve other gods, which neither thou nor thy fathers have known, even wood and stone. And among these nations shalt thou find no ease, neither shall the sole of thy foot have rest; but the Lord shall give thee there a trembling heart, and failing of eyes, and sorrow of mind. And thy life shall hang in doubt before thee; and thou shalt fear day and night, and shalt have no assurance of thy life: in the morning thous shalt say, Would God it were evening! And at evening thou shalt say, Would God it were morning! For the fear of thine heart wherewith thou shalt fear, and for the sight of thine eyes which thou shalt see. And the Lord thall bring thee into Egypt again with ships, by the way whereof I spoke unto thee, Thou shalt see it no more again; and there ye shall be sold unto your enemies for bondmen and bondwomen, and no man shall buy you."

"That's horrible," Joyce said when Earl stopped reading. "I can't imagine such wrath from a loving God."

"I can. Looking back on Jewish history, you'll see that most of the evil came straight from the people themselves, both oppressors and oppressed, and their fallen natures."

"You're saying, then, that this curse of Moses actually came to pass."

"Yes, of course. Look at the Holocaust of Nazi Germany. And that was just a part of the many pogroms and persecutions of the Jews as strangers in strange lands over the past two millennia. Moses' prophecy here indeed came to pass. In living Technicolor. Now I'll continue with the history lesson. After Solomon's reign the kingdom split between the ten northern tribes and the two southern tribes of Judah and Benjamin, and with the split both the Israel of the north and the Judah of the south declined into apathy, corruption and moral degeneration. God held His peace for over a hundred years of decline, but eventually in the eighth century B.C. Israel was conquered by the Assyrians. They were forced to intermarry with their conquerors, which virtually completed their destruction. The northern land became known as Samaria; the Samaritans within were looked down upon by the southern Israelites because of the consequent impurity of their blood. The south held out longer, but they, too, were conquered in 606 B.C. by the Babylonians under Nebudchadnezzar and carried away as a people into Babylon. This ejection from their land lasted precisely seventy years as foretold by Jeremiah—Jeremiah 25:12—after which they were allowed to return and rebuild both their temple and the city of Jerusalem.

That dispersion was only the first, and it was far more limited in scope and time than what followed. Thirty-eight years after the crucifixion of Jesus, Titus' troops laid siege to Jerusalem and destroyed the temple so thoroughly that Jesus' prophetic pronouncement that not one stone would be left upon another was fulfilled to the letter. Four years later the Romans under Flavius Silva battered their way into the Masada fortress to end their siege there. Virtually every person alive at the time committed suicide rather than submit to Roman atrocities. There were also accounts of starvation and cannibalism.

"Over the next two millennia there has been an almost unending series of persecutions against the Jews, ending only recently, in our own generation, as a matter of fact, with the creation in 1948 of the modern state of Israel."

"Are you sure that the new nation was sanctioned by God? It seems to me that there's a lot of animosity against them, both there and here. It's doubtful to me that they'll survive."

"Oh, they'll survive, all right. It will seem impossible, but that's the whole point of the story of Gideon."

"I don't know that one," Joyce said. "Tell me about it."

"It'll have to wait until tomorrow. It's bedtime."

Chapter Sixteen

Earl and Joyce returned to their room after dinner. It was a relief to have a semblance of privacy, at least at night. Refugees had been steadily trickling away over the past week and that, combined with the loss of the original residents due to their transferal to the main facility, had allowed them to have their own room. Once inside the doorway she turned to Earl. "So tell me about Gideon," she said.

"The full story's in Judges Chapters 6 through 8," he replied. "Israel had fallen away from God, and God in turn had disciplined them by sending the Midianites to harass and bully them, and threaten them with starvation. I'll read from the beginning of Chapter 6:

> *And the children of Israel did evil in the sight of the Lord; and the Lord delivered them into the hand of Midian seven years. And the hand of Midian prevailed against Israel; and because of the Midianites, the children of Israel made themselves the dens which are in the mountains, and caves, and strongholds. And so it was, when Israel had sown, that the Midianites came up, and the Amalekites, and the children of the east, even they came up against them; and they encamped against them, and destroyed the increase of the earth, till thou come unto Gaza, and left no sustenance for Israel, neither sheep, nor ox, nor*

ass. For they came up with their cattle and their tents, and they came as grasshoppers for multitude; for both they and their camels were without number: and they entered into the land to destroy it. And Israel was greatly impoverished because of the Midianites; and the children of Israel cried unto the Lord.

And it came to pass, when the children of Israel cried unto the Lord because of the Midianites, that the Lord sent a prophet unto the children of Israel, who said unto them, Thus saith the Lord God of Israel, I brought you up from Egypt, and brought you forth out of the house of bondage; and I delivered you out of the hand of the Egyptians, and out of the hand of all who oppressed you, and drove them out from before you, and gave you their land. And I said unto you, I am the Lord your God; fear not the gods of the Amorites, in whose land ye dwell; but ye have not obeyed my voice."

"God certainly made it clear to the Israelites what their problem was," Joyce interrupted.

"He always does, especially to those to whom He is close. Jesus talked about asking much from those He has given much." Earl frowned, attempting to recall the source of that quote. Finally he went over and picked up his concordance. "Ah! There is is!" he exclaimed. "It's in Luke 12. I'll read it to you:

But he that knew not, and did commit things worthy of stripes, shall be beaten with few stripes. For unto whomsoever much is given, of him shall much be required; and to whom men have committed much, of him they will ask the more.

"There is no excuse for misunderstanding the cause-effect relationship for God's people between good and bad times. It's certainly happened that way in America. Since we who live in America historically have thought of ourselves as uniquely close to God, we also can expect God to demand that we toe the mark. According to the book *The Light and the Glory* by Peter Marshall and David Manuel, God would chastise the Puritans whenever they began to drift away from Him." Earl went over to the bookcase and took a well-worn paperback off the shelf. He leafed through it until he found what he was looking for. "According to the authors of *The Light and the Glory*, it took only one or two generations after they landed before the pilgrims, in experiencing an increasing ease of existence, began to fall away from their daily devotion to God. At first the chastising was mild, and quickly returned to blessing as the people heeded the correction. Here's an example," he said to Joyce.

"Perhaps the most extraordinary chastisement in this vein was the rain of caterpillars which Winthrop reported in the summer of 1646. 'Great harm was done in corn (especially wheat and barley) in this month by a caterpillar, like a black worm about an inch and a half long. They eat up first the blades of the stalk, then they eat up the tassels, whereupon the ear withered. It was believed by divers good observers that they fell in a great thunder shower, for divers yards and other bare places where not one of them was seen an hour before, were presently after the shower almost covered with them, besides grass places where they were not so easily discerned. They did the most harm in the southern parts, as in Rhode Island, etc., and in the eastern parts in their Indian corn. In divers places the churches kept a day of humiliation, and presently after, the caterpillars vanished away.'"

"That's kind of frightening," Joyce remarked. "The more we're committed, the more we have to watch ourselves."

"Well, yes and no. Remember, the more we're committed, the more we have of the indwelling Holy Spirit to help us keep on the path. That's the Christian's unique blessing. The committed Christian simply has a closer relationship with God, so he sees and experiences things that others don't. And there's also two sides to that coin: God shows favor as well to the committed Christian. Listen to another example, a sea story this time:

"Our favorite of these sea stories involves *two* ships in distress. The first, under the mastery of William Laiton, was out of Piscataqua and bound for Barbados, when, some thousand miles off the coast, she sprang a leak which could not be staunched. He crew was forced to take refuge in their longboat. It happened that they had a plentiful supply of bread, more than they could possibly eat, but so little water that after eighteen days of drifting, they were down to a teaspoon per man per day. Meanwhile, another ship, captained by one Samuel Scarlet, was having its own difficulties, being 'destitute of provisions, only they had water enough, and to spare.' They spied the drifting longboat, but as Scarlet made ready to take them aboard, his men '. . .desired that he would not go to take the men in, lest they should all die by famine. But the captain was a man of too generous a charity to follow the selfish proposals thus made unto him. He replied, 'It may be these distressed creatures are our own countrymen, and [anyway] they are distressed creatures. I am resolved I will take them in, and I'll trust in God, who is able to deliver us all.' Nor was he a loser by this charitable resolution, for Captain Scarlet had the water which Laiton wanted, and Mr. Laiton had the bread and fish which Scarlet wanted. So they refreshed one another, and in a few days arrived safe to New England. But it was remarked that the chief of the mariners who urged Captain Scarlet against his taking in these distressed people, did afterwards, in his distress at sea, perish without any to take him in.'"

"I kind of got off the track in responding to you," Earl continued. Let me get back to Gideon."

"I'm still all ears."

"Okay. So God has patiently explained to the nation just why they were being oppressed. He also has decided to show mercy to them, for right after that passage we read of an encounter between an angel and Gideon.

> *And there came an angel of the Lord, and sat under an oak which was in Ophrah, that pertained unto Joash, the Abiezrite: and his son, Gideon, threshed wheat by the winepress, to hide it from the Midianites. And the angel of the Lord appeared unto him, and said unto him, The Lord is with thee, thou mighty man of valor.*

"I love that passage, Joyce. I can picture this angel playing the hayseed, probably with a shoot of wheat sticking through his front teeth, grinning up at Gideon, who at that point is anything but a mighty man of valor. The angel probably startled Gideon, whom I visualize pointing to his chest and saying, 'Who, me?' Anyway, to continue,

> *And Gideon said unto him, O my Lord, if the Lord be with us, why then is all this befallen us?"*

"Boy, if that doesn't sound familiar!" Joyce interrupted again. "It's always God's fault. Sorry. Go on."

"You're right. Okay. Gideon is still talking to the angel.

> *And where are all his miracles which our fathers told us of, saying, Did not the Lord bring us up from Egypt? But now the Lord hath forsaken us, and delivered us into the hands of the Midianites.*

> *And the Lord looked upon him, and said, Go in this thy might, and thou shalt save Israel from the hand of the Midianites. Have not I sent thee? And he said unto him, O my Lord, wherewith shall I save Israel? Behold, my family is poor in Manasseh, and I am the least in my father's house. And the Lord said unto him, Surely I will be with thee, and thou shalt smite the Midianites as one man. And [Gideon] said unto him, If now I have found grace in thy sight, then show me a sign that thou talkest with me. Depart not from here, I pray thee, until I come unto thee, and bring forth my present, and set it before thee. And he said, I will tarry until thou come again.*

> *And Gideon went in, and made ready a kid, and unleavened cakes of an ephah of flour. The flesh he put in a basket, and he put the broth in a pot, and brought it out unto him under the oak, and presented it. And the angel of God said unto him, Take the flesh and the unleavened cakes, and lay them upon this rock, and pour out the broth. And he did so. Then the angel of the Lord put forth the end of the staff that was in his hand, and touched the flesh and the unleavened cakes; and there rose up fire out of the rock, and consumed the flesh and the unleavened cakes. Then the angel of the Lord departed out of his sight.*

Earl looked up from his Bible. "Gideon then was told to destroy his father's altar to the false god Baal, which he did, and, acting under the influence of the Holy Spirit, directed messengers to the various tribes of Israel to gather together to confront the Midianites. Here's where Gideon shows a bit of nervousness about the scope of what he's been asked to do. He's probably overwhelmed by the magnitude of it all, and he reacts about the same as any of us would. I think you'll get a kick out of what he does next:

And Gideon said unto God, If thou wilt save Israel by mine hand, as thou hast said, behold, I will put a fleece of wool in the floor; and if the dew be one the fleece only, and it be dry upon all the earth beside it, then shall I know that thou wilt save Israel by mine hand, as thou hast said. And it was so; for he rose up early on the next day, and thrust the fleece together, and wrung the dew out of the fleece, a bowl full of water. And Gideon said unto God, Let not thine anger be hot against me, and I will speak but this once: let me make a trial, I pray thee, but this once more with the fleece; let it now be dry only upon the fleece, and upon all the ground let there be dew. And God did so that night; for it was dry upon the fleece only, and there was dew on all the ground.

"I'm surprised that God put up with Gideon's lack of faith," Joyce said.

"I don't know about that. Gideon was asked to do something that the entire nation shied away from, even the leaders. And he certainly wasn't a leader. It was a task that went against every molecule of his being. I'm not sure I'd be any different. But the whole situation gets hairier. God really demands the last ounce of faith that Gideon is able to give." Earl picked up his Bible and continued to read.

Then Jerubbaal, who is Gideon, and all the people who were with him, rose up early, and encamped beside the well of Harod, so that the host of the Midianites were on the north side of them, by the hill of Moreh, in the valley. And the Lord said unto Gideon, The people who are with thee are too many for me to give the Midianites into their hands, lest Israel vaunt themselves against me, saying, Mine own hand hath saved me. Now, therefore, go, proclaim in the hearing of the people, saying, Whosoever is fearful and afraid, let him return and depart early from Mount Gilead. And there returned of the people twenty and two thousand; and there remained ten thousand. And the Lord said unto Gideon, The people are yet too many. Bring them down unto the water, and I will test them for thee there: and it shall be, that of whom I say unto thee, This shall go with thee, the same shall go with thee; and of whomsoever I say unto thee, This shall not go with thee, the same shall not go.

So he brought down the people unto the water: and the Lord said unto Gideon, Everyone who lappeth of the water with his tongue, as a dog lappeth, him shalt thou set by himself; likewise, everyone who boweth down upon their knees to drink water. And the Lord said unto Gideon, By the three hundred men who lapped shall I save you, and deliver the Midianites into thine hand; and let all the other people go every man unto his place. So the people took provisions in their hand, and their trumpets: and he sent all the rest of Israel, every man, unto his tent, and retained these three hundred men: and the host of Midian was beneath him in the valley.

"From thirty-two thousand to three hundred. That's huge, Earl. No, I mean that's tiny."

"I know what you mean. Like God said, He wanted Israel to understand that they aren't to rely on themselves. That God is there with them. I think that the situation is prophetic. Look at Israel now, surrounded by vicious enemies sworn to murder them to the last man, woman and child, while the rest of the world stands idly by, allowing the hatred against Israel to build to an inevitable point of ignition.

"Not just idly. I don't think Israel has a friend left in the world. So what happens to Gideon?"

And it came to pass the same night, that the Lord said unto him, Arise, get thee down unto the host; for I have delivered it unto thine hand. But if thou fear to go down, go thou with Purah, thy servant, down to the host. And thou shalt hear what they say; and afterward shall thine hands be strengthened to go down unto the host. Then went he down with Purah, his servant, unto the outermost part of the armed men who were in the host. And the Midianites and the Amalekites and all the children of the east lay along in the valley like grasshoppers for multitude; and their camels were without number, as the sand by the seaside for multitude.

"At this point a man in Gideon's company told of a dream involving the battle ahead that stiffened Gideon's resolve. After worshiping the Lord in thanksgiving, Gideon split the men into three companies of a hundred each, armed with trumpets and pitchers into which lamps had been inserted. At the change of the next watch of the host arrayed against them, Gideon and his three hundred men blew their trumpets and broke the pitchers in their hands, crying 'The sword of the Lord and of Gideon'. As they stood fast, the enemy cried out and ran away in terror.

And the Lord set every man's sword against his fellow, even throughout all the host: and the host fled to Beth-shittah in Zererah, and to the border of Abelmeholah, unto Tabbath.

"So the point of all this," Joyce summarized for him, "is that God is letting modern Israel get boxed in to such a degree that her future would be hopeless if it wasn't for God. Then He enters the picture by saving Israel against all rational expectations. Even if He doesn't overtly show Himself, there will be no excuse left for people not to believe in Him."

"Bingo. But there's more to it than that. God had said that He would bless those that blessed Israel, and curse him who cursed Israel. Remember the problems that the early Americans had when they fell away?"

"Yes. You just talked about it."

"Well, the United States historically has been a friend of Israel. President Truman was the first to recognize Israel as a modern nation.

President Nixon, despite his other faults, helped Israel through massive airlifts of equipment to go from defeat to victory in the 1973 Yom Kippur War. But lately, U.S. policy has been changing for the worse, helped along by a totally misguided and unbelievably cowardly State Department. There was a large policy shift under the presidency of George Bush senior. That was the first time, unveiled during the Madrid Peace Conference in Spain, that the U.S. proposed a parting of the land of Israel, to be given to the Palestinians in exchange for their promise of peace. The plan was called 'The Roadmap to Peace'. It was anything but. In the first place, the land already had been parted in support of the Palestinians, even before Israel had become a modern nation. The plan had been to give what is now Jordan, a large piece of real estate, to Israel, but it was taken away from them. The latest attempt to separate the Israelis from their land would make the remaining area completely untenable for defence in case the Palestinians decided to pursue their original game plan of tossing the Jews into the Mediterranean. And they've never gone back on that ultimate intent. They're simply waiting for the right opportunity. God knows all about their murderous plans. In Joel Chapter 3, for example, he expresses His displeasure with the Gentiles for "parting my land".

"So what happened in Madrid?"

"It didn't happen in Madrid. It happened here. While Bush was in Madrid unveiling the Roadmap to Peace, the Perfect Storm, a very rare event, hit the eastern seaboard of the U.S. You know, the one they made the movie about where George Clooney tries to climb a skyscraper wave. It turns out that the storm generated thirty-foot waves that trashed Bush's Kennebunkport home. That was a first and relatively mild warning. After Israel abandoned Gaza at the insistence of the U.S., the Jewish refugees streaming out of the area were matched by American refugees streaming out of New Orleans as Hurricane Katrina drew near. The number of such incidences is beyond coincidence. Oh, people continue to refuse to see any connection. But they do so because they want to, not from rational considerations."

"It does seem like Israel has God looking after her. But still . . ."

"But still, you were going to say, God's right at the edge on this one."

"Well, yes, I've heard people say that modern Israel has nothing to do with God. After all, it still is a thoroughly secular nation."

"What would you say if I told you that Israel's return as a nation is foretold in the Bible? To the very day?"

"What? You can't be serious!"

"I'm very serious. The late Grant Jeffrey, an in-depth Bible scholar, figured it out. According to him, God had foretold in Scripture not only the return of Israel as a nation into her land in 1948, but the exact date of that event. Dr. Jeffrey claimed that he was given the ability by God to piece together the items of Scripture by which that event was foretold, thus demonstrating two points: first, that Scripture is supernaturally accurate, and second, that God had everything to do with the return of Israel as a modern nation in bold opposition to those who would claim that Israel is no longer the apple of God's eye.

"Before getting into the specifics of Jeffrey's research, I should tell you that his conclusions are corroborated elsewhere in Scripture. The Book of Hosea contains prophecies regarding Israel's lengthy dispersion and her subsequent revival as a nation. While not as precise as the prophecies that Dr. Jeffrey investigated, they are quite remarkable in their own right as to the accuracy of the general timing of Israel's revival after two millennia of dispersion. The dispersion itself is addressed in Hosea 4:4 and 5:

> *For the children of Israel shall abide many days without a king, and without a prince, and without a sacrifice, and without an image, and without an ephod, and without teraphim; Afterward shall the children of Israel return, and seek the Lord, their God, and David, their king, and shall fear the Lord and his goodness in the latter days.*

"Hosea 6:2 addresses the general time frame of Israel's return, in which a day is interpreted as a thousand years according to Psalm 90 and 2 Peter 3:8:

After two days will he revive us; in the third day he will raise us up, and we shall live in his sight.

"That already floors me, Earl. I never knew the Bible spoke of the modern nation of Israel. But there it is, in black and white. How many Christians understand even that much?'

"Not so many yet, but I have a feeling that God is opening the books now to a whole lot of people, so probably many more are coming on board with respect to God's hand in the affairs of modern Israel. Anyway, returning to Jeffrey's work regarding Israel's return as a nation, he received his first clue regarding the nature of Israel's return from Ezekiel Chapters 36 and 37, in which the 'dry bones' connect together, are clothed with flesh, and are given life. Many eschatologists view these chapters as applicable to the Jews having been given new life and a return to their homeland after the Holocaust they suffered in Nazi Germany. Now as to the timing of their return to their homeland, Jeffrey received his first clue from Ezekiel 4:4-6."

"Let me read it, Earl." Joyce picked up her Bible and read aloud:

Lie also upon thy left side, and lay the iniquity of the house of Israel upon it; according to the number of the days that thou shalt lie upon it, thou shalt bear their iniquity. For I have laid upon thee the years of their iniquity, according to the number of the days, three hundred and ninety days; so shalt thou bear the iniquity of the house of Israel. And when thou hast accomplished them, lie again on thy right side, and thou shalt bear the iniquity of the house of Judah forty days. I have appointed thee each day for a year.

"So that comes to, um, four hundred thirty years. From when?"

"Here comes the interesting part. Ezekiel himself was a captive in Babylon, so Dr. Jeffrey assumed that the judgment was to begin at the beginning of Israel's or Judah's captivity. Israel was captured by the Assyrians in the eighth Century B.C., while Judah became captive to Nebudchadnezzar somewhere between 606 and 605 B.C. Dr. Jeffrey attempted to apply the 430 years directly to each of these dates, but came up with no historically meaningful end date. Rather than give up, Jeffrey pursued the topic in greater detail, coming to an astonishingly relevant passage in Leviticus 26, specifically verses 17 and 18, and 27 and 28:

Joyce turned to these passages and again read aloud:

And I will set my face against you, and ye shall be slain before your enemies; they that hate you shall reign over you, and ye shall flee when none pursueth you. And if ye will not yet for all this hearken unto me, then I will punish you seven times more for your sins. . . And if ye will not for all this hearken unto me, but walk contrary unto me, Then I will walk contrary unto you also in fury; and I, even I, will chastise you seven times for your sins.

"Ohmygosh, Earl, so it wasn't four hundred thirty years. It was seven times that, wasn't it?"

"Here is where Dr. Jeffrey demonstrates the power of the Holy Spirit and the depth of his knowledge of Scripture," Earl replied. "He realized in connection with this passage that during Ezekiel's time, the northern tribes of Israel had been under continuous captivity while Judah was undergoing a punishment that, according to Jeremiah 25:11, would last for precisely seventy years. Jeffrey also realized that the passage in Leviticus quoted above was conditional upon the Jews failing to turn back to God after an initial punishment. Judah's captivity did indeed end after seventy years, when the Persian King Cyrus, who was called by name by Isaiah over a century before his birth - that's in Isaiah 44:28, Joyce - decreed at some time between 536 and 535 B.C. that Israelites could return to Jerusalem to rebuild their temple. The fulfillment of that prophetic message is recorded in the Book of Ezra. As a side point, many Christians confuse this prophetic event with the fulfillment of Daniel's prophecy in Daniel 9 regarding the appearance of Messiah 483 years after the commandment permitting the Jews to rebuild the city of Jerusalem. That prophecy was fulfilled in the beginning event by Artaxerxes Longimanus in 445 B.C. as recorded in the Book of Nehemiah and at the conclusion by Jesus' triumphal entry into Jerusalem 32 A.D. Anyway, Jeffrey appreciated that the outcome of Leviticus 26 would depend on the behavior of the Jews following the termination of their captivity in Babylon, which meant that the 70-year period of their captivity must be subtracted from the 430-year period of Ezekiel 4 prior to the application of the sevenfold punishment of Leviticus 26. He subtracted the seventy years that Israel had already served her captivity from the four hundred thirty years of Ezekiel to get to 360 years remaining. Then he multiplied this number by seven from Leviticus 26 to arrive at 2520 years."

"Are you almost finished? My head is starting to spin."

"Just about. Years mentioned in the Bible prophecy are always prophetic years of 360 days. Multiplying the 2520 prophetic years by 360 gives 907, 200 days."

"What? Did you actually memorize that number?"

"Hey, this is a truly important prophecy. Yes, I did. I worked it out, too. I added that number to the date that the Babylonian captivity ended and arrived, just like Jeffrey did, at an end date of 1948 A.D. I didn't go farther that that, but I have a feeling that if I did, I'd have come to the date of May 15."

"That's enormous, Earl. I'm overwhelmed."

"So am I. The prophecy fulfills Isaiah 66, verses seven and eight:

Before she travailed, she brought forth; before her pain came, she was delivered of a man-child. Who hath heard such a thing? Who hath seen such things? Shall the earth be made to bring forth in one day? Or shall a nation be born at once? For as soon as Zion travailed, she brought forth her children.

"I'm speechless, Earl."

CHAPTER SEVENTEEN

Henry and Janet decided not to wait. They were married in the Church attended by Earl and Joyce under more normal circumstances. Earl and Joyce still lived in the temporary shelter afforded by the nursing home, but Joyce was by her mother's side during the brief and informal ceremony. Earl was honored to be Henry's Best Man. Despite remaining pockets of anarchy in Seattle and its suburbs, the newlyweds were able to catch a flight out of the heavily-reinforced Sea-Tac airport directly to Maryland, where they embarked on a cruise ship for a two-week stay. When they returned, tanned and flushed with happiness, Earl picked them up at the airport and returned them to Henry's home near Issaquah, which was relatively free of violence.

Two more months passed before order was fully restored in the Seattle area. Earl and Joyce returned to their home, but when they pulled up into the driveway the broken windows, graffiti and trash that greeted them almost drove them away. Saddened by the rampant destruction, they nevertheless managed to overcome their fear as to what they might find inside and braved the opening of their front door. As she surveyed the damage inside, Joyce leaned against the doorjamb and wept. They immediately saw that anything of possible value was gone and their walls were decorated with obscene and blasphemous words. Beyond that, they were shocked to discover that whatever had occupied their home during their absence hadn't bothered to use the bathroom. A Bible lay on the floor, pages torn from it used as toilet paper and tossed into a corner of the living room. Eventually they gathered the nerve to survey the rest of their home, finding the kitchen reeking of rotting food and their bedroom littered with discarded condoms. The bed itself rested at an odd angle, one leg having been broken off. Clothes were everywhere. The most crushing blow was the sight of her picture of Jesus on the floor, the frame in pieces and the picture itself torn. One piece had been used as toilet paper like the Bible pages in the living room.

"What animals could have done this?" she wailed. Earl put his arm around her and held her tight. "Pray for them, Joyce," he replied. "I wouldn't want to go where they're headed. Come on. I'm taking you out of here. We can face it again tomorrow. At least we'll be prepared."

They checked into a motel room, where Earl managed to reach their insurance agent, only to find that riots weren't covered in their homeowners' policy. Over the next week as they slowly began to restore order and livability to their home, they gradually adjusted to their new circumstances. They now had to contend not only with a different world, but with the changes that had made them different as well. Earl was committed by the needs of the congregation they had acquired for the Sunday services to continuing on as an informal pastor. After finally cleaning up the worst of the mess they insisted upon taking Cathy home with them and received no complaint from the staff at the nursing home. As for the government's threatened intrusion into their lives, the bureaucracy was in such a state of turmoil that they had no fear on that score. For the time being.

As life began to return to a new and uneasy normalcy, Earl found that his collection of refugees also was dwindling. Within another month, his temporary Church congregation was largely gone. This exodus was hastened by the government, which declared for health reasons that the nursing home was off-limits as a permanent shelter for the homeless. A new federal agency had come into being almost immediately in response to the disruption to provide food and shelter for the indigent. Although Earl and George had no way of knowing at the time about the true source of the federal takeover, in actuality it was a pre-planned response to the recent violence, much of which was instigated surreptitiously by government agents posing as unruly rioters. A large tract of land was set aside for their housing, which consisted of trailers similar to those that had been purchased to house the disenfranchised of New Orleans after Katrina. In return for this handout, those who accepted it were required to submit to permanent identification. The devices used were radio-frequency identification microcircuits, more popularly known by the acronym RFID. The ubiquitous cell-phone towers were upgraded to periodically monitor the RFIDs in their sectors, enabling the government to keep track of every indigent person 24-7. Given the loss of his audience, Earl gratefully returned to his own Church, still cared for by Pastor George. But he fretted about the new government control over those whom he had considered to be his flock.

"And well you should be concerned," She said to him one night in the midst of the soft glow that surrounded her gorgeous face.

"Concerned about what? And thanks for coming back. I wish you'd come around just a little more often."

"I've been busy."

"Don't give me that. If you can find the time to speak to me out of six billion people, I don't buy it."

The sound of Her laughter was like a softly-played symphony piece. "Okay. You're getting too smart for me. But you should be concerned indeed over the government control over your former flock. It's going to get worse, too. They're preparing for the long haul, Earl. Setting up classrooms to "teach" the children. Her upraised fingers framed the word "teach" with quote symbols. And, of course, the adults will have to attend their own "schools" for indoctrination. The acceptance of these people of government largesse doesn't come free. It never does. It comes at the expense of control for starters, and ultimately of submission to the government's godless worldview. Both you and Joyce will be getting involved with that eventually. But right now you have a more urgent problem to deal with."

"Oh? Worse than that? Now you're scaring me."

"Remember that you always have Me, even if you're not aware of it. I can even unscare you, if it comes to that."

"That's a huge comfort, Wisdom," he told Her gratefully.

"Well, whatever. You won't be getting off Scot-free. Anyway, this other problem is related to the first. The Agency for Indigents, or AI, has morphed from a two-letter acronym to four. It's now AIDE." She spelled it out. "Care to guess what the extra letters stand for?"

"Oh, no," he breathed. His adrenalin dispenser collected a giant gob and hurled it into his bloodstream. "Disabled being one?" he asked in a small voice.

"Yes. The world doesn't know it yet, but the nursing homes will be extinct here within six months. The same goes for assisted living facilities. The "E" stands for "Elderly"."

"Are these others going to be tossed in with the homeless?"

"For a while. But they won't be sticking around for long. The system they're cobbling up to handle the disabled and elderly makes Hitler's death camps seem half-hearted. They're planning on dispensing death in a real landfill scale assembly-line process. It makes perfect sense to them, being totally immersed in materialism, to make the process of living on earth as efficient as possible. Spiritual issues like selfness, compassion and nobility simply have no meaning to them. They are spiritually dead."

She fondled the back of his head and blew him a kiss. "You'll be resisting this process by rescuing souls. I'll be guiding you all the way, sometimes overtly and other times more subtly. But you and Joyce will do well as warriors for God. Especially when you get a double dose of Me within you."

"How so?"

"On that one, Earl, you'll have to find out for yourself. Just don't expect things to get easy any time soon. For joy you'll have to rely on Me. And Joyce. And Cathy, for a while. 'Bye for now." She blew him another kiss and vanished.

Pastor George had for months now set aside his planned series of sermons on the Book of Revelation in favor of more impromptu sermons delivered in reaction to fast-moving events. Now, with the return of some stability, he was thinking of resurrecting his old notes and resuming his discussion of the big picture behind the events they were experiencing. But this Sunday he had a more urgent call to deliver a warning to his flock.

"My dear fellow Christians," he began, "I've been trying through Scripture to equip you to handle the circumstances that we find ourselves in. I'm doing the best I can, but because things are happening so rapidly I find that I'm simply not enough. Nor is your attendance on Sunday mornings enough. I've added Earl Cook to my deacon staff. He and Jim Preston agreed to help out Wednesday evenings with a beefed-up, in-depth Bible study catering to two age groups, both directed toward helping you cope with life as we now must face it. I expect attendance to grow dramatically as the world situation continues to worsen. Jim's great with the kids, and is looking forward to working with them. Earl has enough familiarity with Scripture to handle the task for the adults. He also has some recent experience in conducting Bible studies, even to the point of assuming pastoral duties, so I'm certain that you'll find that time with him will be well-spent. But you have to go beyond that too and make an effort to read Scripture on your own. It's like exercise—the more you get into it, the more you can do. We need to exercise ourselves spiritually. I'm thinking of an hour a day for starters. There's an urgent reason for this. We've been passive too long, not that I mean you should take up violence. But we're in a time when you, as Christians, must show the light of Christ to a world that is entering the darkness of totalitarian control. You have to become so familiar with the Word of God that you can withstand the coming assault on your faith."

He paused, frowning. "I'm not trying to scare you. The world outside our doors is doing a good job of that. I'm trying to make you understand just how bad it is out there, so you can deal with it effectively as Christians. The trial ahead is coming upon us with certainty. How do I know this? Because the events taking place here and around the world are fitting quite precisely into Biblical prophecy. As I said before, you can put away your guns for this battle. They aren't necessary. It's not that kind of war. As Paul told us, what we're facing is spiritual wickedness, and our only true defense against that is our Lord Jesus, who acts upon our faith and obedience. I'll read to you Paul's commentary about this from Ephesians Chapter 6:

> *Put on the whole armor of God, that ye may be able to stand against the wiles of the devil. For we wrestle not against flesh and blood, but against principalities, against powers, against the rulers of the darkness of this world, against spiritual wickedness in high places. Wherefore, take unto you the whole armor of God, that ye may be able to withstand in the evil day, and having done all, to stand. Stand, therefore, having your loins girded about with truth, and having on the breastplate of righteousness, and your feet shod with the preparation of the gospel of peace; above all, taking the shield of faith, with which ye shall be able to quench the fiery darts of the wicked. And take the helmet of salvation, and the sword of the Spirit, which is the word of God; Praying always with all prayer and supplication in the Spirit, and watching thereunto with all perseverance and supplication for all saints; and for me, that utterance may be given unto me, that I may open my mouth boldly, as I ought to speak.*

"Pray that I, too, as well as you, may speak boldly, to open our mouths with full and unyielding commitment to our God to bring the light of Christ to a world descending into a hell on earth. That we take up the weapons, not of materialism, but spiritual, these being truth, righteousness, faith, love and the Gospel of Jesus Christ, submitting ourselves in love to the indwelling Holy Spirit.

"Most of you have been indoctrinated by the Clint Eastwood or Stephen Seagal kind of movies where the "hero" gets his own back in a variety of clever and wonderfully satisfying revenge scenarios. Shoot-'em-ups like that are very entertaining – but they aren't very Christian, and tactics like that have no place in our battle. It's our lot instead, as Christians, to wage a much more difficult war than our friends Clint or Stephen ever had to face. We are called upon by Jesus to endure persecution with loving hearts – to bless those who curse us, to pray for those who treat us badly, to love indiscriminantly."

Pastor George scanned the congregants and noted the irritated expressions on many faces. "To those who would shout Unfair! is it really? As I recall, my relationship with Jesus didn't begin in a loving manner. I disliked Him for all kinds of perceived shortcomings, all of which were terribly false misconceptions. Actually, I refused to believe that He is God, or that God the Father or God the Holy Spirit even existed. Yet He loved me enough to die on my behalf. Can we do less than return this love in faith and obedience?"

The return of regular television programming brought a new element to the home screen: the demeaning of the religions of "the Book", Judaism and Christianity. Sitcoms were offered that cast Christians as their antitypes: selfish, morally disgusting, ill-tempered, maladjusted, materialistic and, above all, hypocritical. This mockery, despite the coarseness and obvious falsehood of the presentations, succeeded in performing the desired social engineering function of forming a public consensus of angry superiority against Christians, who were increasingly cast in a subhuman light. Joyce turned on the television one evening after she had parked Cathy in front of it, and before she could change the channel, she was confronted with an angry fight in a Church aisle between two women who were in the process of yanking on each others' hair. An altar with a cross was clearly visible in the background. A number of Churchgoers were avidly watching the event with obscene smiles on their faces. One woman was clapping her hands, yelling "Git 'er, Sue!" Horrified, Joyce stood dumbfounded before the evil scene. Before she found the presence of mind to respond, a pink-nailed claw ripped the blouse of one of the fighters, exposing a breast. One of the men, lust on his face, moved in to cup the flesh with his hand. Joyce screamed and turned away. Earl came running into the room as the fight played out, one woman on top of the other, their nearly-naked bodies separated by remnants of blood-stained blouses. The pastor on-screen had come up and stood looking at them with ill-disguised interest. Earl picked up the clicker in haste and switched off the set. Cathy squirmed in discomfort.

"That's not real, Cathy," Earl told her. "It's a lie, what some awful people are trying to make others think of Christians.

"Yeah, and it's working, too," Joyce said, attempting without much success to calm herself and Cathy.

This misinformation campaign worked quite well indeed, as indicated by the body language exhibited by the public when faced with the proximity of Christians, some of whom had responded to one pastor's exhortation by wearing white armbands with cross insignias. The use of these armbands spread rapidly through the Christian community, crossing state lines and continuing coast-to-coast. Christians identified in this way increasingly were getting roughed up. Then they started dying.

Earl watched it happen as in slow motion. In the cafeteria at work the talk noticeably coarsened, with women often bearing the brunt of lewd jokes. Then the women began to respond in kind. At the same time, his personal interchange with co-workers cooled much as it did when he was put to the test with Pastor Wilson over his supposed blasphemy. Most noticeable at first was Patty, who avoided him when possible and was curt when forced to communicate with him. Gone was her light-hearted (and –headed) banter and her sassy friendliness with him. Next to make his displeasure with Earl most noticeable was his boss, Walter, who, after having fired him and then apologetically turned around to re-hire him after the exposure of Pastor Wilson as a reactionary zealot, reverted to his old stance of calculated distance at the increasing popularity of the anti-Christian, anti-Jew mindset. When Earl spoke to Joyce of the darkening situation at work, she surprised him with a grin. "I think you should start looking around for new employment," she encouraged, "and I know just what you should apply for."

"What would that be?" he asked her.

"How about RRT?" The grin widened.

"RRT? What on earth is that?"

"Roadkill Removal Technician, of course. Or maybe Mole Depopulation Expert. She laughed ironically. We might as well face it, Earl, and see the humor in it. We've reached the social stratum of rodents, so we might as well capitalize on our kinship with the little fellas."

"I love you more than you can imagine, Joyce. You've put our situation in the proper perspective and reminded me to keep my sights on Jesus and focus on the spiritual. Thanks."

"You're welcome. This material world just doesn't matter any more. We might as well be happy with what we have and leave the driving to God."

One evening Joyce had a chance to apply this developing attitude to another loved one—and to herself as well. "How's your new marriage?" she asked brightly as she answered a phone call from her mother. She was very happy for them both.

"That's wonderful," Janet replied. "But there's something else that's been on my mind, Joyce," she said. "I'd better tell you the real reason why we sped up the wedding. I was diagnosed with breast cancer two months ago. While I was assured at the time that with the many treatment options available the success rate was steadily growing, Henry and I decided not to take any chances with the time available to share our lives. I'm very glad we did that, because I may not be around much longer."

"What do you mean, mom?" Joyce asked with a lump in her throat.

"I found out today that my health plan has denied coverage for treatment. They said that my age made me ineligible. It's part of the revamped health coverage system. Nobody noticed it was there except the insurance companies. They didn't bother telling the public. Now it's too late to change it."

"Oh, mom!" Joyce wailed. "All I can do is pray, but I'll be doing a lot of that. Please come over this weekend. I want to have as much time with you as I can."

"I'll talk with Henry. I'm sure that he won't mind."

"We'll be expecting you." But Joyce suddenly remembered her conversation with Earl over the deteriorating conditions at his job. "Mom," she added, "don't let this get you down. Maybe even if the cancer is terminal, it's for the best. Remember what Paul said in Romans 8. I'll paraphrase it best I can as I remember it: 'All things work together for good for those who love the Lord, who are the called according to His purpose.' As a matter of fact, God may be doing you a big favor by letting you check out of this increasingly evil world. Just make the most of the time you have with Henry—and with us, too."

"You're probably right, dear. Thanks for putting this situation into a better light for me. We'll be seeing you this weekend."

Earl and Joyce continued to shelter Cathy in their home, refraining from travel with her except when it was absolutely necessary. When the other residents of the nursing home had been carted off to who-knows-where by the AIDE teams, they were particularly watchful for signs that the governmental bureaucracy had sorted out the difficulties brought on by the violence sufficiently to come looking for Cathy.

Chapter Eighteen

"Mother, it's Joyce. Pick up."

Still no response. Joyce bit a nail. This was her third call in less than a day. *What had happened to her?* she worried. Joyce decided to check on her personally. When she arrived and rang the doorbell, she received the same negative response. Her Miata was still in the carport. Henry's car was in the driveway behind hers. She went around to the side of the house, where she slipped through a shrub and stood on her toes to peer in the window. There was no sign of life. She repeated the process around the entire house, with no results. Finally, she lifted up a flowerpot, retrieved the key underneath it, and unlocked the front door.

"Mom?" she called tentatively. "Mom!" she yelled. She went into every room and then down into the basement, but the house was empty. She sat in one of the living room chairs and called Earl. "No mom, Earl," she told him. "She's not in the house and her car's still here. Same with Henry. What could have happened to them?"

"Maybe there was an emergency," he replied. "Why don't you try calling the hospital? They should have a log of who came in."

"Good idea. I'm on it." She terminated the call to Earl and called the hospital, to be confronted with a negative response. Then she called the police, who could add nothing to check her rising panic.

At home that evening, Joyce, hand-in-hand with Earl and kneeling on the floor beside their bed, prayed fervently for the welfare of her mother and Henry. They continued to kneel after they had offered up their concern to God, Joyce sobbing. "Remember, honey, what Paul said in Romans 8: 'all things work together for good for those who love the Lord.' We have to stand on that promise, knowing the faithfulness of our God."

"Of course. I'm exhausted. Let's get under the covers."

"Just when things were starting to return to normal," Earl groused under his breath.

The beautiful face that stared lovingly at him out of the darkness failed to hold the merest vestige of a smile. Her huge eyes were wet with grief. "Hello, Earl," She said in a subdued voice.

"What's wrong, Wisdom?" he asked Her.

She hesitated, wiped a budding tear from Her right eye, and attempted to smile. "Thanks for asking. Don't mind me. I'm just tired of having to deal with so much hatred and evil in this world. I'll be all right."

Earl sensed that She was attempting to hide something. Something about him. He knew that She wouldn't lie to him, but She certainly wasn't being candid. She brightened, and he decided not to press the issue.

"Earl, darling, things won't go back to normal. Not for you. You'll have to accept that, and trust Us with all your soul. You will have some happy moments, but then... we're going to be doing some mining tonight," She said, getting to the point of Her presence. "I'm going to educate you from the depths of Scripture. What you'll learn will amaze you. Later it will make you wonder why, with all the billions of Christians that have lived from the time of Jesus until now, so few ever searched Scripture in enough depth to figure it out for themselves. Some day in the future," she said, her voice quavering and her eyes becoming liquid again, "you'll have the opportunity to share this new knowledge with a Jewish individual. He, in turn, will share it with his brothers and sisters. Out of that sharing a nation will return to their God." She cast her eyes downward and wiped them with the backs of Her delicate hands. He noticed for the first time the prominent calluses on Her palms.

After a lengthy pause, She regained control over Her emotions. "Okay," she said. "Let's get started. Do you remember in the Gospels the accounts of Jesus' feeding of the multitudes?"

"Sure," he responded. "First He fed five thousand men, and then four thousand. There were also women and children with the men, but they weren't counted. I suppose they were fed, though."

"Yes, they were. The numbers are hugely significant, Earl. The Gospel of Mark makes that plain. Let me give you excerpts from Chapter 8 of Mark's Gospel. Jesus has just fed four thousand men with seven loaves of fish and left in a boat with His disciples. You have to go to the account in Matthew to see that the number represented the men alone. He has just warned His disciples to beware of the leaven of the Pharisees and they reason that these words had something to do with their having forgotten to bring bread with them. Jesus responds with a very different message. Think about what He said to them as I quote His words:

> *And when Jesus knew it, he saith unto them, Why reason ye, because ye have no bread? perceive ye not yet, neither understand? have ye your heart yet hardened?*
>
> *Having eyes, see ye not? and having ears, hear ye not? and do ye not remember?*
>
> *When I brake the five loaves among five thousand, how many baskets full of fragments took ye up? They say unto him, Twelve.*
>
> *And when the seven among four thousand, how many baskets full of fragments took ye up? And they said, Seven.*
>
> *And he said unto them, How is it that ye do not understand?*

She searched Earl's eyes for a sign of comprehension. "Well?" She asked.

"He's trying to tell them something, isn't He? About the numbers, I mean. There's something in the numbers that's important to their faith."

"You almost have it right. The disciples were eyewitnesses to the feeding events, so they had a clear understanding of how the men were arranged during the feedings, and the details of how the miracle took place. But there are elements of this truth that had to wait until Scripture was complete. It's essential to note here that just before Jesus spoke these words to His disciples, he had responded to the Pharisees by telling them that no sign would be given to that generation. The bottom line is that Jesus is trying to tell *you,* the reader of Mark's Gospel, something significant about the numbers and their relationship to each other. But We have preferred that those with access to Mark's Gospel would have to dig for that understanding, so that when they did acquire it they would see it for the treasure that it is. Some actually did perceive this understanding, but the medieval Church was in such a dismal state at the time that they were unable to share it with the public at large. No matter, because actually, the sign that the Pharisees had asked for is for *you*. I am giving it to you so that when the time is ripe you and others We have chosen for this task will pass it on to some special Jews, and through those men We have chosen to all Israel, who will see in the details of the feedings that Jesus is truly God, the Messiah in whom they had placed their hope."

"That's a tall order. Are you sure that I deserve it?"

"Oh, yes." A tear leaked out of Her eye and made a channel down Her cheek. "I won't say anything about it now, but when the time comes to share it, you'll understand that it comes with a cost. The price you'll pay will be heavy, but you'll bear it like a man, and your understanding will be a great comfort to you."

"Are you trying to tell me that You—God—actually need us humans to do this?"

"I wouldn't go that far, My dearest one," Wisdom said, smiling sweetly. "It's more like a gift to you. Remember when Jesus made His triumphal entry into Jerusalem, sitting on an ass? Read Luke 19 when you get a chance."

"Yes, I remember."

"He told the Pharisees that if the rejoicing people had held their peace, the very stones would immediately cry out. It's the same thing with you. We're giving you the gift of participating, Earl. There will come a time when you won't think much of the gift, but in the end you'll be grateful."

"Thank you, Wisdom. I trust you."

"Good. Let's get back to the subject at hand."

"I've read some commentaries on the feedings," Earl said. "The writer spoke about Chapter 8 of Mark, insinuating that he was making much ado about something not too important, as if in his lack of intellectual sophistication he attempted to use numbers somewhat inappropriately. After all, with what kind of logic can one perceive five loaves as feeding five thousand, whereas it took two more loaves than that to feed a thousand fewer men? According to this man, the feeding events were pure miracle, and any attempt to make sense of the numbers would be fruitless."

For the first time that evening Wisdom laughed without restraint, indulging in a full-throated, lengthy spell of hilarity. "I know the man!" She exclaimed. "He's in heaven, but only through Our grace. He follows the angels like a dog, continually attempting to apologize to Us for his extreme short-sightedness." She wiped another tear from her cheek, but this one was from the laughter. "Actually, Mark could have been the most sophisticated fellow ever to walk the earth, given the information that I handed to him about the feeding. Now let me ask you a question: given what you do know about the feeding episodes, can you tell me how many fragments were in each basket?"

"Gee, I don't know, Wisdom." He gave the issue some thought, eventually responding. "I can't say. It isn't in the Scriptures."

"Yes, the answer is indeed in the Scriptures, but only indirectly. The question itself, not being directly answered, is intended to lead the questioning individual toward finding an answer. You'll be doing just that some time in the near future, under very different and challenging circumstances. To make certain that you'll be able to handle the job, I'll tell you the approach you'd take if you had the time and resources. It's amenable to an algebraic solution. One would assume first that the baskets of remainders for each of the two events are of the same size, which they are not, so that they'll each contain the same number of fragments. It turns out that each basket contains the same number of fragments from the menfolk, but that's a complicating factor that we'll take up in just another moment. Then one would form equations out of the numbers given in Scripture and seek solutions in the form of n equations in n unknowns, as you, being an engineer, are familiar with doing. To furnish more information, another two feeding incidents can be added to the mix."

"Say what?" he asked in surprise. "They wouldn't be in Scripture."

"Wrong again, Earl darling," She said, softening her contradiction with the endearment. "People tend to wade into Scripture with the most closed-minded presuppositions. Here's a reference; remember it well: 2 Kings 4:42 through 44. I'll give it to you:

> *And there came a man from Baalshalisha, and brought the man of God,' (who, by the way, was Elisha), 'bread of the first fruits, twenty loaves of barley, and full ears of corn in its husk. And he said, Give unto the people, that they may eat. And his servant said, What, should I set this before a hundred men? He said again, Give the people, that they may eat; for thus saith the Lord, They shall eat, and shall have some left. So he set it before them, and they did eat, and left some, according to the word of the Lord.*

Earl shook his head in wonder. "Wow," he said, at a loss for a more appropriate word. "That's huge."

"It's even more significant than you think. It ties Jesus in with the Old Testament in a sign that, as you'll see, identifies Him without ambiguity as the Messiah for whom Israel still waits. Now let's move on to the next feeding event, which ties Jesus in with His Church. This account also is in Scripture. It's in Chapter 2 of the Acts of the Apostles, verses 22 through 41 to be precise, where Peter, newly filled with My indwelling presence, addresses the onlookers:

> *Ye men of Israel, hear these words: Jesus of Nazareth, a man approved of God among you by miracles and wonders and signs, which God did by him in the midst of you, as ye yourselves also know; Him, being delivered by the determinate counsel and foreknowledge of God, ye have taken, and by wicked hands have crucified and slain; Whom God hath raised up, having loosed the pains of death, because it was not possible that he should be held by it. For David speaketh concerning him: I foresaw the Lord always before my face; for he is on my right hand, that I should not be moved. Therefore did my heart rejoice, and my tongue was glad; moreover my flesh also shall rest in hope, because thou wilt not leave my soul in hell, neither wilt thou allow thine Holy One to see corruption. Thou hast made known to me the ways of life; thou shalt make me full of joy with thy countenance.*

> *Men and brethren, let me freely speak unto you of the patriarch, David, that he is both dead and buried, and his sepulcher is with us unto this day. Therefore, being a prophet, and knowing that God had sworn with an oath to him, that of the fruit of his loins, according to the flesh, he would raise up Christ to sit on his throne; he, seeing this before, spoke of the resurrection of Christ, that his soul was not left in hell, neither his flesh did see corruption. This Jesus hath God raised up, whereof we all are witnesses. Therefore, being by the right hand of God exalted, and having received from the Father the promise of the Holy Spirit, he hath shed forth this, which ye now see and hear. For David is not ascended into the heavens; but he saith himself, The Lord said unto my Lord, Sit thou on my right hand, until I make thy foes thy footstool. Therefore, let all the house of Israel know assuredly, that God hath made that same Jesus, whom ye have crucified, both Lord and Christ.*

> *Now when they heard this, they were pricked in their heart, and said unto Peter and to the rest of the apostles, Men and brethren, what shall we do? Then Peter said unto them, Repent, and be baptized, every one of you, in the name of Jesus Christ for the remission of sins, and ye shall receive the gift of the Holy Spirit. For the promise is unto you, and to your children, and to all that are afar off, even as many as the Lord, our God, shall call. And with many other words did he testify and exhort, saying, Save yourselves from this crooked generation.*
>
> *Then they that gladly received his word were baptized; and the same day there were added unto them about three thousand souls.*

"Oh!" Earl exclaimed. "So you're saying that Peter's three thousand have the same significance as Jesus' feeding of the five and four thousand. And Elisha's one hundred," he added after a brief pause. "But where was the feeding? There wasn't any bread at all."

"Do yourself a big favor, Earl," She said, shaking Her head. "Try to rise above the material world. The spiritual world is vastly more important. Do you think that Jesus limited His feeding of the masses to physical bread? The physical side was only symbolic of a much greater Bread, the Word of God. The day after He fed the five thousand, He made this abundantly clear. The account's in John Chapter 6. I'll give it to you:

> *Jesus answered them, and said, Verily, verily, I say unto you, Ye seek me, not because ye saw the miracles, but because ye did eat of the loaves, and were filled. Labor not for the food which perisheth, but for that food which endureth unto everlasting life, which the Son of man shall give unto you; for him hath God the Father sealed.*
>
> *Then said they unto him, What shall we do, that we might work the works of God. Jesus answered, and said unto them, This is the work of God, that ye believe on him whom he hath sent. They said, therefore, unto him, What sign showest thou, then, that we may see, and believe thee? What dost thou work?*

> *Our fathers did eat manna in the desert; as it is written, He gave them bread from heaven to eat.*
>
> *Then Jesus said unto them, Verily, verily, I say unto you, Moses gave you not that bread from heaven; but my Father giveth you the true bread from heaven. For the bread of God is he who cometh down from heaven and giveth life unto the world. Then said they unto him, Lord, evermore give us this bread. And Jesus said unto them, I am the bread of life; he that cometh to me shall never hunger, and he that believeth on me shall never thirst.*

"I hear you Wisdom, loud and clear. You're saying that Peter's feeding the three thousand with the Word of God dovetails right in with Jesus' feeding of the five and four thousand with bread. But can you truly call Peter's speech a feeding in the same sense as Jesus' feedings?"

"First of all," She replied, "Jesus fed the five and four thousand with physical bread only in addition to His feeding of them with the true Bread, the Word. The Word, as spiritual bread, was always primary and the material bread a poor second, which Jesus tossed in because of the materialistic bent of the crowd. As for the equivalence of Peter's speech with feeding, don't you remember what Jesus told Peter in John Chapter 21?"

"Please refresh my memory," he said in humility.

> *So when they had dined, Jesus saith to Simon Peter, Simon, son of Jonah, lovest thou me more than these? He saith unto him, Yea, Lord; thou knowest that I love thee. He saith unto him, Feed my lambs. He saith unto him again the second time, Simon, son of Jonah, lovest thou me? He saith unto him, Yea, Lord; thou knowest that I love thee. He saith unto him, Feed my sheep. He saith unto him the third time, Simon, son of Jonah, loves thou me? Peter was grieved because he said unto him the third time, Lovest thou me? And he said unto him, Lord, thou knowest all things; thou knowest that I love thee. Jesus saith unto him, Feed my sheep.*

"Okay, I do get the picture now. That does make the three thousand of Peter a legitimate member of the feeding episodes. What's great about it is that God once more involved man as an integral part of His saving grace. But why did Jesus say this three times?"

She shook her head with a slight grin. "Well, at least the first part of your reply was perceptive. I guess one out of two isn't all that bad. Don't you remember that Peter denied Jesus three times after His arrest? Jesus was just canceling out that denial. Actually, Peter did feed Jesus' sheep three significant times as recounted in Acts: first with the three thousand, again with five thousand, and finally with the gentiles associated with Cornelius."

"Oh," Earl replied in a subdued voice.

"What you must know is that the feedings of the five, four and three thousand souls was primarily a series of highly symbolic events leading up to a symbolic sign that will be of enormous import to the nation of Israel. In this symbology, the feedings were orderly, as was the miracle involved in the physical bread. Although it is possible to reconstruct the order in the process algebraically, starting with the question of how many fragments each basket contained, I'm going to shortcut the process for you by describing both the nature of the miracle and the pattern by which the feedings took place. Once you see the patterns, you won't need the mathematical proof, because it will be perfectly obvious to you how five thousand can be fed with five loaves with twelve baskets of fragments and seven thousand can be fed with seven loaves with seven baskets of fragments."

"That's awesome. I can't wait. What about the question of how many fragments in each basket?"

"The algebraic solution demands that each basket contains, for both the feeding of the five thousand and the four thousand, exactly five fragments. Now here's an interesting fact: the baskets used in the collection of fragments of the four thousand were much larger than those used in the collection of fragments associated with the five thousand, which were just small handbaskets. But here are some interesting and very relevant facts: first, the numbers four and five thousand were associated with the menfolk only, as I had noted before; second, there were women and children in addition to the menfolk in both feeding events; third, according to Mark 7:31 the four thousand were fed near Decapolis on the south shore of the Sea of Galilee, while, according to Luke 9:10, the five thousand were fed near Bethsaida on the north shore, the implication being that the four thousand were mostly Gentile, while the five thousand were primarily Jewish. Further weight is given to this difference by the fact that the seven baskets of the four thousand correspond to the seven representative Churches that Jesus addressed in Revelation 1:20, while the twelve baskets of the five thousand match the twelve tribes of Israel."

"That's very interesting," Earl responded. After a pause, he continued. "I don't mean to be impudent, but what does the makeup of the audience have to do with the size of the baskets?"

"Everything. The practice of the Jewish faith is patriarchal in nature, with the menfolk almost exclusively being involved in the ceremonial ritual. Also, the faith was exclusive in another sense, being restricted to Jews. Given the symbolic nature of the feedings, then, the sizes of the baskets, which represented the growth of the faith, were exceedingly important. The Jewish women and children were certainly fed along with the men, but it was the menfolk to whom the Word of God was primarily directed, it being their responsibility to interpret and direct this Word to their womenfolk. This changed radically with the birth of the Church at the Pentecost following Jesus' resurrection. For the first time, women and even children were to be directly involved in the spread of the Christian faith. This difference is borne out in Acts 2:16 - 18, wherein the Christian women as well as the men not only were involved in the gift of the indwelling Holy Spirit, but were expected to actively use that gift:

But this is that which was spoken through the prophet, Joel: And it shall come to pass in the last days, saith God, I will pour out my Spirit upon all flesh; and your sons and your daughters shall prophesy, and your young men shall see visions, and your old men shall dream dreams; and on my servants and on my handmaidens I will pour out in those days of my Spirit, and they shall prophesy:...

"The bottom line," Wisdom continued, "is that the menfolk of both the four and the five thousand contributed five loaves to each basket. But the women and children of the Gentile four thousand added their share into the baskets of remainders, but only the menfolk of the five thousand contributed to their baskets of remainders."

"I don't know what to say, Wisdom. I'm amazed at the precision of Scripture, down to details so minute as that."

"It is pretty awesome. But then, being God, We're up to the challenge. Now back to the topic at hand – the feedings themselves. Not only is the miracle an ordered one, but it is very simple to understand. Specifically, during the distribution each loaf of bread became whole after it was broken and passed from one participant to another. In this process, the breaking of the bread quite openly symbolizes Jesus' act on the cross, and its restoration, being of God rather than leaven, speaks of His regenerative power."

"Is that all there is to it—the loaves, after being broken, became whole again?"

"In a sense, yes. That's the entirety of the miraculous part of the feedings. But the patterns are important too. The first pattern you must understand is the arrangement of the men being fed in companies, which is spelled out for you in Mark 6:39 and 40:

And [Jesus] commanded them to make all sit down by companies upon the green grass. And they sat down in ranks, by hundreds, and by fifties.

"The most basic company arrangement is the account in 2 Kings 4 of the company of a hundred being fed by twenty loaves. That description evokes the image of a company being represented by a rectangle of twenty columns by five rows deep. That will be one of two fundamental patterns for all the feeding events. But we note in Mark 6 that there also are companies of half that size, or fifty, which, in line with the pattern of a hundred, consist of rectangles of ten columns by five rows deep. In all the information I'll give you next, you are to keep in mind these two patterns: one hundred in a company arranged twenty by five, and fifty in a company arranged ten by five. Always visualize the companies with a long side facing you and the short sides of five on the left and right sides from your perspective. These companies, as I've described them, will be the basic building blocks of larger patterns."

She paused to let Earl absorb the images of the companies. "Okay," She said presently. Let's first consider the larger pattern involved in the feeding of the five thousand. What we'll do is stack up seventeen companies of a hundred, and make up four similar stacks of seventeen companies of fifty. The stack of hundreds we'll place in the center, and put two stacks of fifties side-by-side on each side of the stack of hundreds. What that gives us is a very large rectangle of five companies wide, or four companies of fifty plus one company of a hundred, by seventeen companies deep. Do the math, Earl," She commanded.

"Okay. The number of people deep doesn't depend on the company size. It's five times seventeen, or, um, eighty five. Then as far as the number across goes, it's twenty plus ten times four, or forty—sixty in all. Let me see, 85 times 60 is, ah, fifty-one hundred. There were fifty one hundred people in all."

"Very good!" She exclaimed. But do you see a problem with that number?'

"Well, it isn't exactly five thousand, but it's pretty close. Besides, the numbers were given in the accounts with the word 'about'."

"Earl, Earl," She said sadly. "Do you really think that's the way We operate? Like in Junior High woodshop? Or 'government work'? No. The numbers are intended to be exact. What are you going to do about it?"

"Gee, then I guess I'd have to remove a company of a hundred."

"Okay, but then the rectangle isn't perfect. What are you going to do about *that*?"

"Replace it, I guess... OH! Ohmygosh! Yes! I'd replace it with Elisha's company of a hundred!"

Her broad grin told him that he'd come up with the answer. He was awed by the precision of the pattern, and of how Jesus had integrated His feeding with Elisha's out of the Old Testament. "What next?" he asked Her.

"Now for the fun part. If you have the pattern of companies fixed in your mind, visualize the five loaves as being distributed one to a frontmost company, to the first man in the front of the company, to your right as you face him. He does three things: first he breaks the loaf and gives it to the next man to his right, who does the same to the man on his right, and so on, until each of the frontmost men in each of the frontmost companies have received a loaf; second, our first man breaks the half-loaf that he retained, which in the meantime has become whole again, and gives half to the man directly behind him; finally, our man eats the loaf remaining in his hand. Each of the frontmost people does the same thing: breaks the loaf again, gives a loaf to the man behind him and eats the loaf still in his hand. Now all the men behind the frontmost row will just break the loaves they receive from the men in front of them, pass a loaf to the men to their rear and eat the loaves that remain. In this way, the bread propagates to the rear of the columns, where the rearmost fragments from each column are collected in baskets. I said before that each basket has five loaves. How many columns are there in all? You have already given Me the number."

"As I recall, it's sixty columns."

"Yes. So how many baskets are needed at five loaves per basket?"

"Sixty divided by five. That's... why, that's twelve baskets! Golly, Wisdom, that's incredible!"

"I thought you'd enjoy that. If you're ready to tackle the feeding of the four thousand, let's proceed. But let me save you a few thousand hours of trying on your own. First, continue to visualize the companies with the long side to the front and the short sides to the sides. I'll just tell you that you can't come up with an arrangement of companies with that visualization that will permit you to distribute seven loaves to the frontmost companies and end up with seven baskets at the rear. You have to do something different than with the feeding of the five thousand. This event will require that all the companies will be of fifty, with eleven columns of companies each stacked seven companies deep. Do the math again."

"Okay. Five deep per company times seven companies is thirty-five deep. Ten wide per company times eleven companies wide is one hundred ten. Let's see, that's.... thirty eight fifty. Four thousand is one hundred fifty men too many."

"So?"

Earl thought for a moment. "I guess we'd have to do something else with the hundred and fifty to preserve a perfect rectangle."

"You're right. Just keep that extra hundred fifty in your head for now, and let's have fun again with the rectangle of thirty eight fifty. This time, instead of handing out the initial seven loaves to the front, they'll be handed to the column of men to your rightmost as you face them, one to the man in each rightmost company who is both frontmost and rightmost. The pattern's essentially the same as with the five thousand, just rotated ninety degrees. The loaves will propagate rearward within each company and after that to the left, and will be collected into baskets from the leftmost man in each row. So instead of proceeding from column to column, the collection will be made from ends of the thirty five rows. How many baskets will be needed for the collection at five loaves per basket?"

"Well, that would be seven times five, or thirty five rows divided by five, which comes out to, gee, seven baskets."

"Now do you understand how five thousand can be fed from five loaves and yield twelve baskets, while four thousand can be fed from seven loaves and yield seven baskets?"

"I do, Wisdom. It's amazing—purely a matter of geometry."

"Good. Now, finally let's consider Peter's feeding of three thousand according to Acts 2:41. The pattern is generally the same as with the five thousand, but with three stacks of companies of a hundred side-by-side, each stack being ten companies deep. As you can figure out for yourself, this produces a rectangle of sixty people wide, like with the feeding of the five thousand, and fifty deep. Sixty times fifty, of course, is three thousand. Now, Earl, what can be done with these three rectangles: the composite of the five thousand plus Elisha's one hundred, the four thousand less a hundred fifty that we'll get to later, and Peter's three thousand?"

"Well, we can stack them up together, like we stacked the companies. I'm doing it in my mind, but it doesn't amount to much."

"Did you preserve the sequence of five thousand first or bottom, four thousand next, and three thousand at the top?"

"Yes, but..."

"Did you preserve the rotation of the four thousand men ninety degrees from the orientation of the other two events?"

"No, but I don't see... Ohmygosh! I get a cross, Wisdom! Is that right?"

"Yes. Now, as to the hundred fifty that were left over from the four thousand. What was hung on the cross?"

"I guess the inscription."

"Right. The Titulus. In three languages, as recorded in Luke 23:38:

> *And a superscription also was written over him in letters of Greek, and Latin, and Hebrew, THIS IS THE KING OF THE JEWS.*

"Oh, my," was all that Earl could say.

"Yes," She agreed. "Each of the three fifties that were left over represented the superscription in one of the three languages."

Earl was awed to silence. "It is this understanding of Scripture which will bring the Jews to their Messiah," She told him. "Partly through you. Specifically, through you to a man, a Jew, whom you'll be meeting under very different circumstances than you enjoy at the present time. His name is Jacob and listen carefully, for now I'm going to give you an important introduction to him."

"He must be a significant person."

"In his own mind. But that's not the real problem, and it'll be taken care of in a different way. He's down on Christianity and Christians, which is what the introduction will soften. Remember the issue about My nature that your postings were all about?"

"How could I possibly forget that? Convincing other Christians of your female gender, actually that you possessed a working gender at all, was a very tall order."

"Yes, and you did good, even though most Christians still stubbornly refuse to accept it, preferring their own traditions over Scripture. Anyway, you'll be approaching Jacob with a proof of My gender that he'll find most difficult to reject.

"I posted several very good reasons for attributing to You a female gender. After all, they really came from You. I suppose that You'd like me to go back and refresh my memory of them."

"No, that won't be necessary. There's one reason that you haven't addressed yet, and it's the most appropriate for a Jewish audience."

"I thought I'd covered all the bases."

"You know Scripture pretty well for a layperson, but your knowledge isn't perfect, Earl. There's certainly more in the Word about Me and My gender than you're aware of. The picture I want to give you now is a perception of a facet of God that is uniquely familiar to the Jews. It's called the Glory of God, and in the Hebrew tongue it's called the Shekinah. The word 'Shekinah' is grammatically feminine, as you can verify for yourself by looking up the word on the Internet. The account of this glory begins in Exodus 40:34 through 38 at the dedication of the Tabernacle:

> *Then a cloud covered the tent of the congregation, and the glory of the Lord filled the tabernacle. And Moses was not able to enter into the tent of the congregation, because the cloud abode thereon, and the glory of the Lord filled the tabernacle.*

> *And when the cloud was taken up from over the tabernacle, the children of Israel went onward in all their journeys; but if the cloud were not taken up, then they journeyed not till the day that it was taken up. For the cloud of the Lord was upon the tabernacle by day, and fire was on it by night, in the sight of all the house of Israel, throughout all their journeys.*

"There was a second occasion, very similar to this first, during the dedication of Solomon's Temple several centuries later. This temple also was filled with the Glory of the Lord upon its dedication. The Scriptural account is given in 1 Kings 8:6-11:

> *And the priests brought in the ark of the covenant of the Lord unto its place, into the inner sanctuary of the house, into the most holy place, even under the wings of the cherubim. For the cherubim spread forth their two wings of the place of the ark, and the cherubim covered the ark and its staves above. And they drew out the staves, that the ends of the staves were seen out in the holy place before the inner sanctuary, but they were not seen outside; and there they are unto this day. There was nothing in the ark except the two tables of stone, which Moses put there at Horeb when the Lord made a covenant with the children of Israel, when they came out of the land of Egypt. And it came to pass, when the priests were come out of the holy place, that the cloud filled the house of the Lord, so that the priests could not stand to minister because of the cloud; for the Glory of the Lord had filled the house of the Lord.*

"So here we have two occasions where the Glory of the Lord – the female Shekinah – indwelt the temple of the Lord. What does that remind you of, Earl?"

"Well, as far as 'indwelling' goes, I usually associate that with the indwelling of the Holy Spirit on Christians, the Body of believers."

"Good. And what do Christians represent?"

"The Body of Christ. The Bride of Christ."

"And something else, another way of looking at the Bride of

Christ. I'll give you a hint from the New Testament, two Scriptural passages, specifically 1 Corinthians 3:16 and Ephesians 2:19 through 22:

> *Know ye not that ye are the temple of God, and that the Spirit of God dwelleth in you?'*
>
> *Now, therefore, ye are no more strangers and sojourners, but fellow citizens with the saints, and of the household of God; and are built upon the foundation of the apostles and prophets, Jesus Christ Himself being the chief corner stone, in whom all the building fitly framed together growth unto an holy temple in the Lord; in whom ye also are built together for an habitation of God through the Spirit.'"*

"Of course, Wisdom! Then You're saying that in indwelling the temples, You—the Holy Spirit—were foreshadowing Your indwelling of believers, the Temple of God made without hands."

"Yes. And that's precisely what you're going to tell Jacob when the time comes."

"It's getting complicated. First the feedings and now the Shekinah. How can I possibly remember it all?"

"Don't worry. I'll be with you to put it back in your mind. I love you. 'Bye for now."

Chapter Nineteen

"How's my bride today?" The light-hearted way in which Henry's question was delivered did nothing to calm Janet's depression. She poked a finger through the chain-link fence, careful to avoid the hot metal. Henry wrapped it with two of his and squeezed tightly.

"All I can say is that I'm one day closer to checking out. At least they haven't withheld the pain pills, but I can tell that I'm getting more tired every day. I'll be happy to have it end."

"Don't talk like that," Henry pleaded.

"Why not? Surely you don't think that you and I will ever be together again. Not in this life. I can understand why they took me – they're saving a fortune in medical bills. But I can't believe that they took you too." The aid vehicle had come promptly in response to Janet's call to 9-1-1. All she had wanted was some help in managing the increasing pain associated with her cancer. Instead, the first responders had belted her into a gurney, placed handcuffs on Henry, and dragged them off into the night.

"That's a no-brainer, honey. I suspect that a lot of Americans have some idea of what the real healthcare plan is all about, but without being directly confronted with it they've been able to ignore the implications. There's a good chance that if witnesses were out and about, there'd be some form of public anger. Ergo, I'm here. It would have been nice if they'd kept us together, or at least gave us visiting privileges." Henry sighed in frustration. "But no." The relocation camp maintained a strict segregation of the sexes, which was why so many of the inmates were arrayed along the fence that separated the men from the women despite the intense heat of the Arizona sun.

"Henry, I'm getting weaker. I'm going to have to go back inside. I'm so sorry." A tear leaked down her cheek as Henry released her finger.

"See you tomorrow?" Henry asked plaintively. The sight of his distress made the tears flow faster. "Yes, of course. Take care of yourself. I love you."

It was marginally cooler inside the hastily-constructed cinderblock building, no doubt to keep the guards from rioting. The idea of guards was ridiculous. As if the sick grannies inside were capable of mounting a revolution. She shuffled over to her 'home'—a five-by-ten space occupied by a cot and a footlocker—and lay on the bed. A doctor went about his rounds several hours later and stopped at the 'home' next door. He applied his stethoscope to the feeble lady's chest and listened intently. He moved on. Within a couple of minutes two burly guards came to her bedside and lifted her up onto a gurney. She was still alive because Janet could see her eyelids flutter. Nevertheless, when they carted her away she never saw the woman again. Within an hour another elderly lady was calling the place home.

"Will I ever see her again?" Joyce asked Her. Wisdom had broken the news to her about her mother's circumstance, and remained at her bedside to comfort her.

"Yes, darling, eventually. But not here. Not in this life."

"It's such a waste," Joyce cried. "How could they do that?" The awful reality of the cruel, heartless treatment of her mother had thrust her courageous attitude into a very distant background.

"It's a very natural process, unfortunately." Wisdom extended her arms toward Joyce and drew her to her breast. "Remember how very much we love you," She murmured in Joyce's ear as she gently rocked her. Joyce eventually relaxed, and Wisdom continued. "Once a society has rid itself of the encumbrances associated with a relationship with God, it's just one more step to its ridding itself of God altogether. When that happens, the degeneration of the society becomes inevitable and all sorts of atrocities spring up as the people sink into self-absorbed chaos. It doesn't take long, either. But it's not a waste, Joyce. Even now, at this very moment, your mother is sharing the Gospel with her neighbor. If she hadn't been carted away, that wouldn't have happened. Not because there wasn't an opportunity – there's always an opportunity for that – but because she wouldn't have stepped up to the plate under normal circumstances. So even there, dear, she's having an opportunity to serve God and, incidentally, to lay up treasures for herself in heaven without even realizing it."

"Oh! Then it's not all bad."

"Of course not. Remember the promise that Paul gave you in Romans 8:28?"

"I do: 'All things work together for good for those who love God.'"

"... to them who are the called according to his purpose," Wisdom finished for her. "You've spoken of it to others. It most certainly applies to you also. Don't take that lightly, Joyce. Comfort yourself with the truth of that, as in all Scripture."

"Oh, Wisdom, thank you so much. It really is a much bigger world out there than we know, isn't it?"

"For sure, honey. And you'll be a part of it. You and Earl and your mother. And Henry too."

"Oh! I didn't even think of him," she said with contrition.

"Just to make you feel worse about it," Wisdom said with a laugh, "he's been praying for you and Earl. It may be a good idea to start praying back for him."

"I'll do that," Joyce said. "Is there anything special that I should pray for?"

"He's a real warrior for God, Joyce. You should be very proud of him, and for your mother's taste in men. He preaches the Gospel like a real trooper. He's been kicked around for it, too, but he won't stop for anything. He has over forty souls to his credit so far, and there'll be many more to come."

"Should I pray for his life? And that of mom?"

"If you did it wouldn't do any good. The cancer will take your mother, but not before she brings in more souls. As for Henry, I'm afraid that he won't last much longer with all the abuse he's taking. But he'll take his end like a man. His attitude reminds Me of one of your dear brothers in Christ, the Apostolic Father Polycarp whom We strengthened when he was being carried off to the stake to be burned during the fourth of ten Roman persecutions. 'Be strong, Polycarp, and play the man', We told him. He did, too. Although pity was shown toward him as an elderly man, he refused to deny Christ, which would have resulted in his release. His reply is famous: 'Eighty-six years I have served Him, and He never once wronged me. How can I blaspheme my King, who saved me?' When the fire was lit beneath him, it left him unburned. A soldier eventually stuck a sword into him, but the blood put out the fire. Finally another fire was started, which consumed him. He endured an agonizing end, but never wavered in his testimony for Jesus. He's going to have a happy eternity with Us. Henry will do the same, and save many souls by the manner in which he meets his death."

"Poor Henry," Joyce said. "He really loves mom. You said they've been forced apart. He really must be in agony over that."

"Yes, he is. But he's using it constructively. Like you and Earl, your mom and Henry and George have been picked to help with the final ingathering of the souls that belong to Us."

"Final? Does that mean that we're already in the Tribulation?"

"Yes, it does," Wisdom said with a smile. What you've been seeing happening in America actually is a worldwide event. You're in the last stages of the formation of the new world order foretold in Scripture by Daniel and John, one government over the entire world."

"I remember Pastor George talking about Polycarp. And Perpetua. Now that things are really happening, it's scary. Will Earl and I have the courage to maintain our faith in the midst of this coming persecution? Like them?"

"Tomorrow morning go over to Church and borrow George's copy of John Foxe's *Christian Martyrs of the World.* It's on the north bookshelf of his study, twelfth book from the left. Your pastor already touched on a few basics, but go beyond that and read the details. Store them up in your heart. As you read, you might also think about how those who suffered received help from heaven and courage through Me to get them through the rough spots. It will help you to know how splendidly other Christians held up under persecution, and give you something to shoot for. If you think you're adventure's over, think again." She gave Joyce a tender hug and whispered an endearment in her ear. "Bye for now," She said, and vanished. Joyce turned back to her sleeping husband and gave him a hug of her own. *Thank you, Lord, for giving me this wonderful man*, she prayed, and fell back to sleep.

"Get away from there!" the guard growled, poking Henry with a nightstick. As Henry turned away, the guard pushed the club into his gut with a vicious thrust. As he doubled over, the guard swung the baton into his face, laying bare his cheekbone. "You're a troublemaker," the guard intoned with indifference. "That'll quiet you down some. Won't be too long before you'll be silent for good. Maybe I'll be the one who pulls the duty. I'd like that real good."

The fence had cooled enough in the evening that Henry could cling to the wire without burning his hands. He had been gazing over at his wife's barracks, one of a huge number that had been erected in the desert. The rules included a prohibition of standing near the fence after six in the evening. Henry already had figured out why: during the early nighttime hours that the dead or near-dead were carted away to their more permanent relocation center, which was a monstrous facility with a smokestack that had the size and appearance of the cooling tower of a nuclear power plant. The smoke from it wasn't obvious at night, but sometimes the moving air brought the acrid stench over his own barracks.

The guard had left him there, but was watching at a distance to make sure he left the area of the fence. Holding his aching gut, Henry rose and staggered back to his building.

As Wisdom had instructed, Joyce visited George at the Church and returned with the copy of Foxe. "You might recall a sermon on Revelation that I'd delivered some time ago," he told Joyce as he handed the book to her. "In there," he said, pointing to the book, "Foxe had listed ten persecutions between A.D. 64 and 303. In choosing to categorize them that way, Foxe was referring to a prophecy by Jesus regarding the Church at Smyrna, the second of seven Churches that He addressed in Revelation Chapters 2 and 3. Wait one."

George left to go into his den and returned with his Bible "As a reminder I'll read to you His message to the Church at Smyrna in Revelation 2:8-11:

> *And unto the angel of the church in Smyrna write: These things saith the first and the last, who was dead, and is alive. I know thy works, and tribulation, and poverty (but thou art rich); and I know the blasphemy of them who say they are Jews, and are not, but are of the synagogue of Satan. Fear none of those things which thou shalt suffer. Behold, the devil shall cast some of you into prison, that ye may be tried, and ye shall have tribulation ten days; be thou faithful unto death, and I will give thee a crown of life. He that hath an ear, let him hear what the Spirit saith unto the churches: he that overcometh shall not be hurt of the second death.*

"The Church at Smyrna was the second of the seven Churches addressed by Jesus in Revelation Chapters 2 and 3," George continued. "Of these Churches, Smyrna and Philadelphia were the only two for which Jesus had nothing negative to say. It has been broadly recognized as the persecuted Church. As I had told you in one of my sermons, according to Foxe and other theologians the ten 'days' spoken of by Jesus were ten periods of overt, usually intense persecution." He put his hand over his eyes, rubbing them for comfort. "Oh, my, Joyce, that seems like a lifetime ago, when we were just starting to wake up to the disasters awaiting us."

Back home, Joyce opened the book and soon was absorbed in its contents. She was particularly moved by the account of Perpetua, who suffered under the persecution which began in A.D. 200. According to Foxe, this was the fifth of the ten persecutions foretold by Jesus that would be inflicted on the Church at Smyrna. Born around 181 A.D., Perpetua lived in Carthage in the Roman province of Africa. As Joyce read Foxe's entry regarding this lovely woman, her eyes watered and tears of emotion dripped down her cheeks:

"During the reign of Severus, the Christians had several years of rest and could worship God without fear of punishment. But after a time, the hatred of the ignorant mob again prevailed, and the old laws were remembered and put in force against them. Fire, sword, wild beasts, and imprisonment were resorted to again, and even the dead bodies of Christians were stolen from their graves and mutilated. Yet the faithful continued to multiply. Tertullian, who lived at this time, said that if the Christians had all gone away from the Roman territories, the empire would have been greatly weakened.

"By now, the persecutions had extended to northern Africa, which was a Roman province, and many were murdered in that area. One of these was Perpetua, a married lady twenty-six years old with a baby at her breast. On being taken before the proconsul Minutius, Perpetua was commanded to sacrifice to the idols. Refusing to do so, she was put in a dark dungeon and deprived of her child, but two of her keepers, Tertius and Pomponius, allowed her out in the fresh air several hours a day, during which time she was allowed to nurse her child.

"Finally the Christians were summoned to appear before the judge and urged to deny their Lord, but all remained firm. When

Perpetua's turn came, her father suddenly appeared, carrying her infant in his arms, and begged her to save her own life for the sake of her child. Even the judge seemed to be moved. 'Spare the gray hairs of your father,' he said. 'Spare your child. Offer sacrifice for the welfare of the emperor.'

"Perpetua answered, 'I will not sacrifice.'

"'Are you a Christian?' demanded Hilarianus, the judge.

"'I am a Christian,' was her answer.

"Perpetua and all the other Christians tried with her that day were ordered killed by wild beasts as a show for the crowd on the next holiday. They entered the place of execution clad in the simplest of robes, Perpetua singing a hymn of triumph. The men were to be torn to pieces by leopards and bears. Perpetua and a young woman named Felicitas were hung up in nets, at first naked, but the crowd demanded that they should be allowed their clothing.

"When they were again returned to the arena, a bull was let loose on them. Felicitas fell, seriously wounded. Perpetua was tossed, her loose robe torn and her hair falling loose, but she hastened to the side of the dying Felicitas and gently raised her from the ground. When the bull refused to attack them again, they were dragged out of the arena, to the disappointment of the crowd, which wanted to see their deaths. Finally brought back in to be killed by gladiators, Perpetua was assigned to a trembling young man who stabbed her weakly several times, not being used to such scenes of violence. When she saw how upset the young man was, Perpetua guided his sword to a vital area and died."

Joyce was so taken by the story that she decided to seek more information regarding Perpetua on the Internet. She Googled "Perpetua" and read the Wikipedia entry. This entry differed in some minor details from Foxe's, but also added some useful information. Perpetua, for example, was identified there as of noble heritage. Felicitas (Felicity), was supposedly her slave. The Catholic Church has canonized her, along with Felicity, as a saint. Her feast day is March 7, the date of her execution.

The perceived nobility of her name has a factual basis in the circumstance of her birth, Joyce noted. But she also reckoned that Perpetua's high birth was of little consequence compared to the nobility of her faith and the beautiful manner in which she chose to exercise it.

When Earl came home she sat him down and had him read the same story. She was satisfied to see that before he had finished the account a tear was dribbling down his cheek.

Chapter Twenty

The government might as well have added a "C" and "J" to their AIDE acronym, for it responded to this new unrest by bringing the Christians and Jews under their umbrella. "For their own protection," the government claimed loudly and often as they began to round up Christians and Jews and transported them to new living quarters consisting of the barracks surrounded by barbed wire in which the elderly and infirm were held captive. A few individual couples, posing as Christians, were set up in rather splendid quarters which obviously offered dignity, privacy and comfort. These false showcases were filmed and disseminated to the public, making it even angrier against these "privileged" Christians.

The mistreatment and incarceration of people of the Book suited God just fine. Historically, the Church has thrived under persecution. The addition of Christians into the mix of elderly, infirm and handicapped served as an unprecedented opportunity to reach out to the unsaved with the Gospel message of love and hope. The guards, under the control of satan, responded to this realization with harsh and cruel treatment of the Christian prisoners. They were quick to invent new ways of entertaining themselves at the inmates' expense. The latest fashion was to force a group of prisoners to form a circle, standing with bare feet under the fierce noontime sun as they ate their sparse midday meal. Their hopping caused them to spill their meals, leaving them thirsty and hungry. The motion also resembled a dance, which the guards found hilarious. Another favorite that persisted beyond the fad stage was to plant a scorpion inside the covers of a bed and watch with glee the surprise and agony on the face of the victim as the insect inflicted its sting. Recipients of this treatment, already weakened by the inadequate food and harsh conditions, inevitably would pay with their lives from this joke.

Nevertheless, the Christians held fast to their faith, becoming stronger with each cruel act they were forced to endure. Mighty in word, they brought many souls into the kingdom of God.

Having belatedly caught on to the deeds of salvation being wrought by the Christians that had come into the camp, the warden separated them from the general population, isolating them in separate barracks. This had little effect, for the others still saw the brave manner in which the Christians endured the pain and humiliation of the guards' recreational torture. Moreover, the Christians were able to leave some scraps of Scripture behind. One person had from memory scratched the complete text of John's Prologue, verses one through eighteen of Chapter One of John's Gospel, onto the underside of a toilet seat. This single item of itself led over a hundred people to a saving faith in Jesus Christ.

The general public wasn't faring as well as it expected to under the increasingly repressive regime. The drastically younger population had something in common: the entire generation had been taught unceasingly in school to embrace selfishness as a natural and wholly welcome trait. That, positive thinking, acceptance of "God" as irrelevant to the real world, sensitivity to self-esteem (when it concerned self), openness to hedonistic sexual experimentation, and lack of discipline left it completely without the moral strength to contend with or influence the direction that society was taking. And the direction was in a rapid downward spiral.

At first the much younger society at large had enthusiastically supported the attrition of the elderly and unfit, being quite pleased with the prospect of living life as they wished with their parents' possessions and wealth but without the intrusion of the care involved in dealing with the diminished capacity of mom and pop. Moreover, they expected the savings in health costs to pay immediate dividends in the form of reduced taxes, free health coverage and general prosperity for all.

It didn't happen that way. Taxes continued to climb under the rationale of meeting costs associated with preparing to enter a more tightly-joined community of nations. Health coverage was indeed free, but as often as not the reason for visiting the clinic was sufficient to place the visitor into the category of the infirm. This of course, to the total shock of the individual who had sought medical attention, meant his removal from society at large. An enormous number of outraged people who knew of the negative connotations of the changes that had swept society but thought of them as applying to others, had to think again. And the thoughts were anything but pleasant, exacerbated by the realization that at this stage there was nothing anybody could do about the horrifying situation.

A tsunami of government regulations, having been enacted with indifference to the normal process of legislation, worked inexorably to disenfranchise people from the ownership of land and to bring them *en masse* into rapidly-expanding cities, where they became apartment dwellers living with minimal possessions and entirely void of property. The final straw for small farmers was the fiercely-enforced regulation against child labor. Without the help of their children, farmers were faced with the necessity of hiring adult laborers at the exhorbitant rates established for the protection of farm workers. They folded instead. They had to. They had no choice. Small business, over-regulated in the same heavy-handed manner, also folded. These too were taken over by their larger brothers, the international corporations.

The land itself, or at least that portion of it that God had not rendered barren through one disaster or another, continued to enjoy full utilization. The farms were taken over by large corporations. Having established the necessary control over the population through draconian 'green' laws, the government no longer bothered with the fiction of environmental concern. Huge strip mines opened up, and the earth was torn asunder to make way for vast oil pipelines and processing facilities. Once again, smog enveloped the large cities as they hummed with the feverish activity of minimum-wage workers who were happy just to continue to survive.

Chapter Twenty One

Eventually the day came when Joyce responded to a knock on the door to face Mildred Black, the mean-spirited woman from the bureaucracy, now a member of the AIDE agency. Joyce's heart fell.

Mildred didn't wait to be invited in. Pushing the door aside, she entered the foyer and removed her coat. "I suppose you know why I'm here," she said. "I know that Catherine's here too," she added with a cat-catching-the-mouse sneer. "We can do this the easy way, or I can call the menfolk. How do you want this to go down?" Obviously, Mildred was addicted to cop shows on the tube. She brushed Joyce aside and headed toward the bedroom area.

Joyce had feared that this day would come. They had done nothing to prepare for it, simply because they didn't have any idea what to do about it. They'd also begun to hear rumors of the wholesale slaughter of the least productive members of society, the handicapped, the infirm, and the elderly. Something snapped inside her, and before she could catch a calming breath she grabbed the coatrack and swung it against Mildred's head, flooring her. She looked upon the now-unconscious face, saw blood trickling from a wound in her head, and knew that she had crossed a bridge dividing one part of her life from the next. She hastily collected some food and water from the refrigerator, rummaged around the bedrooms for changes of clothing, and wheeled Cathy out to her car. Once on the roadway, she drove aimlessly for a quarter of an hour. Collecting her wits, she headed for Pastor George's residence next to their Church.

"I can't hide here any longer than a couple of hours at most," she told George. "Given the amount of information they have on everybody, this will be one of the first places they'll come looking once Mildred comes to her senses."

"Are you sure she will? Come to her senses, I mean. She isn't – ah – dead, is she?"

"No. I'm certain of that. I checked her breathing with a mirror."

"Well, that's something, at least. They can't kill you for murder, then."

"No. Just for being a Christian."

"There is that. I'll call Earl at work, let him know that you're here and that he may want to get here in a hurry. No, better yet, you call him. Mildred's probably still out, and if you call there won't be an obvious connection to me. Not that I'm afraid, it's only a matter of time now before they collect us all. But I'd like to be able to take care of the rest of my flock as long as I can, especially one or two fence-sitters who are starting to come around. It would be best if you met him someplace other than here. I'll take care of Cathy in the meantime."

Joyce called Earl and asked him to meet her right away at the local Walmart parking lot. She didn't have to say anything else. He knew from the tone of her voice that the request was an urgent one.

Joyce arrived first. The inactivity of waiting caused her to think of the implications of what she had done. She began to see flashing lights on the roof of every car that moved. As terror crept in and set her nerves on edge, she put her head on her hands. *What am I going to do?* she wailed. *Lord, please help me.*

Cindy.

It was a single word, a name, that came into her head insistently and repetitively.

Cindy.

Confused, Joyce didn't know what to make of it. She didn't know a Cindy.

Earl arrived before Joyce could make sense of the stray name. When he parked she ran up to his car and jerked open the door. "I'm in real trouble," she said breathlessly. "I hit Mildred Black in the head and left her unconscious on the floor."

"You mean the rude bureaucrat who gave us such a hard time with the adoption?"

"Yes. I've got Cathy at George's. We can't go back home. I just came from Church. We can't stay there. I don't know what to do." Tears leaked from her eyes.

"I like it, Joyce," he said with a grin. "I know we're not supposed to get our own back, but just this once it feels real good." The grin widened. "Did you confront her first - ask her if she felt lucky?" He rushed over to the other car, locked the doors, and returned to her. "Look, we probably have enough time to load up with some basics. Let's go shopping." Earl grabbed a stray cart and the two headed inside the huge store, where they focused so intently on the task at hand that they didn't have time to speak to each other. They returned after the whirlwind spree and loaded up the back seat. They jumped into the car, slammed the doors and he pulled out of the parking lot.

"Anything come to mind yet?" Joyce asked him. "I'm so sorry, honey." Just having Earl next to her calmed her down, morphing her panic into remorse.

"Why? You had to do something, Joyce. You know exactly what would have happened to Cathy if you'd stood there and done nothing."

"Thanks for that. But what would have happened to Cathy might very well happen to the three of us anyway."

"Whatever we do, we're going to need some basic supplies for our young 'un. I'll have to risk going to the nursing home before we pick up Cathy. They'll probably figure that it will be last place we'd go."

Earl continued to plan their next move as they loaded a power wheelchair and more supplies into the already-stuffed car. He and Joyce gave Laurie a heartfelt goodbye and took off.

The two remained silent for several minutes, each attempting to fit this new event into their minds as the car headed to Pastor George's. "Chin-up, darling," Earl told her. "If you could get through the hospital experience like you did. . ."

She stared wide-eyed at him "Cindy!" she suddenly exclaimed. "I do know Cindy!"

"Cindy?" Earl responded. "Cindy who?"

"Cindy Miller. She was in the hospital with me. After our accident. Maggie, my therapist, was helping me and another patient who had a wrist injury. Both of them had wonderful senses of humor and with that and the pain, we became very close. Cindy had a boat. A sailboat. It was the love of her life along with her husband Stephen. Maybe they still have it.

"So? How does that involve us?"

"I'm not sure. All I know is that I called out to God in despair while I was waiting for you in the parking lot, and the name Cindy popped into my head. You figure it out."

"Are you sure that it wasn't just a stray thought?"

"No. It was too insistent for that. It meant something, Earl."

Earl didn't say anything more about it while they continued to drive to George's. When they arrived there, George motioned them into the garage and shut the door behind them. "Under normal times, I'd advise you to turn yourself in to the authorities, Joyce," George said. "But these times are anything but normal. As a matter of fact, we've probably put 'normal' behind us forever. So now I'd say that you'd probably do better on the lam. Too bad I can't give you advice on where to go and how to do it when you get there."

"Do you have a phone book?" Earl asked his pastor.

"Yes. But what good..."

"God's been talking with Joyce," he replied, cutting off the question. We have a name."

George went into his study and returned with a telephone book, which he gave to Joyce. She thumbed through it quickly. "Miller... Miller... Stephen... ah. Here it is, a cell number I'm sure." She recited the number to Earl, who wrote it down.

"Hello, Cindy?" Joyce said into the phone. This is Joyce Cook. I'm not sure that you remember me... oh, you do? How are you?" She listened for a moment. "Oh, that's wonderful," she replied. "Cindy, I'm not sure what's going on, but I've been hearing your name in my head, and right now... yes. Yes, I'm in trouble. We have a child now, Cindy. A darling girl, eleven, but she has cerebral palsy. The government wants to take her away from us. We suspect that they want to euthanize her. I went off the deep end, Cindy. When the government worker threatened to take her away, I lost it and whacked her on the head. Then I ran away... Well, yes, but... Are you sure? I don't know, Cindy... well, okay then. 'Bye."

"She obviously doesn't want to see us," Earl told her. "I don't blame her. Who wants to shelter three fugitives, one of whom has a hard time getting around. And especially with the resources the government has at its disposal. And then. . ."

Joyce put her finger to his lips. "Calm down, Earl," she said. "Cindy said no such thing. She told us to get our butts down to the marina as soon as we can. They've been liveaboards for the past three months waiting for an excuse to sail into the sunset. They're on G dock. Slip G-3. Let's go."

"Oh," was all he could say.

Chapter Twenty Two

"Oh, Cindy," Joyce said in the midst of a warm embrace, "I'm so thankful that you cared enough for our plight to have us aboard. You have no idea what that means to us."

"I think I do. Remember, I wasn't born yesterday. And the black experience in America gave me a few insights about man's inhumanity to man—his absolute willingness to see others suffer and die for the sake of his own ego or convenience—to get the picture about Cathy. But even beyond this ever-present background of evil there seems to be a certain point-of-no-return, a threshold of common selfishness below which society can't recover but inevitably falls apart. I didn't go through the Hitler years myself, but I've read enough about those times to see a parallel with our own. Luckily for the world at that time, the Axis Powers were limited in their control. There were braver and more noble societies ready and willing to oppose them. Unfortunately for us, there's nothing of the sort around anywhere to give us a hand. Stephen and I are hoping that we might find an isolated, backwater part of the world that's of no consequence to the powers that be where we might find some success in losing ourselves. We extend that wish to you as well."

"Well, just know that we're very grateful." She looked at the boat from the vantage of the dock. "So here we are at last, at the scene of so many funny stories. I missed you, Cindy. And your tales."

As the two women caught up with each other's lives, the men had a more urgent agenda. "We're going to need to get rid of your car," Stephen said as Earl picked up Cathy from the rear seat. Cathy's gear was already below, waiting on Cindy's practiced eye for stuffing ten pounds into a five-pound bag. Her battery-powered wheelchair was on the dock, awaiting further disposition. "Let's get Cathy comfortable on the cockpit bench there and head out."

"Speaking of tales," Cindy said to Joyce as they stepped aboard the boat, "You missed a big one just last night," she said, succumbing to a series of giggles. As we've just found out in the last couple of months, our life on the docks as liveaboards is very different than what we had ashore. On land our interaction with our neighbors was limited by the privacy of our homes and the hedges and trees that we put up to mark our boundaries. Those homes were the source of our pride, in our neighborhood at least, and we held to certain standards of conduct. Here there's no sense of pretension. A boat is a boat, whether it's new and expensive, or old, barnacle-encrusted and ready to sink. We're packed pretty close together, and we're much more dependent on each other. There's times when we have to help each other out, and we do it with pleasure. Our dock neighbors are the most friendly, happy-go-lucky, and cheerful bunch that we've ever encountered. Already we've made closer friends in three months than we did in over a decade elsewhere."

"Gee, that sounds great, like there's a lot more emphasis on community than on pride and materialism."

"You've got it. Anyway, I kind of got side-tracked. Back to last night. One of our dock neighbors is somewhat colorful. He finds it hard to commit to one woman. On several occasions he gets likkered up and opens his big mouth to brag about his love life. You'll find out yourself soon enough about him. You'll also find that the halyard – that's a line that raises and lowers the sail – runs inside the mast and bangs like a bell against the wall whenever there's a motion of the boat, like in a breeze. Well, last night around two o'clock this nut climbed to the top of his mast to announce, at the top of his lungs, his latest conquest and quite graphically what that entailed. Stephen and I couldn't help but laugh hysterically. Very soon the halyards of all the boats within earshot of his tirade, including ours, were slapping and creating a ruckus. In our case the cause was our explosive laughter. In others it may have been attempts to try out his latest inventions, which he was kind enough to share with the rest of the world."

Joyce giggled with delight. "Oh, this is wonderful. But what did his poor girlfriend do?"

"I don't know. We didn't see her leave. But then they usually slink away before dawn. Come on. I'll show you below and we'll store your things."

Earl followed Stephen's car in his own. His new friend drove a considerable distance to another vehicular venue altogether, a small airfield. "I chose this spot for a number of reasons," Stephen told Earl as they both emerged from their separate cars. "First off, nobody's going to call the police and complain about an abandoned car. At least not for a good two or three weeks. People will just assume that the parked car means that the owner flew off on a trip. And that leads into the second benefit: when the cops do come, they might get sidetracked into thinking that you went somewhere in a plane, which means they might not be looking for you near here. Third thing is that they'll have aircraft on their minds, not boats."

"Brilliant," Earl said as he climbed into Stephen's car. "I've known you, what, maybe an hour or so? I handed over this problem to you in shorter time than that. So what did you do, chose this spot as you started the car?"

"About then." He grinned at Earl. Then he frowned. "I'm not sure that we'll have room for Cathy's wheelchair," he said as he drove back toward the marina.

"I have other plans for it," Earl replied. "Brilliant ones, in fact," he added, grinning. "Don't you have an autopilot of some kind?"

"Yes, we do, sort of. It responds with rudder commands to our

GPS course settings."

"Perfect. If you can get comfortable with the thought of Cathy helping to manually steer the boat, I think I can manage to make her useful."

"I wouldn't mind at all. I'm sure that Cindy would agree. How would you propose to accomplish that?"

"You may have noticed that Cathy can control the motion of her wheelchair with a joystick on her right armrest. Despite her handicap, she's gotten pretty good with it. I was hoping, with your permission of course, to tap into the GPS-to-servomotor interface. I'm pretty good with electronics, Stephen. I promise not to blow up the system."

Stephen laughed. "Brilliant back to you!" he said. "You can even tap into our battery system. But let's save the one on Cathy's wheelchair. I wouldn't mind having another battery around for backup." He parked the car in the marina lot and they headed to the boat.

"So what made you think of me?" Cindy asked as they unpacked in the forward berth.

"You wouldn't believe it if I told you."

"Try me."

"God - The Holy Spirit - imprinted your name in my mind. The message was clear as day. Call me crazy if you want, but that's just what happened."

Cindy began to chuckle. The chuckle turned into a laugh. "Gee, Joyce, it's a good thing that Maggie didn't come into your head! You'd be wearing leathers now." Their outspoken therapist's tales of biking misadventures had been the source of much laughter during the difficult and often painful process of healing from the amputation of her legs following the auto accident.

Joyce laughed with her. "Yeah. Leathers with silver studs, a bandanna and a sore butt."

"Anyway, I do believe you. About the message from above. You see, I kind of got one too. Except I chose to ignore it. But then I'm not a desperado like you, so it wasn't hugely important to me at the time. But now I see mine as more of a preparation kind of thing, to see in your coming a confirmation that God's involved."

"Isn't God wonderful?" Joyce said. "It's so comforting to know that He's there and He's interested in little ol' us."

"Yeah." Cindy placed the two now-empty suitcases below the bunk, creating a hole that she filled with spare bedding. "There isn't room in the bunk for the three of you," she remarked. "Cathy will have to sleep here. Okay?"

"Sure, it looks comfortable enough."

The girls had brought dinner up to the cockpit by the time Earl, using the numerous tools that Stephen had on board, had managed to strip off the battery, motor and controls from Cathy's wheelchair and returned from carrying the chair itself up to the Dumpster. They ate there in the midst of the forest of masts, taking pleasure in observing the almost infinite variety of trawlers, power cruisers and sailboats. A tall, clean-cut man walked purposefully along the dock, turning to wave at Stephen and Cindy. "Hi there, Commodore," Stephen called. When he passed, Cindy turned to Joyce with a wide grin. "Another tale," she confided.

"Please," Joyce replied, clapping her hands with glee. "Share it with us."

"Okay. Jack owns a very large, very shipshape power boat. He also was somewhat pompous and overbearing until he got pruned back a couple of months ago. He's one of the most illustrious sailors on the dock, an individual whose seamanship is legendary. He's in the Coast Guard Auxiliary, and tools around the harbor on big holidays, arresting each and every violator of boating laws, particularly those who attempt to operate watercraft while drunk. His overbearing manner put others off, effectively depriving him of a dockside social life. To tell you the truth, most of us were just a little nervous around him. One day he decided to do something about his lack of popularity. He invited us all on this dock to a get-friendly barbecue around his boat. He could hold a grand barbecue, all right. His propane device was the latest and of the most majestic quality, its massive stainless-steel presence constantly maintained in a spotless, gleaming shine, dominating not only the stern of his boat but the entire dock as well. As we humbly assembled on the dock about his boat in our flimsy little folding chairs, he arose from his varnished captain's chair on the afterdeck and placed a number of chicken parts on his beloved grille. He then lit a match as he reached to turn the propane valve on.

"Unfortunately, he had turned the propane on earlier. It wasn't the volume of the report, impressive as it was, that riveted our attention. It was the sight of the highly-polished stainless-steel cover attempting to attain to the threshold of space, and the startled look of his eyes, no longer graced with eyebrows or lashes, as they followed its upward progress. The event had a good ending. No longer burdened with unnecessary respect for the unfortunate creature, we welcomed him more comfortably into our group as a true friend."

Joyce doubled up in laughter. "See what I mean?" she said to Earl. He nodded, laughing himself.

That night Joyce thanked God for providing them with Cindy and her husband. Despite the terrifying sequence of events that had brought them here, she felt safe in this new home.

She awoke to the diffuse light and the spectacularly beautiful face, softened now and enrichened with familiarity. "Hi, honey. All settled in, I see," Wisdom said with a kind smile. "This is just the start of a wonderful adventure for your excitement and Our glory."

"Oh, I'm so glad to see You, Wisdom. I've missed you so much. I thought You might have left us for more important tasks."

"I thought you might have understood by this time that I don't get spread thin. Much of Me may have other work to accomplish, but there's enough left over to handle whatever might be happening with you."

"Tell me, please. We could have had a decent life at home with

Cathy. Why did you take that away from us?"

"Take what away? Your comfort? A meaningless existence? We haven't taken. We've given. We're giving you the greatest adventure of your life. But that's not the reason for the change in lifestyle. It's not all about you. It's also about Cathy and Our purpose for her, something that she couldn't do at home with you."

"I'm sorry. I can't seem to see the bigger picture in anything You do, can I?"

"You're doing okay, so don't get uptight. Next you're going to ask why We don't heal Cathy, or why she was handicapped to begin with. The answer, Joyce, is that We do heal. But not always. Often We have a greater purpose for someone less than perfect that's more important than making him whole. Sometimes it's to bring, through their actions, more souls to an understanding and appreciation of Us. Other times it's to develop characters in them and the people with whom they interact that are pleasing to Jesus, their future Husband. Always it's to glorify God, which means that out of these interactions between the handicapped and those able to assist them there emerge instances of nobility and selflessness, rare and wonderful qualities that We take particular joy in developing within you. Look at yourself, Joyce. Thinking back, would you really like to have passed up the uncomfortable and scary things that have made you what you are today?"

"Oh, no!" Joyce cried. "I wouldn't change one thing that You've done in my life."

"There you are, then. You've answered your own question. Sure, We could have healed Cathy a long time ago. We could have healed Buddy too. But then where would you be? You certainly wouldn't be closer to Us. You'd have descended into self-indulgence. Can you accept that everything, and I mean *everything*, has a purpose to Us?"

"Well, I kind of fell away there, but I do think I'm getting closer to a natural acceptance of that."

"You are. Just remember what Paul wrote in Romans 8:

And we know that all things work together for good to them that love God, to them who are the called according to his purpose. For whom he did foreknow, he also did predestinate to be conformed to the image of his Son, that he might be the firstborn among many brethren. Moreover, whom he did predestinate, them he also called; and whom he called, them he also justified; and whom he justified, them he also glorified.

"Think on that, Joyce. It's Our glory to glorify you. When you show nobility, We're beaming like proud parents, and Jesus is like a lovesick teenager. Most Christians just skip right on by that without seeing the significance. Actually, it remains a bit of a mystery. Let me finish that beautiful passage of Paul's. I can attest to its marvelous truth:

What shall we then say to these things? If God be for us, who can be against us? He that spared not his own Son, but delivered him up for us all, how shall he not with him also freely give us all things? Who shall lay any thing to the charge of God's elect? Shall God that justifieth? Who is he that condemneth? Shall Christ that died, yea rather, that is risen again, who is even at the right hand of God, who also maketh intercession for us? What shall separate us from the love of Christ? Shall tribulation, or distress, or persecution, or famine, or nakedness, or peril, or sword? As it is written, For thy sake we are killed all the day long; we are accounted as sheep for the slaughter. Nay, in all these things we are more than conquerors through him that loved us. For I am persuaded that neither death, nor life, nor angels, nor principalities, nor powers, nor things present, nor things to come, nor height, nor depth, nor any other creature, shall be able to separate us from the love of God, which is in Christ Jesus, our Lord.

Wisdom searched Joyce's eyes lovingly. "Burn these magnificent words into your heart, because I'm intending them to be a lesson. What can you say about the man who said this?"

"Paul? That he loves Jesus with all his heart and trusts Him beyond his life."

"Nicely said. But do you remember Paul when he was a Pharisee? He hated Christians, and he hated Christ for so thoroughly stirring up the Jewish religious pot. He participated in the stoning of Stephen. He was a Christian-killer. What turned him from that into such a love of God that as a missionary for Jesus he endured suffering, pain and great danger?"

"I – I guess it was You."

"Yes it was. With God all things are possible. Now think back in that context to what you did to Mildred Black."

"Oh! Oh, my," she breathed. "I am so sorry."

"I'm afraid that I have to agree with you. It was not only regrettable, but it demonstrated a lack of faith, besides which it ignored what Jesus said about loving your enemies. Allow me to refresh your memory from Matthew 5:

> *Ye have heard that it hath been said, Thou shalt love thy neighbor, and hate thine enemy; but I say unto you, Love your enemies, bless them that curse you, do good to them that hate you, and pray for them who despitefully use you, and persecute you.*

"Joyce," She continued, "It was your job to love Mildred in the face of her rudeness to you and evil designs on Cathy. You would have ended up on this boat anyway, but now We have to scramble to get Mildred back in the picture."

As Joyce's shoulders shook with her sobs, Wisdom responded immediately. "Oh, My dear, dear girl, come here." Wisdom opened Her arms and enfolded them around Joyce in a tight embrace. She lifted Joyce's chin and gazed lovingly into her eyes. She planted a sweet kiss on one. Don't think We don't love you any less for that. Remember also that Paul said nothing can separate you from Our love. That includes you and your actions. In fact, you humans do that to Us all the time. Keeps Us on Our toes, is what it does. Just remember that sometimes there are better ways than you might dream up on your own. Scripture points the way. I'm here, too, for backup. Doing it the right way will be important in your future, so how about you and Me doing things as a team?"

"Oh, Wisdom, I want that more than anything in the world."

"I know, my darling. I'll be seeing you soon." She lay Joyce back down and left the berth as Joyce returned to sleep.

A knock on the door awakened Joyce. "'Morning, all," Cindy spoke, peeking inside. Breakfast will be ready in half an hour."

"Joyce threw off the covers and sat up. "Can I help?" she offered.

"How about helping with the cleanup after? Today is special to us. The Johnsons are leaving for Baja this morning, and we want to be there to send them off." Mike and Karen Johnson were among the few very close friends that Stephen and Cindy had. Since they were planning on spending the remaining years of their retirement in Mexico, the prospects were slim that they'd ever see each other again. They were sorry to see them leave but were happy to see them get out of an increasingly over-regulated boating environment in the States, where the threat of confiscation was always present and subject to ever-smaller infractions of regulations. With Cathy now aboard and the object of active search, the discussions Stephen and Cindy had between each other of following the other couple southward had taken on real substance.

When breakfast was over, Stephen and Cindy went topside and headed over to the Johnsons, leaving the three others behind. "It would probably be best if you kept a low profile," Stephen told them. They fully agreed, and Earl took over the cleanup chores while Joyce helped Cathy with the complicated toilet system. They were blessed with a boat that had two heads, which eased the impact on their hosts of Cathy's often lengthy use of the one.

When the Millers returned, the expected desolation of spirit wasn't there. Instead, Cindy kept giggling. "When a dock-bound sailor wants to head out to sea, he has a number of things to think of all at once," Stephen explained to them. "The smarter people create a checklist, but most of us don't. Our friends just paid the price for omitting that step. Funny. Murphy bites us all, even those, like our friends, who are respected for their nautical prowess.

"Get on with it," Cindy told her husband. "Just tell them what happened."

"Well, they very professionally cast off and smoothly backed out as we on the dock gave our final waves. Then, as Mike turned the boat, it inexplicably slowed and came to a dead stop. Then it began to return to the dock under the pull of the severely-stressed electrical cable, which they'd forgotten to release."

"It was kind of funny, all of us there staring at them with grins on our faces as they came back to the dock," Cindy said. "They pulled the plug and left again rather quickly. Their eyes remained focused on things that didn't include us on the dock." She laughed again.

"We have an announcement to make to you guys," Stephen said. "Knowing that it wouldn't be wise for you to hole up here much longer, we made up our minds about something last night. We talked to Mike and Karen before they left, and told them we're going to follow them down to Baja as soon as we can get provisioned and shipshape. We'll meet them there and spend a little time with them, but then we'll have to continue on to some place a little more remote. Any comments?"

"I do," Joyce said. "Are we forcing the issue? Would you have made that decision if we weren't here?"

Stephen gave her a kindly smile. "We eventually would have left with or without you, Joyce. We can see the handwriting on the wall, just like Mike and Karen did. All you did was get us off our lazy rear ends and push the schedule up by a few weeks."

"Thanks," Joyce breathed, very relieved.

Chapter Twenty Three

As *Forever Ours* quietly left the harbor under diesel power, Earl and Joyce remained in the forward berth along with Cathy, who lay in her small makeshift bed below their large bunk. The three of them would share this berth for the journey. The two adults would have preferred a small measure of privacy, but were grateful to their hosts for taking them away from certain imprisonment and, for Cathy, worse. Pulling aside a short curtain, they shared a glimpse of the boat's exit from the harbor through the starboard bow porthole, which wasn't a porthole in the classic sense, but more like a rectangular window. The port was just a few feet above the waterline, which gave them the impression that they were in a submarine that was about to descend into the deep. A rock seawall came into view, and when they passed it the water became noticeably rougher, at times climbing up to the level of the port. The sun was ascending aft to illuminate a new day, coloring the water a deep blue. The vibration of the four-cylinder engine picked up as Stephen at the helm increased power. They continued watching as the United States slowly diminished in size and significance. After another half hour the engine slowed again and they heard footsteps on the deck above them. Soon they heard mechanical sounds and white canvas appeared outside their window to replace the view of water and sky. The boat tilted at such a pronounced angle that one port appeared to be sinking into the water while the opposite port, in reaching toward the sky, let in an abundance of light. The lower port stopped just short of dipping below the surface when the engine noise died to be replaced by the whisper of water along the hull.

A boat under sail rewards her handlers with an ineffable feeling of graceful harmony with the magnificent world of God's design. It's a feeling that is as easy to convey to the inexperienced sailor as describing the color orange to a blind person. The same feeling also extends to passengers, but to a greater or lesser extent depending on their familiarity with sail handling. Yet at that moment of transition from power to sail everyone aboard felt it quite strongly, Cathy sounding a coo of delight. When Cindy knocked on their door and gave the "all clear", the three joyfully went up topside, Cathy in Earl's arms. The air was chilly, causing Joyce to go back down and return with warm coats. Joyce looked behind her at the indistinct pencil-thin line of landmass they'd left behind. She was stricken with a moment of sharp regret at the probability that this would be the last view of her country that she might ever see. The pang soon receded under the certainty that they were fulfilling the will of God. *My life was probably over*, she thought. *Who knows what adventures lay ahead, to be shared with those I love?*

She watched Stephen at the helm for a while, then turned again to stare at the land astern. She could see by the wake in the water that the boat was moving, but marveled that the land appeared to be stationary, refusing to recede into the distance. Only very gradually could she discern that its distance was increasing. Cindy interrupted her reverie by sitting next to her on the bench. "Everything okay?" she asked.

"It's so beautiful," Joyce replied. "I'm beginning to understand why you love it. I—we're so very grateful that you took us along."

"We're happy to have the company, especially when you seem so happy to be experiencing it." She laughed. "We do love it, but it's not without its costs. Know what "BOAT" stands for?"

"What?"

"B-O-A-T. Break Out Another Thou." They both laughed at that. "I'm glad that wind is so cheap," Cindy continued. "Everything else comes dear. First there's moorage, which makes most marinas quite wealthy. There's so much demand for slip space, at least on the West Coast, that they can pretty much charge what they please. One time when we docked at the marina in Everett, I took a stroll over to the office to inquire about slip space. I was curious, and had a hunch that moorage there would be cheaper than our slip at Shilshole Marina. The guy at the desk asked how big our boat was, and when I told him he said he'd be happy to take a reservation. 'It'll be a while, though,' he said like it was an afterthought. 'How long does that mean?' I asked back. He smiled and said that they'd probably have a slip available when my grandson comes of age."

"Wow."

"Yeah. It's that way all over the coast. Then there's the haulout. Every two years our poor lady has to submit to being plucked out of the water by slings fore and aft, get the barnacles scraped off and have her bottom painted. Otherwise the hull starts to make an impressive marine habitat. You can immediately pick out those that don't get hauled out on a regular basis. When they sail, they're trailing a rather large assortment of marine flora and fauna. Very uncool, especially since it has a significant effect on the performance of the boat. Then, of course, is the insurance, which doesn't come cheap. Etc., etc. Oh. And the doctor bills. It seems inevitable that something will happen." She massaged her wrist, then brightened. "Not that I'm complaining. I wouldn't trade this for anything."

"I'm beginning to see why. Your wrist. Did it happen while you were sailing?" Joyce reminisced briefly of meeting Cindy in the hospital while recovering from the car accident that had taken her legs. She and Cindy had shared the same therapist, Maggie, who had entertained them both with stories of motorcycle adventures gone bad. Cindy, she remembered, had been recovering from a mangled wrist.

"Sure did." She pointed to a large chrome-plated drum, used to haul in the sheets, or lines, attached to the sails. "That winch over there. Got my wrist caught between it and a sheet. That's a line—a rope to landlubbers."

"Ouch," was all Joyce could say.

"Honey," Stephen called over to his wife, "how about taking over the helm for a bit? I have to make a head call."

"I'm not surprised," she said as she moved to stand behind the wheel, "with all that coffee you drank this morning."

Stephen rushed down into the cabin. When he returned topside, he motioned to Earl. "Ready for some lessons?"

"You bet."

"Have you ever sailed before?"

"Well, yes and no. I'm not trying to be evasive. I have sailed before, but not on a boat. My sailing was vertical rather than horizontal."

"Oh? Did some sailplaning?"

"Not quite. My rig was more primitive than that. Your sails—they're Dacron, aren't they?"

"Yes, they are. Dacron is a lot lighter than the old canvas."

"So was mine. I had a Dacron wing, some aluminum tubing, and a bunch of wires to keep everything together. Like your mast. It seems to be held upright by wires. Probably stainless, like my flying and landing wires."

"That would be an excellent place to start, Earl. A sailboat has two kinds of rigging: standing rigging and running rigging. In the old days rope was used for both kinds, but like the sails, wire is now used for the standing rigging and some, but not all of the running rigging. Nylon rope is used for most of the running rigging. By the way, rope is a material. When it has a specific function, it's given another name. Same for the wire. If you look at the top of the mast, you'll see wires running down from it in all four directions. That's essentially the standing rigging, at least on this boat. The wires going fore and aft are called stays. The stays in front are called forestays. This boat has two: one coming down from the top and a lower one coming down from the middle. The stays in back are called backstays. This boat also has two of these, one running to the starboard side and the other running to the port side. The wires going to the sides are called shrouds."

"Why port and starboard? It would seem just as easy to say right and left."

"Ah! Got you there. Actually, the terms 'port' and 'starboard' convey more useful information than 'right' and 'left', which is pretty important when you have to say something in a hurry. Suppose that I said to you, 'Quick! Something dropped off the right side of the boat! Grab it!' Now if you're facing aft, the right side of the boat to you is the opposite of what it would be if you're facing the front of the boat. See the opportunity for confusion? Starboard doesn't just mean 'right side'; it means 'right side facing the front. There's no ambiguity in the term – it always means the same side of the boat regardless of how a person is facing."

"Understood. And thanks. That's an eye-opener."

"Well, good. Now, about the running rigging. A halyard is used to raise and lower a sail. On this boat, the halyard is the only running line made of wire. All the other lines are made of nylon rope – half inch diameter. See the lines running into the cockpit from the bottoms of the sails? Those are called sheets. They're used to adjust the shape of the sails – how far out or close into the boat – according to the direction of the wind. I think that I've told you enough for now. Look at those things I mentioned. It probably would be a good idea to write down as much as you can remember. Then you could hold class for Joyce, get her up to speed too, and firm it in your own mind."

"Will do. As a matter of fact, I'll get started on it right away." Earl went below to grab a pad and pencil from the navigation drawer and returned. He busied himself writing. Later he took a break and retrieved the controls to Cathy's wheelchair, which by now probably was residing in a landfill. He started out by drawing a schematic.

Then, after warning Stephen of what he was about to do, collected some tools and busied himself as innocuously as possible with some modifications to the steering system, moving quickly out of the way when he threatened to interfere with Stephen's hand on the helm.

By nightfall his task was complete. With Stephen's concurrence, he handed Cathy her wheelchair control box with its toggle switch. Stephen maintained hands-off as she experimented. She was rough at first, but her determination paid off with increasing finesse. After several days with intermittent watches at the helm, she became remarkably competent.

Forever Ours maintained a constant heel into the steady 18-knot breeze. Joyce lay on the deck on the low side, wedging herself between a railing stanchion and the raised cockpit and dipped her hand into the delightfully warm water. She made a rudder with her hand, allowing the moving water to massage her fingers. Her ear tuned into the whispering flow of the water along the polished fiberglass hull. The water below, a deep midnight blue in the shadow of the hull, was framed above by the graceful arc of the great genoa, billowing out under the pressure of the air coming in off the port bow. Looking up at the blue sky above, and then around at the vast expanse of ocean that surrounded them, she realized for the first time that necessity had offered her a view of one of life's most beautiful experiences. Desperation had brought them to this point, but God once more had turned into pure joy a forced change of lifestyle. She offered God a silent prayer of thanksgiving, fully appreciating the odd fact that, had she had a choice to make in their circumstances, it never would have included a sail to a distant port. And they never would have had the opportunity to experience this facet of life.

"Care for some company?" Earl stood above her with two mugs in his hands.

"Of course. Isn't this wonderful, Earl? Who would have expected something so bad to turn into something so good?"

"I know." He offered her one of the cups and sat cross-legged next to her facing the water. They sipped the hot liquid in easy silence. He looked aloft to inspect the telltales on the genoa and main. Noticing a drooping inboard telltale, he wrapped the free end of the jib sheet around a winch with his prosthetic arm, freed up the jib cleat, and paid out the sheet slightly. The boat responded instantly with a sharper heel. They were maintaining a close reach, a point of sail at which the boat excelled, proudly displaying a bone of white as the hull sliced through the sea.

"You're becoming a real salt," Joyce remarked. "Not a bad job of one-armed paper hanging." They both laughed.

"Somebody else's becoming a salt, too," he replied, looking up at Cathy, who was handling the helm with both intensity and joy. Her small-muscle control over the joystick was nothing short of amazing. Her desire to be useful won over the hearts of the four adults, who gave most of the helmsmanship work to her. She would have been perfectly content to keep at the task 24-7 if her body didn't need sleep.

"Sounds pretty quiet upstairs," Stephen said to his wife as they lay on their bunk together. He and Cindy were down below taking advantage of the relatively calm water to catch up on their rest.

"I just heard one of the sails getting sheeted out. Everything's okay." Apprehensive at first with the delegation of sailing chores to their novice friends, they had become somewhat more comfortable lately with the realization that Earl and Joyce, and Cathy too, which was a big surprise, were becoming valuable shipmates.

Stephen yawned. "We'll have to take baths soon," he said. "I'm starting to notice myself."

"Me too. But the weather's so perfect for sailing right now that I think we'd better wait." Fresh water was too precious to waste on personal hygiene. They would need to douse the sails and let the boat drift slowly while they all jumped into the water and rinsed themselves off.

"Okay by me. But don't complain." He laughed and gave her a tickle under her arm. "I'm getting hungry. Let's make some chow."

"Do you smell what I smell?" Earl commented as he motioned

down below. "I'm famished." Cathy gave a squeal in assent. Most of their meals were eaten cold to preserve their precious propane, but this morning the air was heavy with the smell of frying bacon. "Last of the eggs," Cindy called up. "Enjoy them while you can."

"The clouds look like soft pebbles."

"That's a good way of putting it," Stephen said to Joyce. "A pebbled sky is a harbinger of changing weather. Sometime this afternoon we'll be seeing heavier clouds, and probably some more wind." He ducked below and returned with the logbook. "The barometer's heading down, so we're certainly in for rougher weather." He entered the latest barometer reading into the log along with the time of reading. "We'd best be keeping a good eye out for changing conditions."

Over the course of the next several hours as they maintained their heading their point of sail changed from a close reach to a beam reach, and under a strengthening wind they doused the jib and took in a reef on the mainsail. The clouds built and lowered and the sky darkened. The boat took on a wobbly motion that Cathy found difficult to compensate for, and she vented her frustration in a series of angry moans.

The wind stiffened and the sky darkened. "We'd best head below," Stephen shouted to Earl. "Help me douse the main first." Cindy handed Cathy to Joyce and took over the helm. She steered the boat directly into the wind to luff the main as Stephen and Earl took in the sail and bundled it tightly against the tug of the wind. Earl, having been coached enough to know how to help, fetched a canvas bucket from a bow locker and rigged it to make a sea anchor. Cindy, in the meantime, dogged down the helm to maintain the rudder amidships. "Go on down!" Stephen shouted over the low moan of the wind as Earl tossed the bucket off the bow. Stephen took a final moment to rig a fore-to-aft lifeline in case something topside demanded attention, and then swung himself down below and slammed the hatch shut.

The boat was now drifting backwards to leeward under the force of the wind on the hull. Stephen had discussed this eventuality with the others under calmer conditions. He could have chosen the other available alternative of "lying ahull", or unfurling a tiny section of the jib, strengthened in that area just for that purpose, to serve as a storm trysail, at the same time setting the rudder to a constant turn and allowing the boat to drift without the sea anchor. But, as he had told the others, sometimes the boat will broach while lying ahull, a very dangerous condition that can cause the boat to turn turtle or ship water and sink.

"Of course," he told them as they huddled below, hanging onto whatever they could find to brace themselves against the bucking craft, "it's kind of 'you pays your money and you takes your choice', because nothing is certain in a storm. A rogue wave could catch us broadside and we could broach this way too. Or worse yet, we could come up against a wave so steep that we'd pitchpole, like looping a plane, but a lot more violent. Pitchpoling always stops halfway around and never ends well."

"Gee, thanks," Joyce remarked sarcastically. "All we need right now is a little scare to wake us up." Even Cathy, who was beginning to turn green, croaked a laugh. "Thank God that we have God."

"Amen to that."

Within a few minutes Cathy was terribly seasick. All they could do was place a large bowl in the proximity of her head and clean up the mess with rags where she missed. She curled up into a tight little ball. The smell of vomit threatened to bring the others into the same condition. Stephen took charge: "Right now, we're in the hands of God. We're not solving anything by hovering around Cathy getting sicker by the second." He reached into a deck-level cabinet and brought out a gallon jug of a nondescript red wine. He looked at them. "What?" he asked. "Oh." He laughed. "We do have a more genteel wine for toasting the sunset. Do you see a sunset right now? These are emergency rations." He poured a generous amount into four cups and gave one to each of them. "Drink up," he said. "This is the best seasick remedy available." Despite the urgency of the situation he couldn't bring himself to feed alcohol to a child. He gave her another Dramamine tablet and had her drink it down with sips of water. She continued to retch but brought nothing up. Earl picked her up and held her, straining to dampen out with his legs the rocking of the boat. He watched her as she eventually quieted down and fell asleep, and then placed her gently in her small cot in the forward berth. Despite her fears, Joyce gave him a loving glance as he returned to the saloon with wobbly legs.

The wind died down late the next morning, and by nightfall that waves had subsided. The night was clear; stars shone brightly overhead in a spectacular display, the likes of which Earl and Joyce had never seen on land. "It's the absence of all the lighting and whatnot that one has on land, even away from the cities," he remarked. Later that night the moon came up and gave them a brighter view of the heavens. When they returned to their bunks, Earl and Joyce fell asleep immediately, contented with their new life.

The following morning presented an unlimited expanse of blue sky. They all came topside to join Stephen, who was manning the helm. They reveled in the graceful movement of the boat, relieved to experience once again the absence of violent motion. The air was noticeably warmer. "Your sails are out more," Earl remarked to Stephen.

"Yeah. The wind has shifted a bit. We had to change our point of sail to a beam reach to maintain our course. Which is fine with me, because on a beam reach the wind direction is broadside to the boat. It's the fastest point of sail."

"Oh? That surprises me. The boat isn't heeling as much, and it seems calmer."

"I know. It's a bit counter-intuitive. Sailing closer into the wind creates a lot of force, but less of it is useful in pushing the boat through the water. The boat works harder and makes more of a fuss, creating the illusion that it's accomplishing more."

"Thanks. I just learned something."

"Good. There's lots more where that came from."

CHAPTER TWENTY FOUR

Joyce awoke to the repetitive *thwop-thwop* of a helicopter. It was very close. "Heave to!" shouted a voice from a loudspeaker above the noise of the rotor blades. The boat was buffeted by the downdraft. Joyce went to the hatch and peered up at the United Nations logo on the side of the craft. A man appeared at the open doorway and jumped off, clinging to a line. He descended on deck as Joyce jumped away from the hatch. The helicopter moved off to the side, allowing her to hear what was being said. "I'm an officer of the United Nations Maritime Enforcement Division," he claimed authoritatively and very loudly to Stephen, who was at the helm. "We have reason to believe that you are harboring a suspected felon on this boat." He unholstered a handgun and held it on Stephen. "I'm going below to have a look around. Don't move a muscle or you're dead meat, hear?"

Stephen nodded and the intruder opened the hatch. He had gone down two of the stairs when he saw Earl below with Joyce by his side clinging to an arm. "Well, well, well, he purred with a 'gotcha!' expression. "What have we here? Mrs. Cook, I presume. You have an appointment with the authorities back in Seattle, Mrs. Joyce Cook. Up on deck, both of you." He pointed with the gun. As he retreated back up the stairs he stumbled on the top landing, which gave Earl the opportunity he desperately sought. Earl ran up the steps like a rabid dog and grabbed his arm, wrestling the gun out of his hand. Maintaining his hold on the pistol, Earl noted the length of its barrel. *A real cowboy,* he thought with disgust. Thrusting the barrel between the enforcer's buttocks, he shoved hard, causing the man to yelp in pain and climb back up the stairs to emerge from the hatchway. The pilot of the hovering helicopter processed the drama and flew down to the boat in a threatening charge. Refusing to be intimidated, Stephen took over from Earl, grabbing the man by the hair and prolonging his run from Earl until he moved past the helm over the transom and splashed into the sea. The helicopter was very close, the end of the descent line laying limply on the bench. Stephen reached for the dangling rope and tied it to a cleat. The action panicked the pilot, who attempted without success to lift the helicopter against the straining line. He motioned to another person in the craft, who wielded a knife to cut free of the restraint. A freak gust hit the craft without warning, turning it on its side and tossing the man out, where he screamed down to join the other enforcer already in the water. Now only the pilot was left aboard. Unable to deploy the autopilot under the tether condition, the pilot was helpless. They could see him use his radio for help, but he knew that he didn't have enough time. He eventually gave up and set the helicopter gently down on the water, whereupon Stephen quickly cut the line. The pilot swam free as the helicopter sank, joining the other two men. Joyce pleaded with the men to rescue the swimmers, but Stephen shook his head. "They got off a call, so they'll survive, Joyce. At least they have a good chance to, as help is sure to be coming. That's a lot more than they gave us. Let them be."

The boat continued to drift away. Presently the sails were redeployed and they picked up speed. Within half an hour, the clouds had darkened significantly and the wind picked up. Soon after that the boat was hit with wind and a deluge of rain. "We won't be found in this," Stephen shouted to Earl, who stood with him at the helm.

"Thank God for that. And I mean every word."

The storm continued throughout the night, but behind the frequent gusts the wind was in favor of their direction of travel. When the wind calmed somewhat, Earl voiced his concern to Stephen. "You know that was a United Nations helicopter. International. It won't help to leave the U. S. boundary."

"I have a hunch that we were caught and I.D.'d on satellite. Somehow they connected us with you, maybe caught even as remote a link as Cindy and Joyce being together in the hospital after Cindy smashed her wrist. Anything's possible with a supercomputer."

"Or maybe it was just someone at the dock that supplied the information."

"Could be. At any rate, it's still a big ocean. Every hour that we don't get caught makes it that much bigger. Besides, I'm rapidly developing a pretty good hunch that God's in charge of whether they find us or not. Might as well relax as much as we can in this weather."

"Good point."

Chapter Twenty Five

A bright yellow sun radiated light and warmth out of a crystalline blue sky. Cindy looked upward, her grim face showing displeasure with the benign weather, for she knew that the clear beauty of the new day welcomed forth the violence that she knew was inevitable. Physically uncomfortable as the latest storm was, it had simply been too short-lasting for them to escape the United Nations' enforcement agents. She could picture them drawing an ellipse based on wind direction and strength of farthest possible distance about the longitude and latitude of the pickup point of the waterlogged agents. The clear skies offered a golden opportunity for a grid search within that all-too-tiny ellipse.

Stephen came up to join her and offer moral support, but his consternation matched her own. When the helicopter was sighted before noon, it was almost a relief to have the anxiety about it finally come to an end. Having seen them and relayed their position back to their support vessel, the helicopter turned back toward the land to the east.

Within another two hours they sighted the support vessel coming up fast from the direction that the helicopter had returned. Its hurried pace signaled a relentless determination to execute a pounce-

and-snatch operation. Joyce held Cathy tightly to her breast with a dismal, terrifying anticipation.

The boat slowed abruptly just out of range of any possible small arms that the fugitives might have on board, and davits swung out to deploy a small and obviously expendable pickup boat. It bumped against the hull of the sailboat and agents quickly swarmed aboard in trained, forceful haste. Within seconds the men were shackled and the women beaten. Cathy was ripped from Joyce and tossed onto the deck as Joyce looked on in horror through already swelling eyes at her utter helplessness. The thoroughly subdued group was yanked aboard the other boat to huddle forlornly in the stern.

When the pickup boat had moved a couple of hundred yards away from *Forever Ours* four of the crew began to use the fugitive boat for target practice. Eventually a round hit a propane tank, causing an explosion. Smoke billowed out and then flames. The boat listed and began to sink at the stern. Cindy wept openly at the callous destruction of her cherished dream. A guard turned toward the noise of her wailing and laughed. The sight enraged Stephen, who attempted to rise. His hands cuffed behind his back hampered his movements, and before he could get to his knees he was kicked in the face. His moans of pain shocked Cindy into silence, but Joyce responded by softly singing the hymn *How Great Thou Art*. Earl joined her, and presently Stephen also. Their guards frowned at them, but allowed them to continue. After several more hymns they quieted, each speaking to God in silent prayer.

Chapter Twenty Six

The oppressive heat inside the Spartan bed of the military truck forcefully informed the prisoners that their destination was far from Seattle.

Terrified, Cathy was roughly hauled off the hot metal bed of the military truck and flung onto the concrete floor of a huge barracks along with a large number of other physically and mentally handicapped people, mostly children, both male and female. Looking around, she saw that they were in a space void of furniture or comfort, although they seemed to be surrounded by metal bunks. Closer in, they were surrounded by blue-garbed guards, all wearing expressions of disgust and anger. The anger turned into uncontrollable rage as they approached with their batons and started indiscriminately beating the trapped prisoners. Subjected to physical abuse throughout the night, Cathy's cries for bathroom relief had been ignored as if she didn't exist for any purpose other than as a target to hit. Eventually she was forced to empty her bladder and then her bowels into her tattered clothing. Crying openly, she lay helpless and bleeding on the concrete floor in her own filth. The smell was lost in the general miasma generated from other handicapped prisoners reduced to the same condition. Eventually the blue-clad guards grew physically tired from their violence and backed off, allowing several fit female prisoners to enter the chamber to remove their clothing. After they left, a fire hose was brought in and the high-pressure water applied to the bruised bodies to wash them off, adding to the assault on their tortured flesh. The guards came back then, to drag them deeper into the barracks, where empty bunks awaited them. There were no mattresses, just bare metal springs. Cathy was tossed onto a bunk, the guard shouting "Stay there. Don't move or I'll come back. If I do, I'll be real mad." He emphasized the threat with a shove of his baton into her stomach.

The enormous room was filled with the din of pain-filled wailing, which increased in intensity as the springs and metal straps bit deeper into flesh. The odor of urine and feces returned, strengthening in intensity throughout the endless night. In the morning the fire hoses returned, spraying down the helpless and agonized prisoners. When the cleanup was finished, the guards wandered down the aisles between bunks, beating those who had managed to climb out of their sharp metal cradles until they returned in submission, and observing the others for sign of life given up. Two were found in this condition and tagged on their toes. Later in the endless day two fit prisoners trundled to the bunksides with carts, onto which they tenderly placed the bodies, and left again without speaking.

As the room heated up during the day, variants of the word "water" began to be moaned. But it was becoming plain that neither food nor water would be provided to the inmates.

The cacophony of sounds reached a crescendo in the early evening before the return of the fire hoses, and began to diminish afterward. The next morning a dozen inmates were tagged for removal. The day after that the number grew to over a hundred and the great room became ominously silent.

Cathy succumbed on the fourth day, her passing unnoticed and unlamented by all but God.

Chapter Twenty Seven

Joyce and Cindy stepped off the bus into an oven fuelled by a glaring sun. The red color of the barren, sandy ground contrasted sharply with the blue uniforms of the baton-wielding female guards. They were surrounded by large men holding on taut leashes very large dogs with crazy-looking eager eyes.

The blue-clad women shoved and herded the frightened prisoners into ill-shaped blocks. Several blocks contained women who apparently had their health and intact bodies. Several more were populated by the infirm, who made a pitiful sight in the attempt to create orderly blocks. A few were forced by their infirmities to kneel or lie on their legs. Those began to scream and hop crazily as the hot soil bit into their flesh. One unfortunate creature who could stand it no more staggered away from the block in an aimless attempt to escape. The guards did nothing. They watched until the invalid got some distance away. Then a handler released his leash and allowed his dog to run free. The dog made a beeline for the cripple and attacked a leg from behind. The cripple fell, the dog atop her, and blood flew through the air. The guards let the dog have his way as he tore into flesh and bone. The scene made a good example for the others. When the body ceased making feeble movements the handler clapped his hands. The dog obediently returned to his side.

A whistle blew and an older woman, obviously the camp commandant, strode briskly up to face them.

"Women," she began, "this is not Hitler's Germany. We won't try to deceive you into thinking we'll spare your lives. I'll tell you right now, this is the end of your line. But it's up to you how you meet your end. Handle yourselves well and it'll be easier on you. We don't like whiners. If you'd like to see for yourselves how much we hate them, go ahead and snivel. You're going to work, and work hard. It'll keep your minds off your future. Face up to it and you'll be better off." She pointed to a set of barracks, and then turned to point to another set in a different direction.

"If you're in good health, you'll be heading over there," she said, pointing back to the first set of barracks. "Otherwise you'll go off in the other direction. Now, drop your pants and dresses. All of you. No, not you!" she shouted to an obvious cripple, pointing in the direction of the infirm. A guard picked up on the Commandant's displeasure, clubbing the woman on the back as she hobbled away.

Joyce squeezed Cindy's arm, released it and the two complied with the indignity. A female guard came up to Cindy and palmed her crotch. "You're not bad for dark meat," she said with a leer, and abruptly moved on to face Joyce, whom she yanked out of line. "Over there, girlie," she said, pointing to the first group of infirm people. Joyce went over to the infirm adults with pride, knowing that she'd been betrayed by her prosthetic legs. She waved a tearful good-bye to Cindy as they parted ways. In all probability they would never see each other again.

Her block of people were marched toward one of the barracks, if the hobbling and stumbling could be called that. Eventually they were formed into a single file directed toward the entrance to the bleak, shabby building. Signs of the sun's fierce, unrelenting attack were everywhere. *Maybe I can find Cathy,* she thought. *Please, God, make it so.*

After the passage of much time the line shortened appreciably.

Joyce looked to the head and reeled back in shock. *Mildred! Of all the people in the world to greet me here, it has to be Mildred Black! Why, Lord?* The Lord didn't respond, and Joyce's adrenalin level shot up. As the line grew shorter, her dread increased. Mildred was in an ideal payback position, and, given her personality, she'd use it with gusto. Eventually Mildred saw her and Joyce watched the process of recognition play itself out on her face. First the surprise, then the frown as her memory of Joyce's violence toward her surfaced. After that, the full appreciation of her present position with respect to that of Joyce's, which settled in with a vindictive grin. The line shortened inexorably, and Joyce found herself before the woman. She trembled as Mildred confronted her.

Well, well! What have we here?" Mildred asked with a cat-and-mouse grin. Mrs. Cripple-lover, I presume. You're a cripple too, but I already knew that. I've been hoping to meet you in just this setting, as a matter of fact." She felt along Joyce's leg, touching the joint where the prosthetic device connected to the stump. "Yes, hmmm," she murmured. "We'll have to see about that."

Joyce picked up her bedding and went inside the barracks, passing Mildred with a relief that she knew was all too temporary. She was overwhelmed with the intensity of the heat inside, the sense of deliberate wrongness amplified by the darkness of the interior, which was windowless except for some tiny portals near the top of the high walls. The flimsy structure was stick-built, the two-by-fours standing out from the siding, void of insulation. The roof above radiated the sun's blazing heat downward from the asphalt shingles, bringing the inside almost to a boil. The situation would reverse at night, as Joyce and the others would soon find out to their intense discomfort. She was assigned a bed, nothing more than a canvas cot. She placed her bedding on the cot, and discovered that it consisted of nothing more than a thin, worn blanket. Her arm would have to serve as a pillow, she realized.

A whistle blew. "Form a double line for chow!" the guard shouted.

"Come over here, Joyce. On the double!" Joyce rose from the floor that she was scrubbing and walked timidly toward Mildred.

Her insides felt liquid. When Joyce came up to her, she pointed to a doorway. "In there," she said, ignoring the figures moving past toward the chow line. "I want to have a private conversation with you."

Joyce reluctantly went through the doorway into a small room and heard the door shut behind her. *I knew it would come to this*, she thought with dread. *It was inevitable. Dear Lord, please help my faith.* A vicious kick floored her, and immediately Mildred fell on her and unbuckled her prosthetics. She kicked them away and went to the door. "Out," she said, pointing back to the bigger room.

"You won't need them for the work you're doing," Mildred explained happily as Joyce crawled past her. Your knees are just where you belong." She watched, hands on her hips, as Joyce moved on her hands and knees back to where her scrub brush awaited her. "You look a little heavy around the middle, too. I think maybe we need to cut back on your food intake."

After several hours of unremitting toil, Joyce couldn't take the pain any more. She fell into a prone position on the floor, her hands covering her face. "No you don't, dearie," Mildred said. A sharp toe connected with the back of her head. It was followed by a series of kicks to her back. She turned on her back to avoid more blows, and reeled in shock as a foot smashed into her breast. She turned back in agony and managed to get to her knees. "That's the way, honey," Mildred said. "It's back to work, isn't it, now? Joyce remained silent but picked up her brush and began to scrub.

"That's the way. I'm right here to see that you work."

Try as she might, Joyce was unable to find a comfortable position. Her knees ached with a toothache sharpness, her battered head was swollen and bleeding, and her bruised breasts protested their pain. Nothing helped but her exhaustion, which finally allowed her some release through sleep.

"Cathy's gone, Joyce." The finality of those words stabbed deeply into her heart, overwhelming her intense discomfort. She looked up at Wisdom, who gazed back lovingly. "Why? You could have kept her here. All I wanted was to see her once more, to hold her in my arms and tell her I loved her with all my heart. Was one more time too much to ask?" She began to weep.

"Yes it was," Wisdom replied softly. Her work here is over, and she met her tasks like a saint. Her suffering in the process was at the edge of human endurance, and she needs some eternal R & R. I'm sure you wouldn't really want to keep her here in these conditions with no chance of actually seeing her."

"No, I guess not," Joyce replied. "Is she happy?"

"You can be sure of that. Relieved, too, and jumping up and down on legs that work. She's in heaven, as the saying goes. She's waiting for you, Joyce. You'll have a lot to catch up on.'

"Well, then, how about right now? I'm not exactly going to miss this dirty, filthy, rotten scum-filled pile of - -"

"Whoa, there," Wisdom said, laughing. "All in due time. Relief isn't so terribly far away. I can guarantee you this: when you do finish up here, you'll come out to the joy of heaven itself. Most of all, your divine Husband Himself will be most anxious to greet you and welcome you into His bosom.

"What about Earl? Is he gone too? Are you going to keep me here with nothing left?

"No, he's here. He's not very happy, but through his sorrow and pain he will grow in strength and compassion and serve Us in a mighty way, just as you will. He misses you, of course, and prays for you every day, just as you have been praying for him. But I'll give you some encouragement and hope: you will see him again, Joyce, and you'll be able to hold each other as husband and wife. And I'll be around more to comfort you. Rest with those thoughts, My precious one." She reached over and gave her a tender kiss. Within moments, Joyce was asleep.

Chapter Twenty Eight

Earl stood in the blistering heat looking out into the distance beyond the chain link fence, searching for some sign of their women. Stephen sat on the ground next to him. They could see the womens' barracks, but not, of course, the women inside except when, to their horror, loaded carts were brought out and pushed over to the big building with the smokestacks.

The two men prayed almost continuously for the welfare of their women until, one night, Wisdom showed up by his bunk, Her beautiful face clouded with a frown. On one side of Her face, however, her mouth had the slightest uptick. "Okay already, Earl. We hear you. We're keeping Joyce around, so you can rest your mind on that score. You will eventually be together again, so you can comfort yourself with that thought, too. It's time that you devoted more effort to thinking about why you're here and what you're going to do about it."

"Do?" he asked sharply. "You mean that there's actually a reason for this hopeless, meaningless, horrible existence?"

Her mouth turned upward in a full-blown grin. "That's just the kind of spunk I'm getting from your wife. You really are two birds of a feather. Yes, of course there's a reason for your circumstances, as I've already told you. It ranks as one of the most important times of your life. In short, Earl, it's not all about you. I don't mean that in a derogatory sense, just as a fact, okay? There are others here who are suffering too, as you can see. But at least you know Us. You have that hope of a future with Us, and of Our eternal love for you. Many of them don't have that. It's time that you showed some compassion toward them and helped them to find Us, don't you think?"

"Thanks for reminding me," Earl told Her. "I needed that." She left him alone to figure out how he would accomplish the task that She had laid before him.

The next morning Earl spoke to Stephen about his desire to bring the light of Christ to the unfortunate victims who were incarcerated here with them. Stephen agreed with enthusiasm. "It'll give us some sense of purpose at the least," he said. "And we might as well put our loyalty where it belongs."

"Well said," Earl told him. Stephen left the fence and wandered over to a man who was shuffling aimlessly and weeping, the snot running down his face unheeded. Presently he saw Stephen put a loving arm around his shoulder as he talked to him.

Earl set his eyes on another sad, hopeless individual. As he did so the name *Jacob* entered his mind involuntarily. The name was repeated twice, each time more insistently than the last. Earl headed over to talk with him. "Is your name Jacob by any chance?" he asked.

"Yes, it is," the man replied. "I don't know you. How do you know my name?"

As She had promised, Wisdom was there for him. Under Her guidance, Earl led him into the understanding that the Holy Spirit as presented in the New Testament, and particularly in the spectacular events of Acts Chapter 2, was none other than their Shekinah, foreshadowed not only in the Cloud of Glory upon the dedication of their temples, but also in their ancient feast of Pentecost. When he had finished, he barely had time to see Jacob begin to reflect upon what he had heard when Earl felt his head explode in a sharp flash of incoherent light.

CHAPTER TWENTY NINE

Joyce shifted in her cot, attempting as she did every night to find a position that might lessen her constant pain. After a week of a bleak, hopeless existence filled with torture, she cried herself to sleep. It had become a nightly ritual.

"Look at Me, darling," She spoke to Joyce in silence. Somehow, despite the bruises, Joyce managed to open her left eye enough to perceive a rainbow blur. She attempted to wipe the hardening fluid from her swollen lids, but recoiled at the pain of the touch. She blinked several times, finally seeing the face before her, radiant with love.

The moans, sniffles and sobs surrounding her cot faded into the background at the sight. "Wisdom!" she cried. "Oh, I'm so very, very glad to see you! Is it time, Wisdom? Are you taking me home?"

A tear formed in Wisdom's eye. "Not yet, My dearest one. Your work isn't over."

"But why?" she pleaded. "What's there to do? They took my legs away, so I can't even walk. I'm just a toy for these awful people to play with and abuse. There's no one left, Wisdom. The inmates are so hungry and hurting that they're no longer capable of thinking rationally. I know. I'm in the same position. The guards are beyond saving, oh they're way past that," she said with teeth-baring conviction. They're pure evil." She began to wail, a high, keening cry that eventually broke down into shoulder-heaving sobs. "Take me now, Wisdom. Please," she begged, bubbles forming on her mouth.

"No." Wisdom spoke firmly, but her eyes were glassed over with tears. "Remember the promise I gave you about Earl. Your finest hour is still ahead of you, one that you will cherish for all eternity. Do you remember what Jesus said about loving your enemies? To do good to those who treat you badly?"

"Y-yes" Joyce said in a small voice. She stopped crying and thought for a moment. Anger took over then, shoving her feelings of guilt to the bottom of the stack. Her eyes narrowed, as much as their puffiness would allow. "Right now, Wisdom, I'm finding that a bit difficult to do. How'd you like to fill in for me?"

Wisdom laughed. "Now you're spunk is coming back. You and Earl sure are two of a kind. As for Me filling in for you, you have no idea." She chuckled to Herself. "Here's the key, Joyce: think about Jesus as an example. The free gift of Himself he gave on the cross for those who would accept it. Many of those started out hating Him. Others scoffed and mocked, and yet in His humiliation He extended that gift to them too. You're going to be in a very close relationship with Him. I'm looking forward to the special sharing He'll have with you about both of your white-knuckle moments, especially those of yours that went with the things you did in His name."

"Okay, I hear you. But I'm still having a hard time figuring out what good I can do in this wasteland. It's entirely empty of any semblance of love or humanity. Who's here that I can possibly reach in the name of Jesus?"

"You're wrong about the guards,"Wisdom replied. "There's one who is worth saving, who is one of you. And this place is not destitute of love. You're here, aren't you? And the love of God is here, through you. All she needs is your love."

"Who's that?"

"Hang on to your hat, Joyce. It's Mildred."

"What?" She cried. "Oh, you have to be kidding. That's the most ridiculous thing I've ever heard."

"Careful. Do you think I'm in the habit of making ridiculous statements?"

"Oh. I'm so sorry, Wisdom," she said contritely. I forgot my manners. I really do believe You. And love You."

"I know that, My darling. But you must believe Me with all your heart. I know just what it's going to take out of you to love Mildred. But it's something you have to do. When you've emptied yourself of all your self, and can still love Mildred in your heart despite the pain she's going to inflict on you, why, then, Joyce, We'll be the happiest, proudest Parents the world has ever seen. And some day you'll be able to appreciate a Mildred who most gratefully loves you for what you'll do for her."

"Oh, boy. That I'll have to see," she said wryly, but silently she began to formulate a loving approach to Mildred.

"I see you're already starting to figure out how to reach her, Joyce, so I'll be ambling along. Don't worry, We're with you all the way, and are just waiting to shower you with love and blessings. She reached out and drew Joyce to her, and gave her a tender kiss. Then She was gone.

Joyce lay there thinking of Mildred, struggling with alternating thoughts that ranged from unthinking hatred to godly love. Eventually the love won out, much to Joyce's relief. She gave a prayer of thanksgiving, and was astonished to realize that she was no longer in pain.

The next day, as Joyce was scrubbing the floor, Mildred came and stood over her, indulging in intimidation. Joyce turned to her and said "Good Morning," with a smile. When she turned back to her work, she felt a toe prodding her left breast. She could picture the woman grinning. The toe left her body briefly, and then returned in force. She started to cry out in pain, but kept her peace. "I love you," she said to Mildred.

"What did you say?" Mildred demanded. "How dare you!" Mildred yanked the pads from under Joyce's knees. "You've been having it too soft. No more nice-guy with me." She left, the pads in her hands. Joyce silently continued to scrub the floor, resolving to endure the pain in her knees.

Mildred avoided Joyce for the rest of the week, but the next Monday, as Joyce was on her bare knees scrubbing the floor, Mildred came over. The knee pads were in her hand. "Here, she said brusquely."

"I love you for that, too," Joyce said as she placed them on her bleeding knees."

"There's something else to love me for?" she demanded.

"Of course. God loves you."

"Me? Why me?" she scoffed.

God loves all of us, Mildred. Good, bad and even indifferent. That's why Jesus died on the cross. He did it for us all, because He loves all of us. He did it for you, Mildred, every bit as much as He did it for me. All you have to do is accept Jesus' free gift of love.

Mildred stood there, stunned. "Will you show me how?" she said in a tiny, quavering voice.

Joyce smiled at her. I'd be very, very happy to do that. You might want to come down to my level."

Mildred looked around to see if anybody was watching. For a time she struggled between her old pride and a newly-formed desire. The desire won over, and she got down on her knees. Joyce grasped her hand and said, "Mildred, just pray to God with me with these simple words: "Jesus, I know that you loved me so much that you were willing to die for me on the cross."

"Jesus," she began, her face raised upwards and her eyes shut tightly, "I know that you loved me so much that you were willing to die for me on the cross. Just for me," she continued on her own. Even though I don't deserve it. I'm a terrible sinner, Jesus, but I want to change. Thank you for your offer. I accept it. I want it very badly, Jesus. Oh!"

Mildred opened her eyes in shock. She looked over at Joyce. "What have I done to you?" She broke out in uncontrolled sobs. Joyce reached out an arm to comfort her, but she continued to weep. She rose abruptly and lifted Joyce tenderly in her arms. She carried her over to her cot and lay her gently down. "You've done enough work for now. For a decade. Rest. I'll be back with some food."

As Joyce lay on her bed she began to laugh. "You sure know what you're doing, Wisdom!" she said. Surprisingly, Wisdom appeared in front of her with a radiant smile. "Wisdom!" she cried. "Thanks so much. It really did work! I think from now on I'll be able to endure it here, especially since I'll now have Mildred as a friend instead of an enemy." She grinned up at Wisdom.

Wisdom grinned back. "As a matter of fact, I think that I'll give her a session to remember. Bye-bye."

When Mildred returned with a bowl of soup, she was shocked to see Joyce's inert form. She put the soup down in haste and bent over her. Perceiving that she was lifeless, she attempted to rescuscitate her. After laboring over her body for half an hour, she gave up and sat down next to Joyce's body, weeping bitterly. Presently she felt a soft, warm hand covering hers. Looking up, she was astonished to see Joyce alive and smiling at her. "Oh!" she cried. "Praise God! I thought that you'd died. That I'd killed you." She reached over and gave Joyce a fiercely intense hug. Then she reached down and picked up the bowl. She tenderly fed Joyce.

That night Mildred was awakened from the most comfortable sleep she'd had in years to feel a finger brush her cheek and turned to face a spectacularly beautiful woman bathed in light. "Hello, Mildred," the face said. "It's time we had a chat."

CHAPTER THIRTY

Cindy shuffled back to her bunk, distraught with the inhuman, evil things the female guards had forced her to do over the past two weeks. On their arrival the blue-clad guard who had inappropriately fondled her took charge of her and separated her from the other inmates. She was granted special favors that the rest of the prison population failed to receive: friendly smiles, a pillow to lay her head on, exemption from work, an extra portion at mealtime, even the use of the guards' restroom. As the privileges continued, Cindy's consternation grew, for she knew that these excesses would come at a heavy price.

That night the guard came to collect. Coming over to her bunk, she took Cindy by the hand and led her to a private room, where she politely pushed her down onto the large bed. Cindy could hear her heavy breathing as she undressed them both. Without speaking, she motioned for Cindy to do something that shocked her in its depravity. Cindy refused, causing the sky to fall upon her. A rapid series of open-palmed slaps to her face drove her backwards onto the bed, where a fist was driven into her crotch. She was left alone, crying, while the guard dressed herself, and then was yanked naked from the bed and out of the room. "You know what, whore?" the guard shouted into her face as she dragged her out of the barracks. "You got some meat needs tenderizing." She opened the door to the guardroom of the male barracks and turned on the light. "Got something for you," she told the startled men. "Bring her back when you're through."

Cindy was returned to the female guard the next morning. Strangely, she was ushered back to the comfortable bunk that she had been given the day before, and left alone to recover from her night of terror. That night the guard returned and attempted again to engage Cindy in her unspeakable perversions, to which Cindy again resisted until she was dragged back to the male barracks. As the violent assaults began again, she focused her thoughts on God, praying for the souls of the men who attacked her.

After the fourth night of this continuous attack her ravaged body could endure no more. Suddenly, in the midst of the violence she saw a glowing light framing a beautiful woman. "Your trial is over, Cindy," the face spoke, overpowering Cindy's awareness of the world about her. "You've done a magnificent job. We love you and I've come to take you home with Me."

The guards, perceiving that her soul had departed, responded strangely. Remembering the words of her prayers, they began to weep. Kneeling on the floor as one man, they begged God to forgive them.

Stephen wailed as he heard from Wisdom the words that he had dreaded. "Don't be sad, my love," She said as She cupped his cheeks in Her hands. "That was the bad news. Now for the good part. Your task here is finished. You handled it well indeed. You get to go with her."

Chapter Thirty One

Earl awoke slowly to feelings that gradually strengthened. The first was discomfort, followed by confinement. The feeling of being constrained nagged at his severe claustrophobia, rushing his brain back on-line. He heard voices, conversational and nearby, but he couldn't see. Nor could he move his head more than a few degrees left or right. He pushed his head forward and quickly encountered an obstacle. He moved his head backward with the same result. His arms, in fact, were confined to his sides. In attempting to raise them he found that they, like his head and back, were blocked by metallic walls. Realization struck him like the blow of an axe, producing an instant excess of adrenaline that made his heart leap inside his chest and thrust an agony into his panic-filled mind.

"Nooooo," he screamed as the realization of his condition overwhelmed him. The tape over his mouth kept it inside him. As his heart pumped panic into every capillary of his body, he experienced the pain of a torture more severe by far than any mere physical pain. Each fraction of a second represented an eternity of madness.

Time stretched on. At the edge of insanity he heard a still small voice: *come back.* "My God, where are you?" he wailed. "Why have you deserted me?" *Come back* was the reply. "Come back?

What do You mean by that?" he asked sharply. The voices outside his metal coffin became intrusive, causing him to focus on them. He failed to interpret the words, but the brief respite from his mental agony allowed him to shift his focus back to God. "What?" he asked again, and then he remembered the sorrow in Wisdom's eyes as She told him the story of the feedings, and of how they combined to form the cross, a sign for the generation that would be given to understand. *Was the message for now?* he asked in his mind. *Yes* was the reply.

You'll take it like a man, he remembered Wisdom telling him. The message gave him strength. He strained again to understand the words being spoken outside his coffin, finally coming to the realization that the language was foreign, unknown to him. Slowly, methodically, he sucked at the duct tape around his mouth, finally bringing enough of it into the proximity of his teeth that he could chew a small hole. He worked at it, prying with his lips and tongue and chewing at what came close to his teeth until they emerged into the outside of the tape and he was able to scrape at it, slowly peeling it away from the region of his mouth. Eventually the opening was sufficient to project his voice outside his body. "Help!" he shouted. "Help me!"

The voices ceased. Eventually a rapping sound was made against the front surface of his prison, followed by a voice, quite near. "Hello?" it said. The language was English.

"I'm trapped inside!" Earl shouted. "Get me out! Please!" he pleaded, the new hope forcing the urgency back into his mind.

"We can't," was the innocent but cruel reply. "We're prisoners like you. We aren't in boxes, but we're chained to the walls."

"Who are you?" Earl asked. "Why are you here?"

"We're Jews," was the reply, confirming what Earl had already expected. "They think we're dangerous. Are you a Jew?"

"You're close, but no. I'm a Christian."

"Oh. Well, they've been rounding up you Christians too. I guess you already know that."

"Yes." Silence descended on them as Earl struggled through his agony to recall what Wisdom had wanted him to say. *Something about feeding. . .yes, the feedings.* Suddenly he knew what he had to tell them. "Hello?" he said to get their attention.

"Yes?"

"Jesus was a Jew like you. In fact, he not only is your own Messiah, but he was your Jahweh, the God who spoke to Moses out of the burning bush."

"Oh, right," a man scoffed. He laughed, a short grunt. "He's right where he belongs."

"Did you ever hear the story of how Jesus fed five thousand men with five loaves of bread, and four thousand with seven loaves?" Earl replied, his desperation returning.

"So what?" the scoffer said in a surly fashion.

"No, hear him out," another man said rather more kindly. The man's name was Jacob. "I have," he addressed the coffin. "Go on."

"Well, He wasn't the only one who did that," Earl said.

"You're joking."

"No, I'm not. Your prophet Elisha did it too. He fed a hundred men with twenty loaves of barley. I don't know what you call your Scripture, our Old Testament, and you probably don't have one available, but the account's in Second Kings Chapter 4 if you did."

"I remember reading that!" the voice exclaimed. "A long time ago. I never associated it with what Jesus did. So you're saying – and now I agree – that Jesus wasn't the first to do that."

"There's a reason for that. Jesus was trying to integrate your Scripture into the Christianity that would soon follow His crucifixion and resurrection."

"Okay, but it would be more convincing if a Christian were also to have done some feeding like Elisha. And Jesus. It would be even better if this Christian were a Jew like us."

This remark gave Earl the perfect opening, a heaven-sent opportunity to explain what Wisdom had told him back when he had a life. Agreeing with the kind voice, Earl told him about Peter. First, about Peter's denial of Jesus upon His arrest, and then about Jesus' meeting with Peter after His resurrection, and about how He asked Peter if he loved Him and responded to Peter's reply by telling him to feed His sheep. He capped it off by telling how Peter, when he had received the Holy Spirit along with the other apostles at the birth of the Christian Church during the feast of Pentecost, had gone on to feed the Church with the Word of God. His talk gained the respectful attention of the Jewish prisoners, who remained quiet as he spoke.

"But what truly tied these events together," Earl continued, "is the pattern that the feedings took."

"Pattern?" another voice responded. "How can you get a pattern out of the feedings?"

After first making note of the oddity of the several very specific numbers associated with the feedings, Earl answered his question with the specifics of the feeding patterns, ending up with the rectangles and the differing orientations that the numbers demanded. He finally came to the punchline – how the patterns dovetailed with each other to form a cross.

Silence prevailed for a time after he spoke. "The obvious implication being," the man with the kind voice finally said, "that Elisha's feeding, even back then, was intended to set the stage for Jesus. Can you say anything more as to why you think Jesus was our Yahweh?" he added before Earl could respond in the affirmative to his conjecture.

"Yes, I can," Earl replied. Many of the main characters in the Book of Genesis foretold the unique character of Jesus and the nature of His mission on earth." Earl told them of how the relationships between Isaac, his father Abraham and his wife Rebekah foretold of Jesus' crucifixion and spiritual marriage to His Church. "Genesis isn't the only book to talk about Jesus, as a matter of fact," he continued. "Your own Psalms, written by David, talk about Him and His Godhood. If you were to read Psalm 22, for example, you'd find that David was describing the punishment of crucifixion before it was known to the Jews. And then, of course, are the prophets, who wrote about and described Jesus with precision. Isaiah Chapter 53 very explicitly describes the suffering Messiah, a description that Jesus very thoroughly fulfilled."

"He's right about that," another voice allowed.

"And then there's Daniel, whose prophecy in Chapter 9 of the coming of Messiah was related in time to a decree that would be given a century into the future. The prophecy was spectacularly fulfilled to the very day out of a hundred seventy-three thousand, eight hundred eighty days when Jesus made His triumphal entry into Jerusalem on an ass. There are many more links between your Messiah and Jesus besides those, and those that have to do with events and their timing can't be repeated by any other."

Silence reigned in the prison as the Jews attempted to assimilate all that Earl had told them. Then he heard a man snore, and soon several others followed. A dark depression enveloped Earl. He had fulfilled the task that Wisdom had set before him and his terror of confinement agreed with Her sadness at the time She had given the task to him. Was he now to be abandoned to continue in this awful horror forever?

As his inward darkness grew into an intolerable panic, God gave him an answer. His metal box shook in savage violence as the prison was subjected to a strong earthquake. At first his hope was merely to die from the hammer blows of the ground upon his coffin, but then the box itself rent apart. Slowly, unbelievingly, he understood his sudden freedom. Immensely grateful to God for the relief from his phobia, he crawled out and stood, surveying the wreckage of his barracks. Many prisoners wandered aimlessly, but some, more aware of what had just happened, headed for a collapsed side from which light from outside entered the ruined building. Earl followed them, emerging into the sunlight and immediately looking toward the womens' barracks. Seeing that the womens' building had also collapsed he ran toward it. Occupied by the disaster, the guards failed to see his running figure.

Women began to drift out from between collapsed timbers and rent siding. Earl searched frantically for the woman he loved. *There!* he shouted joyfully in his mind. She saw him as he neared and ran toward him, arms outstretched. They met and clung to each other, sobbing in relief. Behind them, a great company of male prisoners strode purposefully toward their own women. Several of them, having found their mates, drifted back to Earl and Joyce, surrounding the two. Finally, one of them spoke. "You've given us a reason to live, Earl. You may be a *goy*, a gentile, but you're a righteous one. We knew you were suffering in that box, but yet you gave us Jews a powerful reason to believe in Jesus. We must get out of here and return to our homeland. Will you go with us – you and your wife?"

"Yes, of course!" Earl responded joyfully. But do you have any idea as to just how that might be accomplished?"

"I don't," the man admitted. "But thanks to the information God passed on to us through you, I'm certain that He does."

"Hey! Look over there!" one of the men shouted, pointing to a troop carrier lying on its side. Several blue-clad figures were lying haphazardly on the ground nearby, obviously having been flung from the truck during its capsizing in the earthquake. None of them were moving. Earl glanced around, checking every direction for signs of functioning guards. There were some in the distance, but they were preoccupied with the aftermath of the enormous quake.

"What luck!" the man next to Earl said as they ran up to the overturned vehicle.

"There's nothing lucky about it," Earl corrected him.

"Gotcha!" the man replied. It took eighteen minutes for twenty three people with several timbers from a collapsed barracks nearby to right the truck. After another twelve minutes they were wearing the blue uniforms of the former prison employees and sporting government-issue .45 caliber handguns.

"Move out!" the new leader called to one of his men, who now sat behind the wheel. Earl sat in back with Joyce, holding her tightly. "I'm never going to let you out of my sight again," she told him.

"Nor I you," he responded as they jounced along the rutted dirt road at the highest speed the truck could go short of going airborne. "Sorry about the bouncing, after all you've been through."

"Are you kidding? After that hellhole, I feel like I'm drifting on a cloud."

See the preview of *Jacob* starting on the next page. *Jacob* is the exciting next novel in the *Buddy* series by Arthur Perkins

JACOB

"Take a left up that wash!" the new leader of the small band shouted to the driver of the commandeered troop carrier. His name was Jacob and, like the rest of the people on board the lurching vehicle, he was a prisoner less than half an hour before, waiting like the others for his turn to die. His crime, like that of his great grandparents before him who were trapped under the Nazi jackboot, was that he was a Jew. Seventy years later, the evil had migrated to America, where the sick, infirm, elderly, Jew and now even the Christian were no longer welcome. As part of the revamping of society into a socialist state for its integration into a one-world system, a thorough housecleaning had taken place. Spearheaded by a self-serving president who had slowly acquired in his first term the godlike powers he chose to exercise with cruelty in his second, the increasingly repressive regime had begun to divest itself of the less productive members of society. Ironically, it was doing so under the guise of providing more efficient care of the less fortunate.

The public at large had enthusiastically bought into this fiction, but then, having grown indolent, self-absorbed and indifferent to the suffering of others, they perceived that they had much to gain and little to lose by the removal of these creatures, whom the press did its utmost to portray as less than human. The notion that they themselves might eventually join the ranks of the elderly was simply beyond the scope of their shallow mindset. As a consequence, the rejects of this new society had been rounded up and herded into a vast network of holding pens located next to death factories, their brutal efficiency inspired by the depraved minds of Hitler's and Stalin's regimes. Removed from the eyes of society, the new misfits, as defined for the public by its corrupt and evil leadership, simply ceased to exist.

All of the ex-prisoners were wearing the uniforms of their former guards, now dead from the destructive chaos of the super-earthquake that had freed the prison inmates. Having been released by the massive killer quake, they were now grasping for a new chance at life. The commandeered truck swung left, leaving a graded dirt road to climb up a shallow bone-dry draw. The vehicle slowed and the transfer case groaned in protest as the driver engaged the front wheels. The vehicle lurched forward and jounced along the dry streambed as the driver strained to negotiate a pathway through the numerous ruts and boulders. Behind them a lengthy cloud of dust marked their passage from the main camp. So far they weren't being followed. They were too far away now to discern individuals, but they could see the buildings of the camp, or what remained of them. The metal-framed barracks had collapsed, undoubtedly trapping most of the prisoners inside. They had probably either been severely injured or died. Even that untimely end, however, was to be preferred to the living hell that each day represented under their brutal overseers. A low-lying black cloud drifted toward the ruined buildings. Something didn't seem quite right with the scene, and suddenly Earl understood why. The huge smokestacks had collapsed. One lay on the ground almost intact, but the others had been reduced to heaps of broken concrete.

Earl looked over to Joyce, thanking God again for the gift of her life and her presence beside him. She gave him a smile. The truck had crested a diminishing rise above the wash and was picking up speed as it moved cross-country over the flat high-desert grassland dotted with mesquite, ocotillo and occasional saguaro. He turned his head toward the front, observing the gradual rise of the land toward the peaks to their east. Scattered high clouds cast a patchwork pattern of shadows about the desert floor, darkening the prevailing tan color to brown. White boulders jutted out from the red-streaked gray hills ahead.

"Look at that, will you?" one of the women yelled. Earl turned his head toward the direction her shocked face was pointing. At first they looked like sticks scattered along the roadway, then, as he focused, more like pieces of rope. His mind made the identification just as the woman shouted "Snakes! Thousands of them!" The rest of the passengers got to their feet and looked rearward. Joyce clung to Earl for support. He felt her shudder in revulsion, but soon the truck had left the patch behind. She nudged his ribs for attention. "Why so many?" she asked.

"Then I guess it's really true that animals can sense an earthquake long before humans can. This area's full of them, but they're usually hidden from sight. The threat of the earthquake must have driven them out of their holes and dens."

As he continued to watch the road below and behind them, the remains came into view of the isolated guardhouse they had just avoided. Situated next to the dirt road, it marked the boundary of the reservation. The earthquake had leveled the shack; there was no sign of life. Jacob must have noticed its desolate condition, for he spoke to the driver, who angled the truck back toward the road. Once back on the roadway the driver shifted out of four-wheel drive and picked up speed. Darkness fell and the temperature dropped, but in their elation at having escaped the band's spirits remained high. They marveled at the blackness of the sky, pierced only by the headlights of their truck. The earthquake obviously had damaged the power grid. "Hey!" someone shouted, looking at his wrist theatrically. "We gotta turn around. It's chow time! We'll miss roll call!" Laughter rippled through the truck.

We hope you enjoyed reading ***Cathy: Encounters with the Holy Spirit*** by Arthur Perkins.
For further reading including novels and non-fiction titles by this author and others, please go to our online catalog at http://www.signalmanpublishing.com